PLUS

# ONE

by

## Graysen Morgen

2024

Plus ONE © 2024 Graysen Morgen
Triplicity Publishing, LLC

ISBN-13: 978-1-970042-26-9
ISBN-10: 1-970042-26-5

Printed in the United States of America
First Edition – 2023
Cover Design: Triplicity Publishing, LLC
Interior Design: Triplicity Publishing, LLC
Editor: Megan Brady - Triplicity Publishing, LLC

# Also by Graysen Morgen

*Boone Creek (Law & Order Series: book 1)*

*Castor Valley (Law & Order Series: book 2)*

*Never Let Go (Never Series: book 1)*

*Never Quit (Never Series: book 2)*

*Bridesmaid of Honor (Bridal Series: book 1)*

*Brides (Bridal Series: book 2)*

*Mommies (Bridal Series: book 3)*

*New Beginnings*

*Crossed Reins*

*Real Love*

*Playing the Game*

*Mission Compromised*

*Meant to Be*

*Coming Home*

*Crashing Waves*

*Cypress Lake*

*Falling Snow*

*Fast Pitch*

*Fate vs. Destiny*

*In Love, at War*

*Just Me*

*Love, Loss, Revenge*

*Natural Instinct*

*Secluded Heart*

*Submerged*

Special thanks to my editor, Megan Brady.
*Ευχαριστώ*

For my grandmother, who loved me unconditionally.

*κάθε μέρα μου λείπεις*

# Chapter 1

Tracey watched as her best friend of five years walked into her apartment and flopped down in the seat across from her. She tossed an envelope onto the table between them as she brushed her long black curls back over her shoulder.

"She's trying to ruin my life," she huffed with a deep sigh.

"What?" Tracey questioned as she opened the envelope addressed to *Ms. Sharni Dinjavi & Guest*, and slid a thick, white bi-folded invitation out in the process. "Oh ... I know what this is," she mumbled, reading the inscription.

*You are cordially invited*
*to the wedding of*
*Maximos Papadakis & Neesa Dinjavi*
*Epidaurus, Peloponnese, Greece*
*6:00PM*
*12 August*

"I love destination weddings! Damnit, I want to go to Greece, too!" Tracey squealed and pouted playfully.

"Keep going."

"There's nothing else here," Tracey said, shaking the envelope.

"Exactly. No reservation card to send back, and she conveniently sent it at the last minute."

"Well, you *are* in the wedding."

"No kidding. I had my dress measurements taken again this morning, by the way. That's not the point. This is my mother's way of making sure I arrive with a plus one. She added it for me! Do you see how the invitation was addressed, me and my guest! Can you believe her?"

"Sharni, you *did* tell your mother you were dating someone," Tracey eased.

"Almost six months ago, when the wedding planning started!" she grumbled, shaking her head as she turned dark eyes towards her friend. Her bronze skin glowed almost golden under the warm, recessed lighting, contrasting against the lime green, sleeveless blouse, and stark white slacks she wore. Lime green pumps accentuated her taut calves as she crossed her lean legs.

Tracey loved her best friend and envied the Sri Lankan beauty in a lot of ways, but her family relationship wasn't one of them. She pulled her barely shoulder length, dirty blonde hair back in a ponytail and leaned into the crook of the couch, wrinkling her plaid gray slacks as she folded her legs to her side. "Call her and say you broke up," she finally muttered.

"Ha!" Sharni laughed. "You've met my mother. She'd skin me alive if I embarrassed her like that. She already shuns me for not being married. I'm the oldest! Hell no. I'm going with a plus one, no matter what."

Tracey's brow raised. "I guess we'd better find you a date then."

Sharni leaned her head down in her hands, then pushed away the long black curls that fell forward.

"Have you heard of this new app called Favor?" Tracey muttered; eyes glued to her phone.

"What?" Sharni lifted her head.

"Favor. You post something you need done or help with and an amount you're willing to pay. If someone wants to do it, they message your post."

"I don't need sex. I need a date!" Sharni laughed.

Tracey chuckled, "It's not *that* kind of app. My paralegal uses it all the time." She bit the corner of her mouth. "Then again, she's hooked up with two guys she met. One helped her move and the other fixed her car."

"Great." Sharni shook her head.

"Seriously, look." Tracey got up and walked over to her. "You can post you need an actor to pretend to be romantically involved with you and be your plus one to a destination wedding. All expenses paid; plus, whatever else you want to offer."

"Like my ass?"

Tracey laughed and shrugged. "I was thinking more like money ... but, if he's hot, go for it."

"This is insane." Sharni ran her hand through her thick hair and shook her head.

"The wedding's in ten days. When are you leaving?"

"Probably Tuesday or Wednesday."

"That's six or seven days, babe. You don't have a lot of options here."

"I know. Are you sure you can't get out of that trial?" Sharni sighed.

Tracey smiled apologetically at her best friend. "I'm lead council. Otherwise, I'd be deathly ill that week and unable to get out of bed, trust me. I've always wanted to go to Greece. I'm jealous, you bitch."

Sharni laughed. "Alright, I guess I have no choice."

"Give me your phone."

Sharni rolled her eyes as she handed over her device. "Don't put my picture on there."

"Why not? It'll help get some attention."

"I get enough attention as it is," Sharni muttered.

Tracey laughed knowing she was right. A lot of men and some women hit on her best friend everywhere they went. "I think you need to add another incentive then, maybe a couple thousand dollars or something like that."

"As if an all-expenses paid week in Greece isn't enough," Sharni grumbled. "Fine. Add five-thousand dollars. That should bring in someone worth taking with me. Make sure he has acting experience, is between twenty-six and forty, and has a valid passport."

"That's a big age gap."

"I'm thirty-two, that's about as far as I'll go in either direction."

Tracey nodded and grinned as she finished adding in all the details. She wanted to put Sharni's photo but decided to use a gorgeous picture of Greece instead. Finished, she handed the iPhone back to Sharni. "Now we wait."

"For what exactly?"

"If someone answers the ad, you'll get a notification. Basically, it's a brief message from a person who is interested. You reply with a date, time, and place to meet to seal the deal."

"This sounds like a sex contract. I imagine this is how the high-class call girls operate."

Tracey laughed. "Well, you can always hire an escort service. They're not allowed to provide sexual services."

"That feels even dirtier than this app of yours," Sharni said as she stood up. "I need to get going. I have an early meeting."

"New merger?"

"Not yet, but I have a feeling it's coming," Sharni replied, hugging her goodbye.

"Let me know how it goes," Tracey said, referring to the app.

"Oh, trust me. You'll be the only person who knows." Sharni shook her head and smiled at her friend. "I can't believe you talked me into this. I hope it works."

"It will. Have faith."

Sharni laughed and waved over her shoulder as she headed down the walkway to the deep purple BMW waiting by the curb.

\*

Sharni walked into her condo, setting her Gucci bag on the side table by the door on her way to the kitchen to pour a glass of merlot. "R2D2, turn on my surprise playlist," she called out to her Alexa device as she put her phone on the counter and slipped her heels off. *She's a Lady* by Tom Jones began playing through the speaker. "That'll do," she muttered, carrying her shoes in one hand by the heels and her glass of merlot in the other as she headed into her bedroom sashaying her hips and singing along. The city lights sparkled in the night sky through the slits in the blinds, reminding her how much she loved living in Los Angeles. The small space had cost her a fortune, but it was well worth it.

She sloshed the red liquid around in the glass between sips as she put her heels on the shelf in the closet.

After tossing her blouse and slacks into the dry-cleaning pile, she danced her way back into her bedroom wearing a crème colored, matching bra and panties set as the playlist changed to another song. She was about to go into the bathroom and start the shower when she heard a man say, 'You have a booty call.'

"What the hell?!" she said, raising a brow in confusion. She swallowed the last sip of wine and held the glass up as if to attack someone with it, then walked from her bedroom into the open living room. "I swear I heard someone," she muttered.

Suddenly, the man's voice spoke again. "You have a booty call."

She yelped and jumped a foot off the ground, before realizing her phone was lit up on the kitchen counter. "What the fuck," she grumbled as she grabbed the phone and swiped to open the lock screen. She had two notifications from the Favor App. "Damn you, Tracey!" She quickly went into her settings and changed the notification sound for the app and stopped her Alexa device before pressing the call button next to her best friend's name.

"Miss me already?" Tracey answered.

"Booty call, really."

Tracey laughed like a hyena. "That means someone answered your post."

"Two someone's, I think."

"What do you mean? Didn't you go on there and see their replies?"

Sharni blew out a frustrating breath. "I hate this."

"Well, you need a boyfriend yesterday, so ..."

"Oh, for fuck's sake," Sharni grumbled, putting Tracey on speakerphone so she could open the app. "Alright, are you ready for this? The first one is

DanTheMan. He likes to be free with himself and one with nature, whatever the hell that means."

"Hmm."

"Girl, I wouldn't go out with this man if I was Catholic, and the Pope blessed him. His picture looks like Jesus and his reply is, 'I'm down for whatever and wherever the mood takes me. Plus, I love role playing!'"

Tracey chuckled.

"The other one is a guy named CatManJoe. He replied he'd like to meet in person to discuss further."

"Okay, that one doesn't sound too bad. What does his picture look like?"

"It's a cat."

"What?"

"I'm serious," Sharni laughed.

"That's hilarious."

"Meet for coffee. That won't hurt anything. You know what you're looking for. If he isn't it, move on."

"The one thing going for me is, I never told my mother anything about the guy I was dating. I simply said I'd been seeing someone for a little while, it was new, but I was happy. That shut her up. Plus, they've never seen anyone I've dated, so they don't know my type."

"That's good. You could literally take anybody."

"Yeah, I guess I can. If he is respectful, decent looking, and a good actor who understands the deal, this'll be easy."

"Let me know how it goes with CatManJoe," Tracey teased.

"Yeah, fuck you."

"Love you, too," Tracey chuckled as she hung up.

# Chapter 2

"That was a complete waste of time."

Sharni watched as her boss walked into her office and flopped down in the chair across from her desk like a deflated balloon.

"Chris, you know these deals don't close on day one. Give it time. Our numbers are increasing week over week and month over month. It'll happen. Don't force it. Let the deal come to you."

He blew out a sigh, then stood up, seemingly back to normal. "What would I do without you?" He smiled and left the room.

Sharni rolled her eyes and shook her head. "I need a vacation," she muttered, realizing she had to meet CatManJoe at the coffee shop down the street in five minutes. "Damnit." She grabbed her debit card and ID from her wallet and locked her purse in her desk drawer.

Two of her employees tried to stop her on the way out, but she held her hand up and kept walking with her heels making a click-click sound as she headed out the door and down the sidewalk.

A cat-call whistle in the distance made her grin, but she kept on pace with her eyes focused ahead. She was a stickler for being on time, and with thirty-seconds and more than half a block to go, she was going to be late.

The small coffee shop was super eclectic with mismatched furniture and abstract art all over the walls. Sharni glanced around the room with her eyes stopping on a brown-haired man wearing a red polo shirt. He had his back to the door, which she found odd.

"Excuse me, are you Joe?" she asked, walking over to the table.

"Hi, yes," he replied with a smile as he stood and waved for her to take her seat.

"I'm Sharni," she said, sitting and extending her hand.

"Nice to meet you. I wasn't sure what you'd want, but I figured you can't go wrong with an espresso."

Sharni smiled. "I have to agree with you."

"So, your ad said you were looking for a wedding date, am I right?"

"Well, it's a little more complicated than that. It's a destination wedding in another country. I'm looking for someone who can pretend to be my boyfriend for the entire week of the trip."

"I see." He nodded. "What week is it?"

"Next week. I'm leaving on Sunday, actually. It's sort of last minute," she said, scrunching her face.

"Oh ... I'm sorry I can't help you. Buster is having surgery on Wednesday, and Phoebe has anxiety. I can't leave her alone that long."

Sharni slowly nodded in confusion. "And Buster and Phoebe are ..."

"My cats. I also have Felix, Esmeralda, and Fuzzball." He smiled like a parent.

Sharni cleared her throat. "It's no problem. I completely understand. Thank you for meeting with me, and thanks for the coffee."

"It's my pleasure. I wish it could've worked out," he replied.

Sharni shook his hand again and hurried to the door, tossing her empty espresso cup in the trash on the way out. *This is a nightmare come to life.* She pulled her phone from her pocket and swiped to call her best friend as she headed back to her office down the block.

"So? Do you have a plus one?" Tracey answered.

"Hell no. I'd bet my paycheck he's a virgin who lives with his mom and a hundred cats."

Tracey laughed hysterically.

"It's not funny! You can meet the next one."

"How many more do you have?"

"I woke up with two notifications, but I haven't had time to check them. We had our first acquisition meeting this morning. I thought Chris was going to have a heart attack when the buyers mentioned a merger. He's pissed that I won't be here next week. I told him not to bother me unless the place was on fire. Who knows if I'll even have cell service."

"Those tech geeks wouldn't find their way out of a paper bag without you."

"Yep. Oh, get this, my mother called this morning. Apparently, I'm supposed to fly in on Sunday. They have events planned all week, and my guest and I need to be present and participate."

"Did she say it like that?"

"Yes. It's a good thing she left a voicemail. I might've flipped out on her. I have no idea how I'm going to get through next week, not to mention the complete stranger I'm bringing along."

"You'll get through it. Hopefully, there'll be cases of wine."

"At this point, I'd hit the hard liquor."

Tracey laughed. "You and liquor do not mix. Just don't drink tequila; you might wind up married too."

"Ha!" Sharni guffawed, opening the building door. "I'm about to lose you. I'm getting into the elevator."

"Don't give up!" Tracey said before ending the call.

Sharni checked herself in the mirror as the elevator doors closed and the box began its ascent up to the eighth floor. The jacket to her crimson-colored pantsuit was hanging on the back of her office chair, leaving her in a sleeveless black blouse that was tucked into her slacks. Classic black, open-toe stiletto heels gave her an additional four inches of height. Her dark locks hung just past her shoulders in loose, wavy spirals with quarter-sized platinum hoops peeking through.

"There you are!" Chris exclaimed, seeing the elevator open to their office.

"I stepped out for lunch."

"Where'd you go?"

"The coffee place down the road. Why?" she stated.

"That's not lunch. Come on, I'm headed over to that new sushi place to meet Alan Powell."

Sharni raised a brow. "I thought he wasn't interested."

"Change of heart, I guess. He just called and invited me to lunch. Go with me. If nothing else, we'll have a nice lunch on his dime."

Sharni shrugged and grabbed her suit jacket from her office.

*

Chris's Tesla reminded her of the movie *I, Robot*. She was waiting for it to take over control at any moment as she checked the two new notifications for the app. The first was WayneHasGains, a gym rat with biceps larger than her thighs. Sharni sighed and deleted his reply. The second was a dark-skinned guy named RomeoMan, who had acted in local theater and loved crashing weddings. Instead of scheduling a day and time to meet, Sharni messaged him back and asked if he was able to travel the following week from Sunday to Saturday or Sunday.

"I think this is it," Chris said, turning into the parking lot.

Sharni shoved her phone into her jacket pocket and got out before the valet drove off with the sewing machine sounding car.

"After you," Chris said, holding the door open.

A tall gentleman in a dark suit waved them over from the bar. "Sharni Dinjavi, how'd I know he'd bring you along," he said, giving her a polite half hug.

"No deal is ever done without me; you know that." She winked and smiled, immediately going into work mode.

He smiled. "Shall we head to our table?"

"Sure," Sharni and Chris said in unison.

"After you," Alan replied, waving for her to lead the way, mostly so he could admire her tight ass.

Sharni rolled her eyes as she followed the hostess to the quiet table in the back. The phone in her pocket vibrated as she took her seat. "Excuse me a second," she said as she checked the message from the app. RomeoMan had a show callback on Tuesday and Wednesday and wouldn't be able to travel at all during the week.

"Always working," Alan said with a quick smile as he ordered Saki for the table.

"Absolutely," Sharni muttered with a grin as she deleted the message and slid her phone back into her pocket. "Could be competition," she added with a raised brow.

"She's cutthroat, isn't she?" Alan chuckled.

Chris laughed and nodded in agreement; Sharni was sure his knees were knocking back and forth nervously under the table. The waitress filled three small cups with cold Saki.

"Most people toast at the end of a meeting as a form of celebration signifying an agreement or deal of some kind. However, I like to toast at the beginning and start each meeting off positively."

"I agree," Sharni said, holding up her cup.

"I do as well," Chris added, lifting his cup.

"Business is business, no hard feelings. We all win some and lose some," Alan toasted.

"To business," Sharni and Chris said simultaneously.

All three cups met in the center of the table, then everyone took a generous sip.

"Alright, let's get down to why we're here," Alan said.

# Chapter
# 3

Sharni's mother had called at four in the morning, forgetting L.A. was ten hours behind Greece, rambling on about everything that was happening and how she needed to be there for her sister and their family, which made her want to shred her passport. She loved her family dearly and would do anything for them, but they drove her absolutely nuts. Her mother was by far the worst with her nitpicking, guilt trips, and constant reminders of what was expected of her. After falling back asleep, she was awoken again by Chris just before sunup, wanting to discuss the meeting from the afternoon before. She reassured him and reminded him to be patient, before silencing her phone as the sun peaked through the vertical blinds, painting stripes across her bed. The thought of pulling the comforter over her head and closing her eyes sounded great, but she hadn't packed a single thing, and she was leaving in twenty-four hours with or without a plus one; that was still to be determined. With two mid-morning coffee dates planned, she hoped to have her dilemma solved sooner rather than later.

\*

With ten minutes to spare, Sharni walked into the coffee shop freshly showered and dressed casually in a hot pink tank top tucked into high-rise black shorts, with black wedge slide sandals on her feet. Her curls were wrapped up in a loose bun with a few wavy tendrils hanging around her face.

"Don't you look cute. Are those new?" Tracey asked, staring at the platinum bar earrings as Sharni slid into the stool across from her.

"Yeah, these are the ones I ordered from Tiffany two months ago."

"I remember. So, who are these two guys we're meeting?"

"The first, BlackJack, should be here in a few minutes. The other one, HelperJorge, should be here in half an hour. I don't know anything about either of them, other than they are both available to travel next week."

Tracey laughed. "Where do these men come up with these names?"

"No idea," Sharni muttered and shook her head. "I'm going to grab a coffee. Watch for a man who comes in looking around."

"This should be fun."

Sharni smiled a mouthful of white teeth as she sauntered over to the counter to pick up the order she'd placed earlier on the app. When she turned around, a nice-looking man was standing next to their table. She raised a brow and walked over with her hazelnut latte, but he left before she could say anything.

"Was that BlackJack?"

"Nope." Tracey shook her head. "He's an attorney with my firm."

"Can he take vacation next week?"

"He's an asshole. Plus, I'm sure his wife wouldn't be too happy."

"Figures," Sharni mumbled, sipping her coffee. "BlackJack's officially fifteen minutes late."

"What if he doesn't show?"

"The next one will be here in twenty-five minutes," Sharni replied, checking her phone. "So, what did that attorney want?"

"Your number."

"What?"

"I'm serious."

"Asshole," Sharni spat.

"Exactly." Tracey touched her cup to Sharni's. "Is your office going to fall apart with you out for the week?"

"Chris may have a stroke. He called me at six this morning to talk about a meeting we had at one yesterday afternoon."

Tracey chuckled. "He's like a windup toy."

"No kidding. If I don't get the ball rolling soon for this acquisition, he's going to make me crazy." Sharni shook her head. "Speaking of crazy, my damn mother called me at four!"

"This morning?"

"Yes!"

"What the hell?"

"That's exactly what I said after I made sure everyone was okay. Then, she proceeds to tell me how to wear my hair and makeup for the wedding and guilt trip me for not already being there because my sister and my family need me. Plus, this should be *my* wedding. I'm the oldest and it looks bad with my younger sister getting married first. Oh, and at least I'm bringing the person I've been dating because it would be even worse if I showed up alone."

"My God."

"She means well, but she's stuck in traditions handed down from generation to generation and old ways of thinking. Wealth and happiness mean nothing if I'm not married and having children like she did, as well as her mother and her grandmother, and so on." Sharni finished her coffee and tossed the cup in the trash. "I contemplated shredding my passport when I hung up with her."

Tracey guffawed and nearly snorted coffee through her nose. "Why not call her and say you and Joe broke up today. He was cheating on you."

Sharni raised a brow. "The cat dude?"

"Who's the cat dude?"

"Joe."

"What?" Tracey scrunched her face in confusion.

"You said tell my mother he and I broke up."

"Oh ..." Tracey laughed. "I used that name out of the blue."

Sharni grinned and shook her head. "And you're the one with the law degree."

Tracey shrugged and held her hands up.

"My mother would demand I bring him and dump him after, so it looked good for the family. I mean this isn't 1823 and the father of the bride has to offer his prized goat and two cows to get a wealthy boy to marry his daughter."

"What about the black sheep?" Tracey teased.

Sharni laughed.

"What time was the other guy supposed to be here? I don't even remember his ridiculous name?"

Sharni looked over at her phone. "An hour ago."

"Wow."

"I hate men," Sharni muttered. "Come on. Let's go shopping."

"Don't you need to pack?"

"My flight leaves in the morning. I'll pack later."

*

"I feel like Julia Roberts in *Pretty Woman*," Tracey said, swinging her bags and shaking her hips as they walked down Rodeo Drive.

Sharni flung her head back in laughter.

"Shake your ass. Maybe you'll find your plus one out here."

"Yeah, right!" Sharni laughed hysterically as they clumsily entered the Versace store. Their loudness echoed in the silent room like a bull in a China shop. A stiff man in a three-piece suit rushed over to them.

"May I help you ladies? Perhaps, what you're looking for is available online," he said, casually trying to turn them back to the door they'd just come through, causing Sharni and Tracey to guffaw.

As they were going back out the door, Tracey looked back at the old man. "Are you available next week? She's looking for a destination wedding date."

Sharni was about to pee herself, she was laughing so hard. She pulled Tracey out onto the sidewalk.

"I tried," Tracey said, wiping her tear-filled cheeks. "Could you imagine showing up with a guy your parents age?"

"My mother wouldn't care!" Sharni cried with laughter.

"Oh, my god my cheeks hurt!"

"Mine too! Come on, I've spent a months' worth of paychecks. Let's get the hell out of here," Sharni said, leading them back towards her dark purple BMW parked curbside further down the road. They tossed their bags in the backseat when they reached the car and got in. "I might as well delete this stupid app," she muttered, pulling her phone from her slim purse.

"Yeah, a lot of good that did."

Just as Sharni held her finger over the app to open the uninstall box, a notification popped up. "Seriously?"

"What?"

"I was trying to delete the damn app and just got a new reply to the ad," Sharni said as she swiped to open the reply. A black and white photo appeared with what looked like a magazine page filled with a young guy wearing dark slacks and a white dress shirt unbuttoned halfway down. The sleeves were rolled back to three-quarters, revealing tattoos on both forearms. The background was gray, and he was barefooted and sitting in a model-type pose. His short hair was brushed back and styled. Sharni had to force her eyes away from the picture to read the reply.

"Who is it this time, Rico Suave?" Tracey chuckled.

"No ... It's Alex."

"Who's Alex?" Tracey questioned.

"I don't know, but I'm going to find out," Sharni said, showing Tracey the picture. "His reply says he loves to travel and is a professional. He's been a print model and an actor."

"Girl, he is fine," Tracey said handing the phone back. "This is a professional photo. He definitely looks like a model. I know I've seen him before."

Sharni quickly replied asking if he was available to travel for the entire week, and if so, could they meet up this afternoon?

"What if he's unavailable next week?"

"Then, we'll move the fucking wedding date," Sharni muttered, waiting patiently for a notification to pop up with a new message.

Tracey snickered.

The phone screen lit up and Sharni caught a brief glimpse of the message before swiping to open it. "He's available! Hallelujah! He is working and suggested we meet at Noir Blanc around eight."

"Noir Blanc? Is that the new bar on Sunset?"

"Yeah, I think so," Sharni mumbled while replying to the message. She put her phone in the cupholder and started the car. "It looks like I have a date!"

"What are you going to wear? You might be bumping elbows with Leo DiCaprio."

Sharni laughed. "I seriously doubt it."

"Well, if you see Jamie Dornan, don't forget my phone number!"

"Will do," Sharni snickered, pulling out into the traffic as her brain began scrolling through mental images of her closet. Suddenly, Tracey smacked her arm, bringing her out of the fog. At first, Sharni thought she'd hit the car in front of her.

"Look!" Tracey yelled, pointing to the right.

Sharni followed her line of sight and noticed a large ad on the side of a city bus. The black and white image was of an androgynous woman in a sports bra and underwear. They were too far away to get a good look at the model's face, but it was the tattoos that stood out to Sharni the most. She had them on her upper arms, forearms, abdomen, and chest, as well as a few on her lower legs. They were almost erotic in the way they were done in pieces here and there, instead of her being fully covered, as if each one was meant to stand alone like artwork and her body was the canvas.

Sharni was still staring when the car behind them blew the horn.

"Oh, fuck off!" she grumbled, moving up about two car lengths in the heavy traffic.

"Damn she's sexy. I've never been with a woman, but I'd let her do whatever she wanted to me," Tracey murmured as the bus turned the corner, driving away.

"Yeah," Sharni mumbled, thinking about the model in the bus ad a little longer than she should have.

*

After dropping Tracey back at her car with a promise to call her later with all the details, Sharni headed home to get ready. It was already getting late, and the evening traffic was sure to be a nightmare of its own. Noir Blanc was an upscale tapas lounge in Hollywood. Sharni had only been there once, and it was for a charity benefit. She knew patrons weren't allowed in unless you were wearing white, black, or a combination of both, so she pulled a stark white mini skirt out of her closet and matched it to a black spaghetti strap top with a low-cut V embroidered with white lace along the edges. She tucked the blouse into the skirt and added a pair of platinum diamond hoop earrings, before finishing her look with a pair of black calf-high leather boots with a two-inch square heel. She let down the hair she'd been wearing up all day in a twisted bun and shook out her thick waves. She sprayed a little bit of detangler and ran her hands through the long dark strands that fell loosely around her shoulders. Her natural complexion was nearly flawless, allowing her to go without make-up other than a little eyeliner to amplify her dark eyes and light gloss on her lips.

# Chapter
# 4

Alex Mitchell stared into the mirror at her bare torso and the various tattoos on her natural beige skin. All were exquisitely done with black ink only and in a minimalist style, making them look almost like pencil sketches, with each having its own meaning or reason for becoming a piece of her body's artwork. Skin toned silicone pasties covered the nipples of her small breasts. She watched as the woman standing behind her with hot pink hair and a nose ring added some product to her short, dark brown hair and ran her hands through the strands to give it some texture. Then, she lined Alex's lower lids with a dark gel pencil to accentuate her caramel-colored eyes and added some finishing touches to her light makeup to intensify her strong jawline and high cheek bones.

"Good to go, babe," the pink-haired woman said, smiling at Alex in the mirror and patting her shoulder as she stepped over to her toolkit.

"You're a miracle worker, Tilly."

"Please. When my canvas looks as good as you, there isn't much for me to do."

Alex smiled and got up from the chair wearing nothing but pasties and a pair of black briefs with Indigo written on the waistband in white. Her modesty was long gone as she pulled on the last of her outfits for the photo shoot, a tailored black suit. She checked the fit of the ankle-length slacks and notched lapel jacket in the mirror, then pulled the front closed over her breasts while leaving it open to her bare torso with parts of some tattoos peeking out. Sexy club thumping music started playing as she walked over to the gray backdrop and took her position in front of the camera.

"Last one," the photographer said before giving her the signal. Alex immediately went into model mode, pushing everything in the room out of sight and out of mind. She was one with the camera and completely alone. "Seduce me, Alex," he urged with a thick Italian accent while snapping shot after shot.

She varied her facial expression and body position with each new pose, staring into the camera lens with slightly parted lips like a begging lover, then playfully biting her finger and grinning, before moving one hand up into her short hair and the other down her bare torso to the waistband of her pants, taunting the lens once more. If there was such a thing as making love to the camera, Alex did it ... over and over.

\*

When the shoot finally ended, the photographer walked over and hugged Alex. "Marvelous, as always," he said with a smile.

"Thank you, Dante." She grinned and stepped over to her agent, who was talking with the shoot manager. "Jean-Pierre, I think I'll wear this one out," she said, looking at herself in the nearby mirror.

"You are dressed to kill, my love," he replied with a smile and a kiss on her cheek.

Alex slipped her slim metal wallet into the left flapper pocket of her jacket, grabbed her keys from the counter, and walked away.

With her nearly ten-year career as a model coming to an end, she'd begun the transition to acting, following the path of other high-profile models. She was agentless, unable to sign with anyone until her modeling contract officially ended, and this left her to find work in the acting world on her own. Taking some acting classes, joining social media groups, and signing up with the Favor app had led her to her only acting gigs so far; she'd performed with the local theater and was a speaking extra in a low budget film. Nothing had manifested from either performance, which was why she was on her way to a meeting with a woman who'd placed an ad looking for an actor to pretend to be in a relationship with her and accompany her to a destination wedding. It wasn't Alex's ideal job, and the woman was more than likely looking for a male actor, but she was intrigued by the ad and needed as much acting experience as she could get. Modeling had paid her handsomely, but the $5,000 payday was more than she'd made in her two acting performances combined, so it was worth taking a shot.

"The face of Indigo for nearly ten years, and now you're moonlighting as an escort," she muttered, shaking her head as she got into her Jaguar.

# Chapter 5

Sharni didn't see anyone who resembled Alex when she walked into the lounge. Although the picture wasn't a close-up, she was sure she'd know him when she saw him. She chose a table facing the door and ordered a dirty martini. Her mind drifted back to that Indigo underwear ad on the side of the bus. There was something about the model's eyes and strong jawline that reminded her of the picture of Alex on the Favor app. Both were grayscale, leaving hair and eye color, tattoo features, and even skin tone to the imagination. Still, there were subtle similarities. "There's no way," she mumbled to herself, sipping her drink, and feeling the gin go straight to the empty pit of her stomach. *I need to eat before I get delirious.*

She waved her hand to get the waitress's attention, but all eyes were on the person who'd just come through the door. Sharni raked her eyes over the fitted suit, landing on the expanse of bare torso under the jacket and teasing tattoo lines as the person moved closer and closer. Her breath hitched, nearly choking her as the person stopped next to her high-top table. *Dear God, it's her!*

"I'm Alex," the mysterious person said, flashing a soft smile as she held her hand out. "I assume you're the person I'm here to meet."

Sharni was completely lost in the caramel swirls of the eyes locked onto hers and the fresh and crisp, aquatic scent of light cologne enticing her like a pheromone as their hands met. "Sharni ..." she mumbled, slightly nodding.

"I apologize. You were probably anticipating a man." Alex winked and sat down across from her. "While I'm not a man, I'm an actor. More importantly, I can be anything you want me to be."

Sharni was still trying to compose herself when the waitress walked over, setting a lowball glass half full of dark liquor and ice in front of Alex. "I'm pretty sure I saw you in your underwear ..." Sharni blurted.

Alex grinned. "Most of the world has."

"So, that *was* you ... on the side of the bus!"

"Buses, billboards, magazines, Time Square, you name it. I'm the worldwide face of Indigo," Alex replied, sipping her drink as she took in the beautifully exotic woman in front of her. "Why does a woman as beautiful as you, need to hire an escort?"

"That's not ... I don't need one of those!" Either the gin was going directly to Sharni's brain, or it was this mysterious, gorgeously androgynous woman in front of her, but her head was spinning.

"I wasn't referring to a call girl." Alex smiled.

"It's a long story," Sharni sighed. "So, you're a model?"

"I thought we'd covered that?" Alex sipped her drink once more and grinned.

"This is crazy," Sharni muttered, trying to avoid getting lost in the caramel swirls of the eyes staring back at her.

"What's crazy about it?"

"My sister is getting married next week in Greece and my family thinks I've been dating the same person for the past eight months. They're expecting me to show up with this person ... tomorrow."

"Oh." Alex nodded. "That sounds like a lot to unpack."

"I haven't packed anything, much less unpacked." Sharni ran her hand through her long curly locks frustratingly. "I've met with every person who answered my ad and showed up. This is it. You're the last one," she sighed.

"Let me guess, you need a boyfriend, not a girlfriend."

"Yes and no. When my mother and sister started planning the wedding, I mentioned I'd been dating someone and left it at that. As the months went by, I sort of forgot about it. Now, I'm expected to show up with this person. However, my family is Tamil, originally from Sri Lanka. Showing up with a woman would ... I don't even know what it would do."

Alex nodded.

Sharni locked eyes with her, swimming in the caramel swirls as warmth covered her body. Realizing it wasn't the alcohol, she quickly pulled her gaze away and cleared her throat.

"I'm sitting here with a stranger who placed an ad for a fake boyfriend to accompany her to a wedding in another country. I have to give it to you. That's pretty bold."

"Bold or insane? And it was my best friend's idea." Sharni sipped the last of her drink and slid the glass to the side. "Why *did* you answer if you knew I was looking for a man?"

"I guess Dove Cameron said it best. I can be a better boyfriend than him," Alex said with a smirk and a wink.

"You're very confident," Sharni replied with a raised brow.

"You said it yourself, there are photos of me in my underwear plastered all over. I certainly can't be modest."

"If you're this big-time model, why are you answering Favor ads?"

"I've been doing some acting in the last few months and that app is how I found the lead for my gigs," Alex replied, finishing her drink.

Sharni nodded.

"Which brings me to why I actually answered your ad. It sounded like a great way to gain more acting experience on multiple levels."

"What have you done so far?"

"I was in a show for the local theater that ran for four weeks, and a low budget film."

"What makes you think you can convince my family, who has a very different way of thinking about pretty much everything, that you and I are in love and have been dating for several months?"

Alex looked into her beautiful dark brown eyes. "It's simple. We can pretend to like or dislike each other, but chemistry is a very real thing. You either have it or you don't."

"And according to you, we have it?"

"I'd hope so. Otherwise, it would be an epic failure."

Sharni laughed. "I can't believe I'm saying this, but are you free for the next eight days?"

Alex nodded.

"I'm sure your passport has more stamps than mine," Sharni laughed, causing Alex to smile at her. "Okay, before I come to my senses and change my mind, our flight leaves tomorrow morning from LAX. I'll be at the Emirates counter at five."

"I'll be there," Alex replied with a soft smile.

# Chapter 6

"This is crazy," Alex muttered, looking through her closet. She and Sharni had parted ways sometime after ten without so much as exchanging last names or phone numbers. "You're going to Greece with a beautiful woman on your arm. Quit bitching," she told herself and began packing. She'd been to Europe multiple times and figured casual chic with a touch of class would be a good look. She owned every collection and piece that she'd ever modeled and was highly encouraged to wear them and promote the brand she worked for, leaving her with two closets full of clothes, shoes, hats, and jackets. She'd also been given cologne and perfume from the fragrance lines she'd promoted over the years. She kept the things she would wear again; everything else went to charity and friends.

After packing enough clothes and toiletries to last ten days, she closed her suitcase. She slipped her slim metal wallet, passport, and phone charger into the outer pocket before texting Jean-Pierre.

*Sorry it's so late. I'm headed to Greece for a little last-minute R&R. I'll be back next weekend. And before you text me back, I know. Wear sunscreen! Seriously though, if you haven't heard from me by next Monday, send a search party.*

"What are we talking about?" Tracey said, trying to understand what her best friend was going on and on about over the phone at midnight.

"I'm trying to figure out what to pack," Sharni said. "I've never been to Greece. I'm sure she has ..." she mumbled, pulling various pieces of clothing from her closet.

"What? Who?"

"Alex," Sharni said, trying to put outfits together on her bed.

"Wait, so it worked out! You found a plus one!" Tracey exclaimed. "Is this why I didn't hear from you for hours? What does he look like? He's a model, isn't he? I knew that was a professional photo."

Sharni sat on the ottoman at the foot of her bed to gather her thoughts. "Definitely a model. Do you remember that bus we saw earlier today with the underwear ad on the side?"

"Yeah. I'm not a lesbian but damn it's hard to forget that body."

"That's Alex."

"What? But ... no. Are you serious?"

"As a fucking heart attack. You should see her in person."

"Holy shit!" Tracey squealed, slightly stunned. "Wait, are you taking her with you?!"

"Yep."

"Whoa. First, I'm confused. Since when are you into women? Second, damn girl. Third, your mother is going to have a stroke."

Sharni laughed. "I'm hoping this makes my mother let me live my own life, my way. Obviously dating men has gotten nowhere. Otherwise, I'd have an actual boyfriend to take with me. Besides, it's not real. We won't be having sex or anything like that. We'll just hang out together for a week."

"Hang out as a couple who has been dating for months. You'll have to be affectionate."

"I'm affectionate with you. Holding hands or hugging here and there will be nothing. The hard part is getting to know enough about each other to make them believe we've been together ... I guess it would be eight months by now."

"Well, you have a sixteen-hour flight. Make the best of it, and maybe make out with her so it's not a complete shock."

Sharni laughed. "I'm starting to think you might be a little more lez than you think."

Tracey guffawed. "Says the woman taking her fake girlfriend to a sexy destination wedding for a week."

"Fake is the keyword here."

"Uh huh. Send me a pic when you land ... make sure she's in it! I can't believe you're taking the hot underwear model to Greece with you as your fake girlfriend to meet your family. Even saying it sounds insane. Now, I really wish I was going."

Sharni laughed. "Hopefully, my family doesn't pay attention to print and digital ads. Could you imagine if one of them recognized her?"

Tracey cackled like a hyena, causing Sharni to laugh with her.

"I think I'm delirious at this point. I still need to finish packing and be at the airport in four and a half hours."

"I love you. Travel safe and have loads of fun ... with Alex."

Sharni smiled and shook her head. "Love you too. I'll be in touch during the week," she said before hanging up. She tossed her phone into the clothes scattered around her bed and went to work putting her outfits together. By the time she'd finished, she had enough clothes for a month crammed into her suitcase and it was well past one in the morning.

"I'm going to be a zombie. Shoot me now," she mumbled, flopping down onto her now empty bed.

# Chapter
# 7

The soft jazz playing in the Uber was lulling Sharni back to sleep as they drove along the freeway towards the airport. "Excuse me, could you turn on something a little more upbeat?" she asked.

"Oh, sure. Most people don't want anything exciting this early." The purple-haired girl smiled.

"I need to stay awake, so knock your socks off," Sharni replied, scrolling through the news on her phone.

Suddenly, the music switched to *River* by Miley Cyrus. Sharni found herself tapping her foot along to the beat and grinning with a raised brow at the risqué lyrics. The playlist quickly changed to *Boyfriend* by Dove Cameron and Sharni dropped her phone.

"Shit," she mumbled, bending down to try and find it in the dark as the song played. The bold lyrics conjured the image of Alex in the bar, scantily dressed in her designer suit. Sharni fought to shake the vision from her head as she felt around the floorboard. Suddenly, the car lurched to a stop at the arrival terminal. She swung the door open and immediately saw the phone when the interior lights illuminated. She snatched it up and shoved it into the outer pocket of her suitcase before getting out of the car.

\*

Alex stood off to the side, dressed casually monochromatic in dark gray chinos and a light gray linen button down, with black loafers and a matching belt that had a platinum buckle. Her sleeves were rolled back to the elbows revealing her tattoos on both forearms, and the top three buttons of her shirt were undone and spread open, exposing the edges of her collarbone tattoos and the top of the tattoo in the center of her chest. She looked up from her phone in time to see Sharni striding towards her in dark gray chino shorts with a fitted white top tucked into them, a black blazer with the sleeves rolled back, and pointed toe shoes with a low heel. Her long dark curls were bouncing loosely over one shoulder. Alex couldn't take her eyes off the slim, golden-tanned legs coming towards her, until she looked up and caught the smile and what seemed to be a sigh of relief when Sharni found her in the crowd. *My god, she's beautiful. Jesus, Moses, Jehovah ... whoever you are, give me the strength to get through this week.*

"You're here," Sharni said, stopping in front of her with a rather large suitcase. The couple inches of heel on her shoes put her at eye level with Alex.

"You look tired," Alex said, studying the dark eyes staring back at her.

"I was up most of the night packing. How are you not half asleep, too?" Sharni replied.

Alex nodded towards her smaller suitcase. "Didn't take me all night," she muttered.

Sharni rolled her eyes and Alex reached out, grabbing her hand. Sharni pulled back in surprise, both at the gesture and the softness of her hand.

"Are you sure you want to do this?" Alex questioned softly. "If you can't hold my hand, how are you going to convince your family that we've been dating for several months?"

Sharni took a deep breath and sighed audibly. "This is new to me. I have to get used to it ... to you," she said, meeting the gaze of Alex's enticing eyes.

"My being another woman or a stranger?"

"We literally just met hours ago, I haven't dated in what feels like forever, and now I have to pretend to be in love with you. That's a lot to take in."

"The line's moving. It's now or never," Alex said.

Sharni grabbed her hand. "Come on."

Alex grinned and went along with her.

*

Sharni settled in next to the window with Alex beside her in the aisle seat. The same crisp cologne she'd smelled the night before lingered in the air, causing her to glance at the woman next to her.

"Everything okay?" Alex asked, studying her eyes.

"Yeah." Sharni nodded. "I hate long flights," she muttered, turning her head towards the window, watching the plane push back.

"They don't bother me. I guess I've gotten used to them over the years," Alex said as the flight attendants stepped into the aisle and began the safety briefing.

"How often do you travel?"

"It depends on the month and the collection. I'm a print model, so my work is done in the studio and on location. I've been all over the world, but never stayed anywhere longer than a couple of days. We fly in, get the shot, and fly right back out."

"Do you model underwear only or ..."

"Whatever Indigo is advertising. The brand is a lot like Calvin Klein. They started in underwear; that'll always be their backbone. They also have multiple clothing, fragrance, and accessory lines. I've been involved in all of it over the years."

"Ten, right?"

Alex nodded. "Next month. I signed my contract with Indigo when I was eighteen. Everything changed for me overnight and before long, what was supposed to be two years wound up being a decade."

"Why are you quitting? It sounds like you enjoy it."

"It wasn't my choice. My contract hasn't been renewed, which is a fancy way of saying I'm aging out." Alex shrugged. "That's why I turned to acting. I know a few models who have made the career change successfully."

"Seriously? At twenty-eight you're too old to model?"

"Yep."

"Wow." Sharni shook her head.

"What made you decide to do it in the first place?"

"I needed a way to pay for college," Alex said with a shrug, then she sighed. "It was my ticket out." Dark eyes met hers in the dimly lit cabin.

"Out of where?"

Alex turned her head, pulling her eyes away.

"You don't have to talk about it," Sharni said softly.

"It's fine. I'm not used to talking about myself."

"You're supposed to be acting, so technically you could make up an elaborate story."

Alex leaned her head back against the seat and rolled it towards her, mimicking Sharni's position. "I come from a royal family, and it wasn't for me, so I left and became a model." She smiled.

Sharni smirked. "So, you're a princess?"

"What do you want me to be? You're writing this story."

Grinning, Sharni shook her head and turned her eyes to the window and the blue sky passing by.

"I was adopted by my maternal grandparents when I was four. We'd never met. My mother was estranged from them after getting pregnant with me. I was born in California, which is where we were living when she died in a car accident. Her parents took me in and moved me to Utah. The next fourteen years were miserable. They're extremely religious, to the point of it being cult-like. They refused to talk about my mother. I was too little to understand and keep anything of my mother's, including photos, before they threw her stuff in the trash. Just like her, I left and never looked back," Alex sighed. "I guess I'm a little like Cinderella." She smiled, meeting Sharni's eyes when she turned back towards her.

"Oh, Alex. I'm sorry. You didn't have to tell me."

"It's fine. I've moved on. Look at me now. I'm in a fake relationship with a beautiful woman and about to spend a week in Greece." She grinned.

Sharni rolled her eyes and laughed.

"What about you? I don't even know your last name."

"I don't know yours either."

"Mitchell. Alex Nicole Mitchell." She grinned. "Your turn."

"Sharni Dinjavi," she replied. "I'm thirty-two and vice president of a solar energy start-up. I have an MBA from UCLA."

"Wow. That's impressive."

"Thanks. So, my family is Tamil. We're originally from Sri Lanka. Our grandparents fled with a large group to the UK before emigrating to Canada, where my parents were both born. Then they finally made it to the US, where they all became citizens. My parents had me and my sister when they were finishing medical school. We were both born in Boston."

"That's crazy."

"Yeah."

"So, they're both doctors?"

"Yep. My sister, too." Sharni nodded. "As is her soon to be husband."

"I sense some resentment."

Sharni shook her head. "Not from me, but yes. I left medical school to go to business school in my second year. Since then, I've taken multiple start-ups and built them into companies that sold for millions, but it doesn't compare to being a doctor ... in their eyes. I'm also the oldest and unmarried, which is frowned upon."

"Do you want to get married, one day?"

"Sure. I think most girls want that, but I haven't met the right person and I've been busy building my career. What about you?"

"It's just me, so I've definitely thought of getting married and creating my own family one day."

Sharni's heart broke at the sentiment. Her family drove her crazy, but she loved them and couldn't imagine not having them in her life.

"Do they all practice together? Your family," Alex asked.

"No. My mother is a dermatologist, my father is a neurologist, and Neesa, that's my sister, she's a pediatrician, and your age. She graduated high school and college with her BS degree at the same time, which allowed her to complete medical school and her residency by the time she was twenty-five. She joined Doctors Without Borders after residency; that's where she met her fiancé."

"Wow. Talk about dedication."

"She had it all planned out by the time she was twelve. Me on the other hand ..." Sharni shook her head. "I wasn't sure, but I knew I had to go to medical school. That was a given. The first year of college was fine, but by the second year, I hated every minute of it. Biology wasn't for me. A friend on campus was talking about start-ups and I sort of migrated towards the idea of taking nothing and building it into something big. I thought my parents were going to disown me when I told them I'd changed my major. I know they're still disappointed, no matter how much money I make, or how many magazines write articles on the companies I've worked with."

"No one else can live your life. Your family may try to control the direction, but at the end of the day, it's your life and yours alone."

"I agree." Sharni smiled. "I do what I want, how I want, and when I want. It's made me the black sheep, but I love my life. I wouldn't change it."

"What's it going to be like showing up with me?"

Sharni laughed. "I honestly don't know." She shook her head. "My mother may have a coronary."

"Then, why do it?"

"Because I'm tired of the constant put downs. I'm not married. I'm not a doctor. I don't live in Boston. I don't let my Tamil culture dictate everything I do. I'm happy. I have a great life. Maybe this will open my mother's eyes and she'll see that," she sighed, pursing her lips.

Alex met her eyes and smiled softly. "Tell me about *you*."

"I don't know where to start." Sharni rolled her head to the side and stared out the window once more.

"How about what inspires you?"

"I don't know. Success, a challenge, competition, freedom. What about you?"

"I'm extremely competitive, but I'm inspired by my work. At first, I was shy about it, never talked about my job or what it was like to be this face of a brand, plastered all over everything. Over the years I learned to embrace it. I'm driven by watching that creativity come to life," Alex replied. "What's your favorite time of day?"

"Sunset. I think it's romantic and magical. I love the sun and the water. I'm a summer baby for sure." She smiled.

"I like sunset, too."

"What's your favorite food?" Sharni asked.

"I think it depends on where I am. I like to try the cuisine of different countries and cultures. You?"

"I like a lot of different things, but I'd take a pastry over just about anything."

"Cream or chocolate filled?"

"Cream for sure," Sharni replied, flashing a bright smile. "What about movies or TV shows?"

"Hmm ... I'm not much of a TV person. I love going to the theater though. I've seen quite a few plays, musicals, and ballets. I will say I've seen all the 007 movies."

"I'm partial to the theater myself. I also like comedies. I hate reality TV. My best friend, Tracey, she loves the Bachelor and Bachelorette and drives me crazy with them. I'd rather watch paint dry."

Alex laughed. "What about relationships?"

"My love life has been pretty nonexistent lately. The last relationship I had was over a year ago and it barely lasted two months."

"Have you only dated guys?"

Sharni nodded. "I did have a closeted relationship with a girl in college that lasted a couple months."

Alex raised a brow in surprise. "Do tell."

Sharni chuckled. "It's not as exciting as it sounds. We were just two friends that sort of experimented together for a bit. What about you?"

"I wasn't allowed to date until I left home, but I've only ever dated women. Being in the fashion world you see a lot of gay men, bisexual women, and so on. Everyone is comfortable in their skin. I learned a lot about myself and the world pretty quickly. I think Indigo has used gender fluid campaigns over the years because they like the mystique. I know they've marketed me as such and I'm fine with it. Let's be honest, sex sells. And what's sexier than a woman in a fitted suit or wearing nothing but underwear and a men's button-down dress shirt that's open and barely covering her breasts?"

"That suit you were in last night was certainly something." Sharni grinned.

"I'd just finished my shoot for the day. That was the last piece from the collection, so I kept it on and left as soon as we were finished."

"It definitely turned a few heads."

"Was yours one of them?"

"I'm pretty sure I had to pick my jaw up from the table."

Alex laughed.

"Seriously, you have to know earlier in the day, Tracey and I were shopping on Rodeo Drive and saw a city bus go by with a huge picture on the side of you in underwear. Then, you walked into the bar and sat down at my table. I was tongue tied."

Alex smiled brightly. "So, you've seen me in my underwear."

"As you put it, so has most of the world."

"I know. I'm teasing."

"Does it bother you?"

"The first time I saw a picture like that out in public I nearly had a panic attack, but our ads are tastefully done. To be honest, I've done so many, I don't even notice them anymore."

"Do people recognize you?"

"Not often. Indigo has launch and wrap parties for different campaigns and they are usually at places like Noir Blanc, so the employees there see me and know who I am, but out on the street, it's pretty rare. I think most people are more taken by celebrities."

Sharni nodded.

"We should probably get a feel for what we're comfortable with. How are you with PDA?"

"If someone has to use the phrase 'get a room' that's too much. Hand holding, hugging, those are innocent gestures. I'm sure we'll have to kiss eventually; I mean we're supposed to have been dating for about eight months at this point. I guess whatever feels natural in the moment, you know what I mean?"

"Yeah, I agree," Alex said as the plane started the slow descent into Newark for their hour-long layover.

# Chapter 8

"Are you hungry?" Sharni asked as they stepped into the terminal and began looking for the screen to find the gate for their next flight.

"Starving," Alex replied. "And, I have to pee."

"Oh, me too."

Alex grabbed her hand, interlacing their fingers as she led them through the massive crowd towards the signs for food and restrooms. Sharni didn't have time to think about the hand holding hers as she was whisked away.

"Did you happen to catch the gate?" Sharni asked over the noise.

"Yeah, D12. We came in at A4. We leave in 56 minutes."

"Great," Sharni muttered, careful not to let go of the hand leading her.

Alex pulled Sharni to a stop next to a wall with a large advertisement on a digital screen. "Look, I'm not in my underwear," she teased, posing next to the picture of herself wearing a white blouse and slacks with nothing under them and soaking wet with a wave crashing against her back. The image was done tastefully without showing her breasts under the clothing clinging to her skin.

"You might as well be naked." Sharni laughed.

Alex smiled and shook her head.

"What is the ad even for?"

"Cologne," Alex said, pulling her close to smell the fragrance on her neck.

"Oh ..." Sharni mumbled, picking up the same captivating scent from the night before in the lounge.

"It's called Wet," Alex said, catching her eyes for a split second, ignoring the onlookers gawking at them, before tugging her away to keep moving towards the food court.

\*

After a quick bathroom stop, Alex and Sharni were able to grab a coffee and pastry from the food court and rush to their gate in time to board the plane. Once again, they were seated on the side with Sharni near the window and Alex in the aisle seat.

"So, what is it exactly that you do? I know you said you were the VP of a solar energy start-up, but what does your day look like?" Alex asked as she sipped her coffee and unwrapped her raspberry and cheese Danish.

Sharni smiled apologetically with her cheeks full of food after having just bitten into her blueberry scone.

"I'm sorry," Alex chuckled.

"I should be the one apologizing for eating like a rabid baboon." Sharni shook her head and sipped her coffee. "Anyhow, basically I get involved with the start-up companies in the very beginning, sort of like when you have a tech guru who forms a company because he has this great idea but isn't quite sure how to get it off the ground. My job is to pull in resources and funding in the beginning, then market the company to the highest bidder once it takes off. So, say you have this idea for a lawn mower that works like a Roomba. It comes out of a charging base, mows your yard, goes back into the base when it's finished. It's programmed to do this twice a week, understands when it is raining and adjusts its schedule, and is fully powered by solar energy. You've built a few prototypes and have enough personal funding to form a company. This is where I come in and take what you have and turn it into a company worth millions of dollars. Together, we sell to the highest bidder and walk away. I make a profit off the sale of the company."

"That's interesting. How many companies have you done this with?"

"I'm currently on my sixth. I've made a lot of connections over the years, which has helped tremendously."

"Are they always solar related?"

"Efficiency is what drives people and solar energy is the future. If you're not inventing concepts based on both of those variables, you're already years behind your competition. When I graduated with my MBA, my thesis was on the future of solar technology and how efficiency will drive the business model."

"I'm impressed. All I do is stand in front of a camera."

Sharni smiled. "I'm pretty sure you do a bit more than that."

"I wear the clothes and cologne and make sure I'm seen schmoozing with people. I go to the fashion shows and fashion weeks all over the world, but mostly I pose in front of a camera."

"See, you're the face of the brand. You said it yourself."

Alex grinned and shook her head. "Okay, change of subject. What do you drive?"

Sharni went to answer, but Alex cut her off.

"Wait, let me guess ... a Tesla or some other EV."

Sharni chuckled and shook her head. "BMW and it's not an EV. I haven't found one I like, otherwise I might make the switch. Let me guess, you drive a Porsche."

"Jaguar." Alex grinned. "I did an ad a couple of years ago that was a collaboration with Indigo and Jaguar. The shoot was done with a Jaguar F-Type, and I fell in love with the car."

"Nice ride."

"Thanks."

"So, what's your favorite color?" Alex asked.

"Purple."

"Let me guess, your beamer is purple, isn't it?" Alex laughed.

"How'd you know?" Sharni giggled. "Yours is black."

"Favorite color or car?" Alex questioned.

"Both."

"My car is all black inside and out, wheels included. However, my favorite color is blue."

"Hmm ... when is your birthday?" Sharni asked.

"February fifth. You?"

"June fourteenth."

Alex leaned her seatback and rolled her head to the side, smiling when she saw Sharni mimicking her position and looking back at her. "What are some things that are absolute deal breakers for you? Or things you can't stand?"

"In a relationship or otherwise?"

Alex shrugged. "Both."

"Untrustworthy people for sure. Immaturity is definitely a deal breaker. What about you?"

"I agree with both of those. I really don't like people who chew with their mouth open or talk over you constantly. Also, unreliable people. That's a huge pet peeve of mine."

"Oh, yeah. That's a good one, too. Also, don't take my food. I'll share or let you try it, but don't assume you can just jab your fork onto my plate without permission."

Alex guffawed. "I hate that! If you wanted to try it, you should've ordered it. Now, if we agree to share, then go for it."

"Exactly!" Sharni exclaimed. She watched Alex reach up to scratch her ear, and her eyes went straight to the tattoos on her arm. Instinctively, she reached out, running her fingers over the markings when Alex put her arm back down. "How many tattoos do you have?"

Alex smiled, gazing at the fingers gently tracing the ink on her skin. "Oh, I don't know. I've lost count. Each one was done for a different reason. They all have their own meaning for me. I look at my body like a canvas, telling the story of my life." She shrugged. "I never wanted to be covered with them, which is why none of them connect."

"Interesting," Sharni said, meeting her eyes as she removed her hand.

"Do you have any?"

She shook her head. "I used to want one when I was younger, but I never did it."

"We should probably come up with our love story," Alex murmured, still fixated on the dark eyes looking back at her.

"They won't care."

"Are you sure about that? Even if they see you in love and happy with someone?"

Sharni shrugged. "What would you say if they asked?"

"That I walked into a lounge to grab a drink with a friend, and you were there sitting at a table alone, waiting for a friend. With one look you took my breath away. I had no choice but to walk over and introduce myself."

Sharni smiled.

"We canceled on our friends and spent the rest of the night talking."

"I like that."

"On our first date we took a walk and got caught in the rain. We laughed and danced in the rain like kids. I pulled you against me and kissed you as water ran off our faces."

"Damn," Sharni murmured.

"I knew I was in love with you early on, but you said it first."

"Oh, really?" Sharni raised a brow and grinned.

"We'd had a petty disagreement over something mundane. Instead of continuing the argument or walking away to cool off, I pulled you against me and lay back on the couch because I'd rather make love with you than fight. You straddled my lap, forgetting all about our argument, looked me in the eyes and said, 'I love you,' before bending down and kissing me."

Sharni bit her lower lip between her teeth. "You sure pull me against you a lot."

Alex grinned. "You like it."

Sharni smiled and rolled her eyes. "You've certainly thought it all out."

"I feel like we'd have a very passionate relationship with a deep connection and great chemistry. We'd fall fast and hard."

"You think so?"

Alex nodded. "I don't think either of us would have a choice. It would be unlike anything we'd felt before ... with anyone. At least, that's how I see it. Feel free to make any changes, or leave it to mystery, if you choose. It's your story."

"I like what you've created. It's a beautiful love story," Sharni said softly, still gazing at the caramel swirls in her eyes as she placed her hand on Alex's and linked their fingers together.

Alex smiled tenderly.

"I still don't think my pretentious family will think twice about it, much less ask."

"Well, it's there if we need it." Alex squeezed her hand. "And I'm there if you need me."

"Thanks." Sharni smiled.

"Pardon my interruption," the flight attendant said, squatting down in the aisle beside Alex; Sharni automatically let go of her hand. "I'd like to know your dinner order for tonight. We have a vegetable stir-fry option or chicken with penne pasta."

"Chicken and pasta," they said simultaneously.

The flight attendant smiled and checked the menu list for their seat numbers. "Also, may I just say you are the cutest couple. Are you going to Greece for vacation?"

"Wedding, actually," Alex answered.

"Oh, wow. You're getting married! That's so romantic!" she squealed as she stood up and walked away.

Alex looked at Sharni and they both laughed.

"We went from not knowing each other twenty-four hours ago to dating for eight months, and now we're getting married." Sharni giggled and shook her head.

"Time flies when you're having fun."

"Yeah, I'd say so."

"Here you are, ladies, compliments of Emirates. Congratulations!" the flight attendant said, appearing with two glasses of champagne.

"Thank you," they both replied with smiles as they took the glasses.

"To us, babe," Alex said.

Sharni laughed and tapped her plastic glass against Alex's.

# Chapter
# 9

Sometime in the night Alex woke up with Sharni curled beside her with her head on Alex's shoulder. A thin airline blanket was draped casually over them. She hadn't remembered falling asleep and by the stiffness in her back, she'd been stuck in one position for quite a while. She needed to get out of that airplane seat and stretch out, but Sharni was too peaceful to move.

At first, Alex thought she'd made a huge mistake by agreeing to this craziness. Now, she couldn't imagine not doing it. There was something about Sharni Dinjavi that intrigued her, stirring something unfamiliar. She rolled her head to the side, inhaling the floral scent of the dark curls resting on her shoulder. *You're working. This is a job you're getting paid for. Don't forget that.* She chastised herself, shaking away the thoughts of the beautiful woman lying against her when the flight attendant appeared in the aisle.

"Can I get you anything?" the woman asked quietly.

"Coffee."

She smiled and nodded towards Sharni. "Anything for her?"

"Do you have any pastries?"

"I believe so. I'll see what I can find."

"Thanks."

"No worries. I just ... you two give me so much hope," she said with another smile before walking away.

Graysen Morgen

"If you only knew," she whispered.

\*

Sharni cracked her eyes open, glancing around the dimly lit plane cabin, slowly realizing she was lying against Alex when she felt the subtle rise and fall of her shoulder as she breathed. She casually pulled herself back to her seat, slowly turning her gaze to the caramel eyes staring back at her.

"Good morning," Alex said softly.

"I'm sorry for using you as a pillow," Sharni replied, smiling sheepishly, and stifling a yawn.

Alex grinned. "It's fine."

"Are these for me?" she asked, turning back towards the coffee and pastry on the tray table.

"Yes. I ate about a half hour ago," Alex said between stretches as she carefully stood. Her body was stiff and sore and in need of a massage. "We should be landing in about two hours."

"Great," Sharni muttered after a long sip of coffee. "I didn't think to bring a carry-on bag with a change of clothes and toiletries."

"I didn't either because I'm used to getting off a private plane and being shuttled to a shoot location."

"Your clothes aren't even wrinkled," Sharni teased. "How do you wake up looking like a ..."

"Model?" Alex laughed.

"Yes!" Sharni exclaimed, shaking her head. "Meanwhile, I could use a hairbrush, a change of clothes, some moisturizer, and most definitely a toothbrush."

Alex shrugged and smiled as she sat back down. "So, what's the plan when we land?"

Sharni finished her pastry and sipped the last of her coffee. "My sister and her fiancé are supposed to be at the airport to get us."

"When did your family get here?"

"My sister's fiancé is from here, so his family is all here. He and my sister travel all over working with Doctors Without Borders and call a few places home. My parents were part of the wedding planning, so they came over about a week ago. They live in the Boston area."

"I see," Alex said, buckling her seatbelt. "So, is there anything I need to know that you haven't told me? Any last-minute details?"

"Like what?"

Alex shrugged. "Your uncle was a serial killer, or you have a crazy ex-boyfriend who might try to kill me."

"What!" Sharni guffawed. "Um ... no. None of the above. What about you? If my family Googles you, are they going to find a sex tape or a psycho ex-girlfriend?"

"Most definitely not," Alex laughed, shaking her head.

"We're good then."

Alex gave her a thumbs up.

*

The plane landed effortlessly and taxied to the gate. Alex and Sharni disembarked with the rest of the passengers and made their way towards the signs for baggage claim. As they started down the escalator, Sharni saw her sister standing off to the side with a man, smiling and laughing.

"Here we go," she said, grabbing Alex's hand.

"Are they here?" Alex asked, searching the people milling about until her eyes landed on a young woman with the same exotic bronze skin tone and dark hair as Sharni, except her long locks were much straighter. The man next to her had dark brown hair and a cheeky smile with a slight five o'clock shadow on his jaw. He was casually dressed in jeans and a gray button down with the sleeves rolled back, and she was wearing white slacks and a pink blouse.

Before Sharni could answer, they reached the bottom of the escalator and stepped off right in front of her sister and soon to be brother-in-law.

"You made it!" her sister exclaimed, wrapping her arms around Sharni.

"Longest plane ride ever," Sharni joked. "Neesa, this is Alex. Alex, my little sister, Doctor Neesa Dinjavi."

Neesa took in the person standing with her sister, holding her hand. Her brows shot up into her hairline when she realized Alex was not only a woman, but a woman with stunning features and the most gorgeous eyes.

"It's nice to meet you," Alex said, holding out her free hand, which Neesa accepted in a slow, confusing shake.

"Max, it's good to see you again," Sharni said, half hugging him.

"Oh, you as well," he replied.

"I'm sorry," Neesa muttered. "I'm still trying to wrap my head around this. Forgive my manners. Alex, this is my fiancé Doctor Maximos Papadakis."

"Just call me Max." He smiled, shaking Alex's hand.

"Now that that's all settled, we need to get our bags and head over to the hotel. I'm sure we're both dying for a shower and a change of clothes," Sharni said.

"All of the family is staying at our estate in the countryside. That's where the wedding is taking place. It's about an hour's drive. You'll love it. The massive stone mansion has been in my family for four generations, including my brother and me. It sits on about three hundred acres near a hillside cliff and overlooks the rolling hills of the vineyard, orchard, and olive trees."

"Wow," Alex replied.

"It's very enchanting, especially at night when it's all lit up," Neesa beamed.

"Can't wait to see it." Sharni smiled, grabbing her suitcase as it went around the conveyor belt. Alex quickly grabbed hers as well.

"Please, let me get those," Max said, taking their bags before either woman could say anything. "So, what is it that you do, Alex? I'm afraid I haven't heard much about you."

"I'd say the same thing," Neesa added, looking at her sister.

"I'm a model."

"Like on the runway at fashion week?" Neesa questioned.

"No. I do print work. Mostly magazine ads and things like that."

"She's the face of Indigo. If you see one of their ads in a magazine, on a billboard, Times Square, the side of a bus, you name it, she's the model in the picture," Sharni said, smiling at Alex, who grinned and shook her head.

"Wow! That's impressive."

"Thank you, but I hear the two of you are doctors who travel around the world doing humanitarian work. That's extraordinary."

"Aww, thanks. So many people in the world are suffering and have nowhere near the resources we have. This was just us doing our part," Neesa replied.

"We've actually taken time away to plan the wedding and so on. I'm not sure we'll be going back after. It may be time for us to settle down and start a practice or something somewhere," Max stated.

"Are you thinking Greece or the States?" Sharni asked.

"Not sure." Neesa shrugged.

When they reached the small SUV Max stowed the bags in the back and Neesa encouraged Alex to ride up front with him. Everyone got into the vehicle and Neesa immediately grabbed her sister's arm and pointed to the seatback in front of her, deadpanning her with a stare.

"When were you going to tell me that you were dating a woman?" she whispered. "I mean, I see the appeal. She's very attractive."

Sharni shrugged and grinned.

"Our mother is going to flip out. I'm pretty sure I'm still in shock."

"Neesa, I'm thirty-two years old. I'm allowed to date whomever I choose whether our parents approve or not. Alex and I fell in love. She's ..." Sharni smiled. "She's amazing."

"You must really love her to bring her here ... now."

Sharni nodded. "You'll like her once you get to know her."

"I already do because she's here with you. I know anyone you allow into your life is special," Neesa said, squeezing her sister's hand. "I've missed you."

"I've missed you, too."

"This is so exciting. We have so much planned for the week," Neesa squealed like a little kid. "Wait until you meet Max's family. They're so different. His parents are so kind, and his brother is sweet. His grandmother is wonderful."

Sharni smiled. It warmed her to see how happy her sister was.

"So, I'm dying to hear how this all happened," Neesa said, waving her hand from her sister to the back of Alex's seat.

Sharni smiled. "Completely by surprise. I was meeting Tracey for a drink when Alex walked in and took my breath away. I couldn't take my eyes off her. Our eyes locked when she went to walk by, and she stopped and introduced herself. She'd been there to meet a friend as well. We quickly ditched them both and spent the rest of the night talking about anything and everything." Sharni's gaze shifted from her sister to Alex as she continued. "We went for a walk on our first date and got caught in the rain. We were soaked to the bone, laughing and dancing like kids. Then, she pulled me against her and kissed me. I fell in love in her arms right there in the street with water running off my face."

"Wow," Neesa murmured. "Attractive and charming. Is she really a big-time model?"

Sharni nodded and pulled out her phone, quickly Googling Indigo. Multiple ads popped up with Alex in various forms of dress, including the underwear ads.

"Holy shit," Neesa whispered. "Look at all those tattoos."

"Sexy as hell," Sharni muttered.

"I bet she's really good in—"

"Neesa!" Sharni squeaked, cutting her off and putting her phone away.

"Well?" She shrugged.

Sharni raised a brow and grinned.

*

"So, Alex. Is this your first time in Greece?"

"No." She shook her head. "About five years ago we shot a collection in Mykonos."

"Oh, wow. That's awesome. Do you like it? Being a model?"

"For the most part, yes. I love what I do. It has its drawbacks like everything else. It's allowed me to travel the world and meet a lot of people over the years."

"How long have you been doing it?"

"Ten years next month," she answered. "What about you? If I remember correctly, you're a pediatrician?"

He nodded and smiled. "I am. We both are, actually. We met through Doctors Without Borders."

"Love at first site?"

"No," he laughed. "She drove me crazy. But she's so genuine and kind, not to mention beautiful. We were fast friends and before long, head over heels in love. What about you and her sister?"

"We met unintentionally and were drawn to each other like a moth to a flame."

"Sounds like kismet."

"Yeah, you could say that. She's gorgeous with the most beautiful smile. I knew I had to talk to her when I saw her eyes were as fixated as mine. We were both supposed to meet with friends at the same bar, whom we completely ditched after I sat down at her table and introduced myself."

Alex shrugged. "We spent the rest of the night together talking like old friends."

"Maybe yours will be the next wedding," Max said with a smile.

Alex smiled.

# Chapter 10

The SUV turned down a private, tree-lined road that eventually opened to a beautiful expanse of land with a majestic view of rolling hills and valleys all around. A massive stone mansion was situated in the center.

"Wow," Alex whispered.

"Oh my," Sharni said. "Max, this is stunning."

"Thank you." He smiled and brought the vehicle to a stop. "Welcome to the Nikolaidis Family Estate."

Everyone quickly got out. Sharni and Alex stood together, immersed in the breath-taking view as Max got their luggage out of the back. Once they walked around towards the front of the house, they noticed the people outside waiting to greet them.

Alex swallowed the lump in her throat and smiled politely at all the eyes staring back at her. She felt Sharni grip her hand tightly.

"This is my family," Max said. "My parents, Orphea and Thaddeus Papadakis. My brother, Leonidas Papadakis. And my grandmother, Persephone Nikolaidis."

Alex took in his parents as they stepped forward, hugging her and Sharni in welcome. She noticed his mother's stylish shoulder length hair, similar to her own shade of brown. Her thin lips were stretched into a bright smile. His father had thick dark hair long enough to touch his shirt collar in the back and slightly thinning up top. Big bushy eyebrows were over dark brown eyes, and a thin smile was spread across his face. Max's brother Leo resembled their father much more than him but had their mother's lighter hair. He also hugged the new guests, taking extra time with Sharni which didn't go unnoticed by Alex.

*

Sharni never let go of Alex's hand as she stepped over to her parents. "Mom and Dad, this is Alex ... my girlfriend."

Her mother immediately went off in Tamil, leaving everyone but the Dinjavi family out of what she was saying. Sharni replied in the same language as both women seemed to square off. Suddenly, the matriarch of Max's family, who'd been standing off to the side, stepped over, grabbing both Alex and Sharni's hands. She spoke briefly in Greek, then English.

"Welcome to my family home. We are happy to have you both." The sunlight catching the streaks of grey in her shoulder length brown hair, made them glisten. She had black framed glasses accentuating the friendly, beady eyes staring up at Alex and her lightly tinted lips were turned up into a smile.

"Thank you," Alex said, smiling and nodding at her.

Sharni's mother saw the gesture and instantly changed her demeanor to match.

"This is my mother and father, doctors Preet and Ganesh Dinjavi," Sharni said.

Alex noticed right away where Sharni got her assertiveness, and it was clear she and Neesa also inherited their beauty from their mother. Preet was a strong woman who stood with her head held high and her chin forward.

She had long black wavy hair pushed back over her shoulders, revealing dangling earrings and the same golden skin tone and dark eyes as both of her daughters. Her lips were pursed together, refusing even the slightest smile. Their father had short dark hair combed to the side and a thick mustache. Unlike his wife, he had a smile on his face at seeing his oldest daughter.

"It's nice to meet you both," she said.

"Please, everyone come inside and have tea," Orphea interjected, smiling at her son and Neesa.

Sharni's mother stepped to the side, thinking her daughter would go with her, but she hugged her father, kissing his cheek instead.

"They're good people, once you get to know them. Like any family, they take their culture and values very seriously," Max whispered to Alex, patting her on the shoulder. He turned to Sharni. "Come, let me show you both around."

They followed, entering through the massive double wooden doors. The interior was like walking through a palace with multiple open rooms decorated mutedly in various shades of crème, mauve, and light blue. Some of the floors were polished wood and others were polished marble. Each woman took in her surroundings and listened as Max explained all the different spaces from the parlor and drawing room to the tearoom, sitting room, and dining room. They finally ended upstairs in front of a door at the end of the hall.

"This is one of the best bedrooms in the house. You're both going to love it," he said, opening the door and stepping inside with the suitcases he was carrying. Alex and Sharni walked in together behind him, both gasping as they glanced around the exquisite room. The wall behind the king-sized bed was the same antique crème as some of the other rooms, but the rest of the walls were ornate floral wallpaper. The wooden floors were polished and matched the same dark coloring as the vintage desk and nightstands. An elegant crystal chandelier hung in the center of the room, and a narrow pair of French doors opened to a small balcony that overlooked the rolling hills and valley on one side.

"It's very beautiful," Sharni exclaimed.

He smiled and set their suitcases down together near the bed.

"We're sharing?"

"Of course. My family is traditional, but it's the twenty-first century." He grinned, patting her on the shoulder as he walked back towards the door. "The bathroom is through that door over there. That's why this one is quite special. Only a few of the rooms have an en suite."

"Wow. Well, thank you for the upgrade," Sharni said.

"I'll leave you to it. We'll be having lunch soon. I'm sure you want to get freshened up from the long plane ride."

As soon as the door closed, Sharni sat down on the edge of the bed and let out a huge sigh.

"I have no idea what was said, but it was pretty clear your mother wasn't happy," Alex said, sitting down next to her.

"She said I embarrassed our family, but honestly it was her. Everyone welcomed us ... except her, which I pointed out. I knew she was going to flip. Hopefully, that's the end of it."

"Hey," Alex murmured, grabbing her hand. "You're not here for her. You're here for your sister, who clearly loves you."

Sharni smiled. "It looks like we're sharing a bed for the week," she said, looking around the room. There was nothing else for one of them to sleep on, other than the floor.

"Yep." Alex nodded with her brows raised. "I'll shower first, if you don't mind," she said, letting go of her hand and standing.

"No, go ahead," she replied, watching Alex pull her suitcase towards the bathroom door.

\*

Alex stood in the hall outside of their shared room, adjusting the thin platinum bracelet on her wrist. She'd freshened up quickly and changed into a light gray pair of chinos, a white, short-sleeved button up with the top three buttons open, and the same black loafers she'd had on earlier.

"Do you love her?" a female voice called from nearby.

Alex spun around to see Neesa, Sharni's little sister, standing a few feet away.

"Because if she brought you here, she loves you with everything she has. I don't want to see her heart get broken, not by you. It'll destroy her."

Alex swallowed the lump in her throat just as the door swung open and Sharni appeared, freshly clean and dressed in an olive-green spaghetti strap dress that stopped right above her knees. The front dipped down in a low V and the back was fully open. Her luscious dark curls were pushed back over her shoulders.

"You're breathtaking," Alex whispered, wrapping her arms around her.

The feeling of Alex's hands running up her bare back sent shivers down Sharni's spine. She backed away slightly, putting some space between them. "Is everything okay?" she murmured, looking into the caramel eyes staring back at her. For a split second, she was sure Alex was about to kiss her.

"Yeah. Good," Alex said, clearing her throat as she looked around. Neesa was long gone. "We should probably head downstairs," she added, grabbing Sharni's hand, and interlacing their fingers.

*

All eyes were on the two women as they came down the stairs hand in hand. Preet Dinjavi turned away, choosing to show her back to her eldest daughter. Neesa locked eyes with Alex before giving her sister a big smile.

"Lunch is served," the groom's grandmother said, inviting everyone into the dining room where an array of tapas style food covered the long rectangle table. She took her place at the head, with her daughter, the groom's mother, to her left and her grandson, the groom, to her right. Everyone else filed in, taking a seat. Alex and Sharni wound up across from her parents, with Neesa sitting between her sister and fiancé.

Alex smiled politely but avoided eye contact with the two people across from her. Sharni's father was busy eating and chatting with the groom's father, but her mother was staring daggers at Alex so strongly, she was sure she could feel their icy tip penetrating her skin as she tried to eat and maintain conversation.

"We've put together some fun family activities for this week," Orphea, the groom's mother said. "The first is a romantic scavenger hunt through the nearby towns starting tomorrow morning. There are three teams of two, couples of course." She smiled. "You'll have five hours to check off as many items on the list as possible."

"Come again?" Sharni muttered.

"It's going to be so much fun," Neesa exclaimed, squeezing her arm. "It'll be me and Max, you with Alex, and Leo with his girlfriend, Penny."

"Hey, we're not exclusive," he said with a grin from the other end of the table.

Neesa laughed and rolled her eyes.

"Anyhow, the cars will arrive at nine, so we'll have breakfast and you all will be off on your adventure," Orphea continued. "Once that is over, everyone will have the afternoon free. We'll come together for a family dinner at seven."

Sharni glanced to her right and Alex smiled softly at her, knowing this was probably going to be anything but fun.

"Sounds great," Sharni said, giving her sister a big fake smile. "What about the rest of the week?"

"On Wednesday we're having an afternoon family bocce ball tournament on the south lawn," Orphea answered.

"Thursday you and Alex are going with Max and I to our dance lessons," Neesa added.

"I believe Leo is going as well," Max said, looking at his younger brother who nodded.

"Peachy," Sharni muttered under her breath.

"Sounds like a fun-filled week. Thank you for including me," Alex said.

"A toast to our family, old and new," the grandmother said, picking up her small glass full of cloudy liquid and a few ice cubes. Everyone followed suit, picking up their identical glasses. "Nikolaidis, Papadakis, Dinjavi ..." she said, then paused. "Alexei, I'm afraid I do not know your family name."

Alex stared at her.

"Mitchell," Sharni replied with a smile.

"Yes, Mitchell," Alex said.

"Ah ... to the Nikolaidis, Papadakis, Dinjavi, and Mitchell family," she continued, holding her glass high.

Everyone held their glasses up with her, then clinked them together, except for Sharni's parents who avoided Alex, before taking a nice long sip.

The licorice flavored drink tickled Alex's senses. "Is this ouzo?" she asked.

"Yes," the grandmother answered. "Over a hundred years ago, my late husband's great-grandfather planted rows and rows of grape vines, olive trees, and fruit trees, which still produce wonderfully to this day. We make wine, ouzo, and olive oil that is bottled and sold all over the world. We also maintain a reserve section of our crop that is solely used for our family." She finished with a small smile and a wink.

"Word of warning, the ouzo will sneak up and bite you, if you're not careful," Max said with a grin.

"I can attest to that," Neesa laughed.

# Chapter 11

"You two should take a nice walk," the grandmother said, patting Alex on the arm as she passed by her and Sharni when lunch ended.

"That's a great idea. Shall we?" Alex said, holding her hand out to Sharni.

"Sure." She smiled and interlaced their fingers. Once they were out of the house she let go of Alex's hand. "What happened at the table?"

"Huh?" Alex muttered, looking out at the rolling hills surrounding the valley.

"You forgot your last name."

"Oh, that," she sighed. "I didn't forget. I was thrown off a bit. Did you hear her call me something different?"

"I thought she said Alex."

"I'm pretty sure she said Alexei."

"That's probably Greek for Alex. Her accent's quite thick."

"Yeah." Alex nodded. "So, what do you think about our itinerary for the rest of the week?"

"A scavenger hunt? I could smack my sister. I literally took vacation this week because it was demanded I be here early for pre-wedding stuff since I'm in the damn thing." Sharni shook her head. "Don't get me started on dance lessons. What the hell does that have to do with anything? We're not the bride and groom."

"Have you ever had any lessons?" Alex asked casually as they continued down a path that led towards the vines.

"No. You?"

"Oh yeah. My grandmother forced me to take dance and piano lessons from four to fourteen. I can't tell you how many times I had to perform."

"Wow. I'm sorry. I'll give an excuse to my sister."

"I'll be fine." Alex smiled and grabbed her hand, pulling her into the vines.

"I don't think we're supposed to be out here," Sharni muttered, looking down at the dirt under her designer heels.

"Let's live a little."

"What do you mean by that?"

"You said it yourself. You're on vacation."

"Yeah," Sharni muttered.

Alex plucked a grape from one of the vines. "Open your mouth," she whispered.

Sharni raised a brow, then obeyed when Alex moved close enough for their bodies to touch. She parted her lips, taking the grape between her teeth as Alex fed it to her, casually grazing Sharni's lips with her finger and thumb. Sharni sighed inwardly, her breath caught in her throat and her eyes locked on the mystical caramel swirls staring back at her as she bit the sweet fruit in half.

Alex watched her lips delicately part after she swallowed. Movement out of the corner of her eye caught her attention, and she closed the distance between them, pressing her mouth to Sharni's in a soft kiss.

Sharni pulled away, gazing back at her in confusion as her brain tried to escape the fog clouding it, until the sound of someone nearby clearing their throat brought her careening back to reality. Alex's eyes had shifted and were looking past her. She quickly turned around to see her sister standing at the edge of the vines.

"I'm sorry. I didn't mean to interrupt," Neesa apologized with a crooked smile.

"It's fine," Sharni replied, shaking her head as she walked away from Alex and approached her sister.

"We're leaving soon for our final dress fitting," Neesa said. "Well, technically, it's your first."

Sharni smiled. "My measurements were taken and sent over twice, so hopefully there are no issues. Do our mother and Max's mom have to go with us?"

"They've been at every one of them."

Sharni frowned and sighed.

"Also, Max and I are going out for dinner and drinks tonight. I wanted to invite you and Alex to come with us."

"I'm okay with whatever you want to do," Alex said, stepping up behind Sharni. "I need to go up to the house and make a quick call." She winked at Sharni and walked away.

Sharni's eyes were glued to her back as their kiss replayed in her head.

"Hello!" Neesa said, waving her head in front of her sister's face.

"Huh?" Sharni muttered.

"I've never seen you like this."

"Like what?" Sharni huffed, raising a brow at her little sister.

"In love."

"What?"

"I see why. She's sexy as hell. I've never been interested in another woman, but she could make me think twice."

"Seriously, Neesa?" Sharni shook her head.

"Calm down," she laughed. "You two are great together. You're happy and I'm happy for you."

"Thanks. I think." Sharni grinned.

"It's so beautiful here," Neesa said, looking around at the rolling hills. "The countryside is so different from the city and the coastal beaches."

"It's peaceful, despite our mother being here."

Neesa chuckled. "Max's grandfather was born and raised here. The operation runs itself, but the family is all very much involved."

Sharni nodded. "Is this where you and Max would live, if you chose to stay here?"

"None of the family lives here full time anymore, but there is always someone from the family here. They also gather here quite often. All the holidays, big birthdays, and other events are held here. Max and I have an apartment in Athens, not far from the airport. I also still have my place in Boston," Neesa said as they walked around the house. "Do you and Alex live together?"

"No," Sharni blurted. "Uh ... it's only been about eight months. We're both very independent. Plus, she travels a lot," she added, mentally kicking herself. *Alex is so much better at this.*

\*

Alex was happy to stay behind and thankful to not have to deal with Sharni's parents as everyone scattered into vehicles and headed out for last-minute wedding preparations. The men headed off for final tux fittings and the women to their final dress fittings. With nothing to do, Alex walked around the grounds a little more. Then, she made a few calls to her agent and manager before deciding to take her own tour of the massive house. The bone-colored grand piano in the tearoom was too beautiful to simply pass by. She sat on the bench and pushed the cover back to expose the keys. Since no one else was around, she placed her fingers over the keys and began playing the first song that came to mind, *I'll Stand By You* by the Pretenders. She started slowly, surprised at how easily the hours and hours of training came rushing back to her. She picked up the pace as she progressed the song, singing the lyrics in her head.

When she finished, she pulled the cover closed over the keys and stood up.

"You're very talented," the groom's grandmother said.

Alex spun around, shocked to see her sitting in a nearby chair. "Uh ... thank you." She smiled. "I'm sorry. No one was around ..."

"Never be sorry for sharing a gift, Alexei."

Alex felt the hair on the back of her neck stand up at the woman once again calling her by the Greek name. She was sure she could see her mother's image in her head when she closed her eyes. She shook away the strange feeling as she walked over and sat on the couch adjacent to the grandmother's chair.

"My husband and son are the only people to ever play that piano. It's nice to hear it again in this house. Thank you," she said, reaching out and patting Alex's hand. "Tell me about yourself? I hear you're a big-time model."

"Yes." Alex smiled and nodded. "There's not much to tell, really. My grandparents adopted me when my mom passed away. I left their home when I turned eighteen and started modeling."

"Oh, my. I'm sorry to hear about your mother. How old were you?"

"Four. She was killed in a car accident."

The older woman shook her head.

"It was a long time ago, but when you call me Alexei, it reminds me of her."

"Alexei is the Greek form of Alex. It is also my son's middle name. You remind me of him."

Alex smiled. "Why isn't he here?"

"He passed away."

"I'm so sorry."

"Thank you, but it was a long time ago, like your mother." She smiled. "Come, let's have tea. Then, I'd like you to play again."

"Sure," Alex replied with a smile.

\*

"Do you think we could go to dinner a little earlier? I barely slept on the plane and I'm jet lagged. If you want me to go traipsing all over town tomorrow for a scavenger hunt, then I need to get some sleep," Sharni said as they pulled up at the house. She was thankful they'd taken separate cars from the mothers who apparently had other stops to make before heading back to the estate.

"I promise it'll be fun. It's supposed to be romantic and exciting. Max's mother came up with the idea and our mom helped lay it out. I know nothing about it except it took a few days for them to put it all together."

"Great," Sharni muttered as they walked through the front door. The melody of the piano echoed through the mansion, causing both women to pause and look at each other before following the sound until they reached the tearoom, which was really a small sitting space off to the side of another larger area. It was used for morning tea, which is why someone in the family had dubbed it the tearoom generations ago.

"Is that Alex playing?" Neesa whispered.

Sharni nodded and pointed to Max's grandmother sitting in a chair behind Alex, her head swaying softly to the beautiful music.

Neesa shrugged. In the dozen or so times she'd been to the house, she'd never seen anyone play the piano. It seemed more like a glorious antique decoration than anything else.

Sharni wanted to close her eyes and get lost in the song, but she couldn't peel her gaze from Alex's back, realizing right away the song was *Unchained Melody*. She listened intently, unable to help the couple of tears that slid down her cheeks at witnessing something so beautiful.

When she finished the song, Alex turned around, her smile faded from the older woman wiping away tears as her eyes landed on Sharni and Neesa, who began clapping like two kids at a concert. The grandmother twisted around and smiled. Then, she stood and grabbed Alex's hands.

"Alexei, you have a very precious gift. Thank you for sharing it with me and bringing back such wonderful memories."

Alex smiled and nodded. She watched Sharni walk towards her once the older woman was gone. She searched the dark eyes gazing down at her as Sharni's hands reached for her face. In a split second, Sharni's soft lips were against hers. The kiss ended just as her lips parted, inviting Sharni in for more. Her heart thumped in her chest as her cheeks cooled after Sharni's warm touch.

"You play beautifully," Neesa said, walking over to them.

"Thank you," Alex replied, pulling her eyes from Sharni and smiling at her sister. "I'm a little rusty, but I guess it's like riding a bike."

"Did Max's grandmother ask you to play for her?" Neesa asked.

"Not at first. I actually didn't think anyone was around, so I sat down and started playing. I turned around and she was sitting right there. She said her late husband and son were the only ones who ever played it. Then, she asked me to play *Unchained Melody*. It's her favorite song, and they used to play it for her."

"Wow. I wish the rest of the family had been here."

"Yeah, where is everyone?" Sharni asked. "I figured they'd all be back by now."

Neesa shrugged. "We'll be leaving for dinner in about an hour. I'm going up to change."

As she walked away, Alex grabbed Sharni's hand and tugged her over to sit down beside her on the piano bench. "Hi," she said, giving a cheeky grin to the intense dark eyes staring back at her.

"Hi," Sharni replied with a wide smile and slight shake of her head.

"So, how did it go at the dress shop?"

"Not bad, surprisingly. My mother won't dare embarrass herself in front of Max's mother. She kept her mouth shut as far as you and I are concerned."

Alex nodded.

"I forgot to tell you the wedding is semi-formal; not exactly black-tie, but—"

"I brought a black suit very similar to the one I was wearing when we met the other night."

Sharni raised a brow and bit her lower lip. "I'd love to see you in it, although I think a few people might have heart attacks."

"It's a good thing they're all doctors," Alex replied, her eyes never leaving Sharni's. For a brief second, she thought about kissing her, but with no one in the room with them, there was no reason for the affection.

Sharni laughed. "You're like this magical creature that mystifies at every turn. I'm not quite sure what to do with you."

"I can think of a few things," Alex mumbled.

Sharni chuckled. "For the record, my very straight sister thinks you're sexy."

"She's going to be heartbroken when she finds out this isn't real."

"I know," Sharni sighed. "But, after the wedding and everyone goes back to their lives, they'll forget about us and move on. I'll casually mention we broke up, and that's that."

"Sounds like you have it all planned out," Alex said as she stood up.

"It was a long plane ride," Sharni said, standing as well. "Do you want to head up and get ready to go to dinner?"

"I was just going to freshen up a bit. I don't see the need to fully change or anything."

"Yeah, I agree."

Sharni led the way and Alex followed, taking one last look at the piano before it was out of sight.

# Chapter 12

The upscale restaurant had a rooftop bar, which was where the two couples found themselves as they waited for a table.

"What is everyone drinking?" Max asked.

"A glass of wine is fine with me," Neesa answered and turned to her sister and Alex. A sensual song was playing over the speakers and the two of them were tangled together, swaying side to side. "Uh ... I think they're good," she muttered.

\*

"Is it working?" Sharni whispered.

Alex glanced back over Sharni's shoulder at the two people leaning against the bar, nursing drinks, and watching them dance. "Yep," she murmured, grazing her lips over the delicate skin of Sharni's neck.

Sharni stiffened. Her head was spinning as she leaned back to look into Alex's eyes. Her body was screaming to kiss her, but her brain was hard on the brakes. *This isn't real,* she kept telling herself. "You're quite the actor."

"You make it easy," Alex said, her lips curling into a smile. "I thought you said you don't dance."

"I wouldn't really call this dancing. I mean, we're barely moving."

Alex shrugged.

"I think we've put on enough of a display. We should join them," Sharni said, beginning to pull away, but Alex held her closer.

"Look," she whispered.

Sharni turned her head to see her sister and Max, slow dancing a few feet away. "I thought they needed lessons."

"I thought you said *this* wasn't dancing?" Alex replied.

Sharni rolled her eyes. "Come on," she grumbled, pulling away from Alex and grabbing her hand when she saw the hostess call their table number.

Alex watched multiple men give Sharni the once over as they walked past. She held onto her hand and gave each one a sly grin.

\*

"I'm so glad you are here," Neesa said between bites of food. "And I'm really glad you two came out with us tonight."

Sharni smiled and raised her glass to her sister. "So, why are we going to dance lessons? It looks like you two know what to do," she replied, changing the subject.

Max and Neesa both chuckled. "We can barely sway together without stepping on each other's feet," Neesa said.

"That is true," Max added. "Our lesson is more formal with actual dance steps."

Sharni nodded and glanced at Alex, who shrugged.

"I'm going to the restroom. Sharni, do you want to go with me?" Neesa said as she stood up and placed her cloth napkin on the table.

"Sure," Sharni replied, doing the same before brushing her hand over Alex's shoulder as she walked away.

*

"Our mother cornered me earlier and told me to pick a new maid of honor," Neesa said as she washed her hands and checked herself in the mirror.

"What did you say to her?" Sharni asked.

"I told her it was my wedding and I'll do as I please. There is nothing wrong with seeing you happy and in love with someone, no matter who the person is."

Sharni smiled into the mirror at her sister. "Who are you, and what have you done with my little sister?"

Neesa laughed. "I am still here. I love my culture and my family. It doesn't mean my values and views can't change. I think spending so much time with Max's family has rubbed off on me a little bit. They are wonderful people."

"Yes," Sharni agreed, nodding her head. "I think you're marrying into a great family."

Neesa hugged her. "I'm so glad you're here."

"Me too," Sharni replied.

*

"Are you having a good time?" Max asked.

"Absolutely. Your family estate is stunning. I've always found Greece to be romantic in its own way. The countryside contrasts beautifully with the beaches."

"Thank you. I wish you two could stay longer. Maybe you can come back again for a visit that isn't so chaotic."

"Yes, that would be nice. I'd love to show Sharni the coast."

"I know you travel quite a bit for work. Is this your first trip out of the States with Sharni?"

Alex nodded. "Yes, it is actually. My work travels are usually chaotic with quick turn arounds. This is more like a vacation." She smiled. "Are you going anywhere special for your honeymoon?"

"Tuscany."

"Oh, wow. I've been to Milan a handful of times, as well as Rome, but never stayed long enough to see or do anything."

"We're going for a week. Then, we leave from there to join our DWB group in Thailand to finish out the year."

"It's really amazing what you both do. I bet it's nice to be able to travel and work together."

"It's a dream come true," he said. "Although, this may be one of our last trips. We're thinking of settling down and opening a practice. We're just not sure where. We've talked about going to another country altogether instead of choosing between the States and Greece."

"That's interesting. How do your families feel about that?"

"We haven't told them," he laughed.

"Good man," Alex chuckled, raising her glass to him.

"What is all this?" Neesa said with a smile. "We leave for five minutes and you two are best pals."

Max and Alex smiled and shrugged.

"Shall we head back? I'm sure Leo is pouring ouzo as I speak," he said.

"Don't we have to be up early?" Alex asked as they headed out of the restaurant.

"Exactly, so go easy," Neesa replied. "Otherwise, Sharni will be scavenger hunting by herself."

"I don't think so," Sharni said with a raised brow, causing Alex to laugh.

*

Max pulled the SUV into the underground garage of the Nikolaidis Family Estate and killed the engine.

"So, this is where the cars are stashed," Alex muttered, looking at the covered, antique car parked in the corner.

"This used to be the working area of the vineyard, as well as the rest of the basement," he said, pointing to the door they were about to enter. "My grandfather redid all of this when he moved the day-to-day business away from the house years ago."

Alex and Sharni followed as he and Neesa led them into the basement. Massive oil paintings hung on the walls around the room with curtains surrounding them as if they were windows. Couches and tables were in the middle of the room with a pool table and card table on one end and a full bar complete with stools and taps on the other.

"Wow," Sharni muttered.

"This is my favorite room," Max said. "Here, we can let our hair down." He smiled when he saw his brother and a young blonde woman over by the bar. "Come on, let's have a toast."

"My big brother and his bride!" Leo said cheerfully as he poured multiple mini glasses of ouzo and passed them around.

"Penny, this is my sister, Sharni, and her girlfriend, Alex."

"Nice to meet you," they all said in unison.

"Alex, what's your game of choice?" Max asked, waving his hand towards the card table and pool table.

"Poker?"

"My kind of girl." He grinned, grabbing the ouzo bottle from the bar, and headed towards the card table.

Everyone followed, taking their seats at the eight-person round table. Each couple was split up, with Sharni winding up directly across from Alex and Max and Neesa on either side of her. Max set the ouzo bottle on a nearby hutch and pulled the cards and poker chips from a drawer underneath. He began passing out the colored stacks while Leo ran the cards through the automatic shuffler.

"Texas hold 'em. Ante is one chip, and the minimum bet is two. There is no maximum bet," Max said, waiting for each of them to ante up before dealing two cards to everyone.

Alex had a feeling this table had seen quite a number of high stakes games. She wasn't a card shark by any means, but she knew how to play, and more importantly, how to bluff. Sitting to Max's left meant she was first. She grabbed the edge of her cards and tilted them up, noticing a pair of kings. She pushed her cards back down and tossed two chips into the pot in the center of the table.

Neesa was next, sitting on Alex's left. She saw her ace and ten of hearts and tossed in two chips to meet Alex's bet.

Leo glanced at his cards and quickly folded on his turn.

Sharni was beside him. She looked at her cards and saw a pair of queens. Careful not to make eye contact with anyone, she met Alex's bet and raised two more before finishing her glass of ouzo like a boss. She raised a brow at Alex when she caught her staring at her.

Penny folded just as quickly as Leo had.

Max was the last to go and had waited until this point to see his cards, a jack and a nine of clubs. He paused for a second, then tossed four chips into the pot, bringing play back around to Alex. She winked at Sharni as she added two more chips to the pile, meeting her raised bet.

Neesa followed, also meeting the new bet.

"Ladies and gentlemen, the flop," Max said, dealing three cards face up in the middle of the table: a five of diamonds, a jack of spades, and a ten of clubs.

Alex tossed in two more chips and finished her glass of ouzo, all without breaking eye contact with Sharni.

Neesa met the new bet without skipping a beat. Sharni also tossed two chips in, keeping her raised brow in Alex's direction.

Leo began refilling everyone's glasses as Max dealt the turn card: a two of hearts. Everyone checked.

"Here we go," he said, placing the river card on the table: a two of spades.

Alex placed four chips into the pile and took a long swallow of ouzo. Neesa met her bet but pushed the glass of ouzo to the side.

Sharni grinned at Alex, then she picked up four chips and dropped them into the pile one at a time.

"I meet your bet and call you," Max said, putting four chips into the pot.

Alex flipped over her cards and said, "Kings and twos." Everyone at the table sighed as they each turned over their cards, revealing her as the winner. She leaned in, pulling the large pile of chips towards her.

"I'm glad I folded like a cheap hat," Leo muttered.

"Everyone's so serious," Max laughed as he gathered the cards and put them into the shuffle machine once more. Then, he cut the cards and handed the deck to Alex. Everyone tossed a chip in for the ante.

"You two seem pretty competitive," Penny said, glancing from Alex to Sharni.

"Nah," Alex muttered and winked at Sharni as she dealt two cards face down to everyone and placed the deck to the side.

Neesa checked her cards and bet two chips on her pair of fours. Next to her, Leo glanced at his five and jack and met her bet with a smile.

Sharni peeled her eyes from Alex long enough to look at the king and queen sitting face down in front of her. She met the bet of two chips and raised it two more as she gave a sly grin to the caramel eyes staring her way.

Penny and Max both folded, leaving Alex for last. She turned the corner of her cards up, revealing a pair of twos. Without meeting Sharni's eyes, she put four chips into the pile.

Neesa put in two to meet the raise while Leo folded.

Alex dealt the flop: a king of hearts, a nine of diamonds, and a two of spades.

"I'll check," Neesa said.

Alex shifted her eyes to the woman staring back at her.

"I check as well," Sharni added.

"I'll raise you two," Alex said, placing two more chips in the pile.

"I'm out," Neesa said, pushing her cards away.

"I see your two," Sharni replied confidently as she placed the chips into the pot.

Alex dealt the turn card: a queen of spades. Then, she turned her eyes to Sharni, who was placing four more chips into the pile and raising the stakes even higher. She finished her second glass of ouzo and slid four chips into the middle. "The river," she said, turning over the final card and placing it in line with the others: a seven of hearts.

"I call you," Sharni said.

"Are you sure you don't want to raise again?" Alex teased.

"Come on, let's see it," Sharni replied with a grin on her face.

"It's just a simple pair ..." Alex said, flipping her cards over, revealing her three of a kind.

"Motherfucker," Sharni grumbled, turning her cards over.

"Three twos beat a pair of kings and queens." Max shook his head.

"We should call it a night. The scavenger hunt starts early," Neesa said.

"I'm excited," Penny added.

Sharni stood up and the booze rushed to her head, causing her to sway a bit. Leo grabbed ahold of her, wrapping his arm around her quickly to steady her. "Thank you," she said, smiling at him.

"Oh man, you guys are going to be hurting in the morning," Neesa muttered, scrunching her face.

Max smiled sympathetically.

Alex's head was a little cloudy when she stood, but she shook it off. *Maybe I should just sleep on one of the couches down here*, she thought. Instead, she walked around the table and reached for Sharni's hand. After beating her twice at cards, Alex wasn't a hundred percent sure Sharni would take her hand, but she did, gripping a little tighter than usual.

*

As soon as Alex closed the bedroom door, Sharni sat on the edge of the bed and kicked her heels off. "You're a shark," she mumbled as she began unzipping her dress. The material fell off her shoulders, gathering at her waist as her black satin and lace, strapless bra was revealed.

Alex turned her head, but not quick enough to have the image burned into memory. She cleared her throat and kicked her shoes off. "What did you call me?" she asked, still turned away from her as she began unbuttoning her shirt.

"Shark," Sharni muttered.

"Do you mean card shark?" Alex questioned, turning around in confusion. Her unbuttoned shirt was open and untucked, revealing the white plunge style sports bra covering her small breasts. Indigo was scrolled over and over across the bottom band in black.

"Maybe," Sharni replied, swaying a little as she stood up yawning.

Alex sighed in frustration as she wrapped her arms around her to steady her. The rest of Sharni's dress fell to the floor in a pile of fabric as she reached up, interlacing her arms around Alex's neck and laid her head on her shoulder. Alex picked her up in one swift motion, carried her over to the side of the bed, and laid her down on her back. Sharni's eyes were closed when Alex removed her arms from around her neck and backed away. Her eyes skimmed down the beautiful bronze body lying on the bed, stopping on the bikini cut black lace panties that matched the strapless bra. She quickly turned away and rummaged through her suitcase. Finding what she was looking for, she walked back over and sat on the edge of the bed beside Sharni's limp body. She reached down pulling the sleeping woman up against her and began putting the old t-shirt up her arms and over her head. When she finished, she held onto her with one arm around her while the other hand pulled the shirt down to Sharni's waist. Then, she reached under it in the back, unclasping the bra to remove it before laying her back down.

"You're going to be as mad as a wet hen in the morning," she whispered, kissing her cheek softly before pulling the blanket up over her. As she walked away, she re-buttoned her shirt, but left it untucked as she quietly left the room and padded downstairs barefooted. Her head was still slightly foggy from the alcohol, which she was sure would linger in the form of a hangover in the morning. She ran into Max and Neesa when she entered the kitchen.

"Everything okay?" he asked.

"Yeah. She's out. I came down to get some water and ibuprofen."

"Aww, poor Sharni," Neesa murmured.

"I think she had a little too much to drink, as did I, but I think it's exhaustion more than anything."

"Here," Max said, handing her two glasses of water and a couple of pills. "Also, a little hair of the dog ... for the morning," he added, giving her a small flask of ouzo.

"Thank you. What time do we need to be down here?" she asked.

"Hector will have breakfast ready at eight. I believe we leave on our adventure at nine," Max replied.

"Do you need help taking that up?" Neesa asked.

"No, I've got it. Good night." Alex smiled.

Neesa stepped over, kissing her on the cheek. "I'm so happy my sister has you in her life."

Alex smiled again and walked away. When she got back to the room, Sharni was still sleeping peacefully. She set the alarm on her phone, then brushed her teeth, and washed her face, before changing into a tank top and pair of shorts. "What a day," she whispered to herself as she lay down on top of the covers, careful not to disturb the sleeping woman next to her.

# Chapter 13

*Where is it coming from?* Sharni thought, cuddling further into the warmth as the sound of the insistent beeping gradually increased. "No," she murmured in protest.

Alex pried her eyes open, staring around at the unfamiliar room. The warm body pressed up against her back and the hand resting casually against the bare skin of her torso caused her to freeze in place. The last thing she remembered was going to bed ... on top of the comforter. Having no idea how she wound up under it, or with Sharni wrapped around her, she slowly snaked one arm out from under the blanket, reaching for her cell phone to quiet the alarm.

Sharni groaned disapprovingly when coolness enveloped her skin as the warmth peeled away. Sighing, she opened her eyes and quickly realized Alex's body was the warmth she was tangled in. She quickly backed away.

"Good morning," Alex said, sitting up and turning back to look at her.

"What happened last night? And what am I wearing?" Sharni grumbled, noticing the t-shirt she was wearing wasn't something she owned.

The steady thumping between Alex's ears was a telltale reminder that she'd had too much to drink. Thankfully, the room wasn't spinning, and her stomach wasn't doing backflips. "That's my shirt. You dropped your dress on the floor and passed out on the bed in your bra and panties."

"You changed me?!"

"Well, I couldn't let you sleep like that," Alex replied, her feet finding the floor as she stood up. Her body sent all the signals it could, letting her know it required food, water, and a bottle of ibuprofen ... now.

"Where's my bra?"

"Over there with your dress," Alex said, pointing to a chair. "And before you flip out, I put the shirt on you with your bra still on. Then, I unclasped it from the back and removed it ... all without seeing or touching anything."

Sharni sighed in frustration, then groaned as she sat up and tried to stand. "My head feels like it's going to explode."

"We need to get moving. Breakfast is being served, then we're off on that scavenger hunt thing," Alex said as she went into the bathroom to splash some water on her face.

"Damnit. I could kill my sister," Sharni muttered, walking to the sink beside her.

"Do you feel sick at all?" Alex asked, cautiously.

"No. My body feels like shit, and my head feels like there is a drummer between my ears. The last thing I want to do is go gallivanting around, playing some stupid game!"

Knowing they both needed to get it together and fast, Alex went back into the bedroom in search of the flask Max had given her the night before. "Here," she said, taking a swig and handing it to Sharni.

"What is it?"

"Hair of the dog."

"Excuse me?" Sharni stared at her with a raised brow.

"Just drink some of it," Alex mumbled as she began brushing her teeth.

Sharni shook her head and took a sip, immediately spitting it out all over the sink. "This is ouzo! Why in the hell would I drink more of it?!"

Alex wiped her face on the nearby towel as droplets of clear liquor began sliding down the mirror. "Didn't you go to college?"

"Of course, but I wasn't a drunken frat girl."

Alex sighed in frustration. "When you're hungover, the best medicine is to drink a little of what made you drunk. It's called: the hair of the dog that bit you. It helps to take the edge off the hangover as your body recuperates. Everyone knows this."

"I certainly don't. I've never done that. And I'm not doing it now."

"Okay, fine. Feel like shit all day." Alex threw her hands up and walked by her to get dressed. "We need to be downstairs in ten minutes."

"I'll go down there when I feel like it."

"Great," Alex replied sarcastically as she pulled a pair of dark blue khaki shorts from her suitcase, along with a light blue, short-sleeve button up shirt. She quickly got dressed with her back to Sharni while she continued complaining at the sink. When she was finished, she sprayed some cologne onto her wrists and touched them to the sides of her neck. Then, she put some gel in her hair and ran her fingers through it. With one last glance at Sharni, she slipped a pair of dark brown, leather boat shoes onto her feet and put a black pair of sunglasses up on her head.

\*

"You certainly don't look hungover," Neesa said as Alex walked down the stairs looking like she owned the place.

Alex grinned.

"How's my sister?"

"Hungover and as mad as a wet hen."

"You poor thing," Neesa laughed.

"I feel good ... thanks to Max."

He bumped knuckles with her as he passed by.

"Okay?" she questioned, staring from one to the other.

"Call it intuition," he said, smiling at his bride-to-be.

"Breakfast is served," the grandmother called.

"Where is your sister?" Neesa's mother hissed under her breath.

"She wasn't feeling well. She'll be down soon," Alex said, overhearing her.

"I told you kids to go easy on the ouzo," Max's mother added.

"Kids?" Leo chuckled, walking into the dining room with Penny.

"Let me guess, you're both hungover, also," his father muttered.

"Nope. Remedied that situation a while ago. Now, we're just hungry." He grinned.

Alex's stomach rumbled and her mouth watered as she waited in anticipation, staring at the various platters that were scattered around the table. She had no idea what some of it was, but that didn't matter. She'd eat a skinned rat covered in hot sauce at this point.

At the head of the table, the grandmother spread her hands out and was about to allow everyone to start eating when she paused.

Alex looked up to see Sharni standing in the doorway, freshly dressed in a red top with a beautiful Indian pattern and a lowcut V in the front and black shorts. Her dark curls flowed wildly around her shoulders. A natural smile spread across her face.

"Come, sit. We're just about to eat. I hope you're feeling better, my dear."

"Thank you," Sharni said, smiling politely as she took her seat next to Alex.

Everyone began passing platters and filling up their plates as the chef walked around with fresh cups of steaming black coffee.

"Did you all sleep okay?" Max's mother asked.

"Yes, thank you," Alex replied, and Sharni nodded with a polite smile. She leaned closer to her and whispered, "Are you feeling any better?"

"You were right," Sharni replied.

Alex's brow furrowed in confusion.

"Hairless dog or whatever you called it."

Alex laughed and Sharni rolled her eyes.

# Chapter 14

After breakfast, everyone gathered in the main parlor. Max's mother handed an envelope to each of the three couples, who were ready to go with whatever belongings each couple thought they might need.

"Inside you'll find the nine quests to complete for the scavenger hunt, along with a Visa gift card to cover all your expenses, and the keys to a Fiat 500 that is parked outside. You must locate each destination and take a selfie or video completing the task, and don't forget to add a kiss. This is a romantic scavenger hunt, after all. Then, email it or text it, along with the location, and move onto the next task. Once you've finished all nine, make your way back here. The first couple to return with their hunt fully completed wins. I'll give you one hint: everything revolves around history and was particularly planned. You have five hours. Your time starts now," she finished, pressing the button on a timer.

Sharni tore open the envelope she was holding as the three couples rushed outside to the yellow, blue, and red cars. She handed the paper inside to Alex as she pressed the lock button on the key fob to see which car was theirs. The lights and horn on the blue car began flashing and beeping. "Come on!" She grabbed Alex's hand and snatched her in that direction.

Alex pulled her sunglasses down from the top of her head and jumped in the car. She began studying the paper. "The first task is to Serenade Your Love: karaoke sing a duet love song in the theatre."

"What the hell?" Sharni questioned as she fought with the stick shift to get the car into reverse.

"Are you good?" Alex asked, carefully putting her seatbelt on.

"Peachy," she grumbled, grinding the gears, and stalling the car.

"I can drive."

"I've got it! Find out where the hell this theatre is!" Sharni spat as she finally got the car going. The other two teams were already out of sight.

Alex was glad Sharni's eyes were hidden behind dark sunglasses because she was sure the look she gave her would cut glass. Shrugging it off, she went on Google and began looking for the nearest historical theatre. The first place that came up was the Ancient Theatre in Epidaurus. She put the address in the GPS and turned the volume up while holding on for dear life as Sharni careened around sharp turns, nearly running over the curbs of the tight streets, all the while, grinding the hell out of the gears and lurching the car around. *I'm either going to puke or die ... perhaps both!*

"Are you sure that's it?" Sharni questioned.

"Yes. It has to be."

Twenty minutes later, after missing a turn, redirecting and stalling, the little blue car pulled into the parking lot for the Epidaurus Archaeological Site and careened into a space. Alex thought about kissing the ground when she got out.

"Where do we go?" Sharni asked, looking at the signs.

"It's all Greek to me," Alex laughed. "We're in the right place," she added, pointing out the yellow and red cars parked nearby.

"Come on!" Sharni grabbed her hand and headed to the ticket booth. "We're looking for a theatre," she said to the man behind the glass.

He began going on and on in Greek, waving his hands and pointing to things on a paper map.

"I don't know what the fuck he is saying," Sharni grumbled to Alex, who simply held up two fingers and slid the card through the slot at the bottom of the glass.

The man smiled, printed a pair of day tickets, and passed them back with the card and a map.

"I have a feeling we'll be here for a few things. I read ahead while fearing for my life as you drove."

"Oh, you're funny," Sharni deadpanned.

Alex and Sharni walked down the sidewalk, following the map towards the ancient theatre.

"Sharni!" Neesa called, full of excitement as she and Max rushed up to them, heading in the opposite direction. "This is so much fun!"

"Yep. Loads of fun," Sharni replied, hugging her sister before parting ways. "Come on, they've already finished the first task!"

"And I thought *I* was competitive," Alex muttered.

Alex saw the back of the massive stone structure up ahead. It looked like something off the page of a history book. She wished she had more time to explore the details of this beautiful site.

"We're here. What are we supposed to do?"

"Record ourselves singing a love song duet together and share a kiss from the stage."

"Oh, for fuck's sake." Sharni shook her head. "The whole song? Half the song? A couple bars?"

"No idea," Alex said.

Thankfully, it was Tuesday and not the weekend. There were a lot less people milling about as the two of them walked up to the stage.

"Wow," Alex murmured, looking out at the giant, half-circle shaped stone seating, large enough to fit a couple thousand people. "This is amazing."

"We don't have time to sightsee. Pick the shortest song you can find on YouTube that has the lyrics. I'll do a selfie video with my phone."

"Uh, excuse me," a nearby man said. "Are you with the other singing couples? I'd be happy to video for you. I helped them as well."

Alex shrugged and Sharni handed him her phone.

"What songs did they sing?" she asked.

"I'm not sure," he replied.

"Here," Alex said. "Tell me you've seen Dirty Dancing."

"Of course."

"We're singing *Stay* from the movie soundtrack. Press record," Alex said, pulling Sharni close so they could both read the lyrics on the screen.

When the music started, Alex began singing the first verse. She trained her eyes on Sharni as she belted the words and swayed around dancing. Sharni sang the second verse a little shyer, but they finished the rest together, smiling and literally singing to each other. As soon as it was over, Sharni kissed Alex quickly, then grabbed her phone from the man.

"Thank you!" they said in unison as they rushed off.

"Oh my God that was embarrassing," Sharni said, shaking her head.

"Nah, it was a little fun."

"For you maybe. What's next?" Sharni said.

"You need to email or text that video. I'll see what else we can do here."

"There's no signal," Sharni grumbled as Alex opened the letter and began scrolling through the quests. "Bless Your Love: pray for a blessing of health from the sleeping gods. I saw some kind of god sanctuary on this map." She quickly switched papers and began searching around. "Here! We'll find a signal later. Come on!" She grabbed Sharni's hand and rushed down the walkway.

"I really hate my sister," Sharni muttered, causing Alex to laugh.

Sure enough, they were entering the Sanctuary of the Egyptian Gods when the other two couples were leaving. Neesa and Max waved like little kids.

Sharni shook her head as she watched the others walk away. "What are we supposed to do here?"

"Pray for health and take a picture of us kissing," Alex answered. "This whole area has to do with the first doctor ... ever."

"It makes sense now. The bride and groom are doctors. They've probably been here before."

"Come on. We can do our little ritual over here," Alex said, pointing to a cluster of large stones.

Sharni held Alex's hands and said a prayer for good health in her cultural Tamil language. Then, they snapped a selfie of them kissing, before rushing off towards what was left of the Temple of Asclepius.

"What is this?" Sharni asked.

"The temple of Apollo's son, according to the map. Expand Your Love: seek the birthplace of Apollo's child and wish for one of your own."

"Oh, hell no!" Sharni shook her head. "You can do this one."

"We have to do it together and take a picture, remember?"

"Goddamnit."

"That's probably not the best thing to say," Alex laughed as they walked up to the massive pillars that were still standing among the ruins of the temple.

Sharni sighed.

"We seek the Asclepius and wish for a child," Alex said.

"For my sister Neesa!" Sharni added.

Alex guffawed as Sharni held out her phone. Their lips met in a hasty kiss, almost barely touching before they parted and headed off down the trail.

"This is the last thing we can do here, unless you see a tall tower we can climb up on or a fountain we can get into," Alex said.

"Nope."

"Look!" Alex shouted, pointing at the red car leaving the parking lot. She and Sharni ran as fast as they could, but the car was long gone by the time Sharni got their car out of the parking space after stalling it and grinding the gears. "Would you please let me drive?"

"I've got it," Sharni growled, squealing the tires. "See if you can find a damn signal!"

Alex rubbed her temple and checked her phone. Having a signal once more, she texted the videos and pictures, along with their locations as requested, then went back onto Google to figure out where to go next. "I think we're heading to the coast. There's something about the middle of a water city."

Sharni navigated the light traffic to get back onto the main road.

"Sunken City!" Alex exclaimed. "Here," she said, plugging the address into the GPS as Sharni careened around a corner and stalled the car at the stop sign that she nearly skidded past. "You drive like Cruella De Vil!"

"Oh, shut up," Sharni grumbled, restarting the car, and taking off, once again grinding through the gears, and popping the clutch.

"I think we left the transmission back there."

"Do you want to walk?" Sharni spat, staring at her with a raised brow that appeared over the frame of her dark sunglasses.

Alex simply sighed and held onto the 'oh shit' handle as Sharni followed the GPS directions for the next twenty minutes, finally ending with them near the water. Sharni pulled into the parking lot for the Sunken City and killed the engine.

Alex said a silent prayer, thanking Apollo and his son for keeping her alive as she got out of the car and looked around. "I don't see anything."

"Me neither," Sharni added as they walked out of the parking lot and headed down to the beach. Several people were sitting on towels, and a few were on kayaks out in the water.

"Excuse me? Do you speak English?" Alex said, stopping a woman who was passing by.

"A little," she replied.

"Where is the sunken city?"

The woman pointed out to the water. Alex followed her line of site but didn't see anything but the kayaks.

"You have to see it from above," she said, before walking away.

"I guess we're going kayaking," Alex muttered.

"Wonderful," Sharni spat.

Alex walked further up the beach to the small hut with kayaks lying in the sand. She handed him the Visa card. When he held up one then two fingers, she briefly thought of getting them separate kayaks, but with the way Sharni drove, she thought she might drown, so she explained she needed a two person.

Sharni was off to the side waiting for her when Alex waved her over.

"I'll drag the kayak; you carry the paddles. Have you ever done this before?"

"Kayak over an ancient city? No. Have you?"

"I meant kayak in general, smartass."

Sharni chuckled. "Obviously not."

"I have. Just get on and do what I say. Otherwise, we're going for a swim."

"Can't wait," Sharni sighed in frustration as she pulled a hair tie from her pocket and threw her long flowing locks into a ponytail.

Alex pulled the yellow sit-on-top kayak all the way to the water. Then, she took her shoes off and put them inside. Sharni did the same. "Okay, you sit in the front. We're supposed to go to the middle of the city, so you'll be the guide. When I paddle on the left, you paddle on the right and so on. If we're not opposite, we'll just go in a circle."

"Aye-aye, captain," Sharni muttered as she climbed onto the front seat of the kayak.

Alex pushed the plastic boat until she was almost knee deep in the water, then she got on, settling in the backseat. Sharni shrieked and grabbed the side as it rocked back and forth.

"Calm down. You're fine. Start paddling!" Alex spat. "Start on your right side!"

It took a couple of minutes for the two of them to get in sync. They began going in a circle at first. Then, they wobbled around until they nearly tipped over.

"I see it! Straight ahead!" Sharni called as they paddled further and further from the shore. The ruins of an ancient city were visible in the clear water, sitting about six feet below the surface. "Oh my God!"

"Wow! This is incredible." Alex used her paddle to spin them around in what looked like the center so they could take it all in.

"It's unbelievable," Sharni said as she began snapping photos with her phone, seemingly forgetting why they were out there to begin with.

"We're supposed to make a wish in the middle," Alex said.

"With what?"

"There's a coin in the envelope!" Alex exclaimed. The kayak rocked forcefully as she shifted positions to get the envelope out of her pocket, causing Sharni to freak out and nearly fall into the water.

"Are you crazy!"

"It takes a lot for this thing to tip over. You're fine. Besides, you can swim, can't you?"

"Yes, I can swim! That doesn't mean I want to!"

"Carefully slide yourself back to me."

"What? Why?" Sharni turned around.

Alex couldn't see her eyes because of her sunglasses, but she was sure dark eyes were staring back at her.

"We have to make a wish and toss this coin in together and take a kissing selfie."

"Oh, for fuck's sake with the kissing pictures," she spat. "I can't slide back."

"Yes, you can. Just do it easily. I promise we won't tip over."

Alex flattened her paddle, using it to press down in the water on either side to steady the boat as Sharni slowly slid herself backwards until she was between Alex's legs. "See, that wasn't bad," she said, inhaling the floral scent of her shampoo.

"There's no way I can move back up."

"It's fine. Here," she said, holding out the coin. "We're supposed to wish for luck."

"Here's to good fortune!" they said in unison as they held hands and tossed the coin behind them.

Sharni held her phone out in front of her and turned her head to the side. Alex wrapped her arms around her from behind and met her lips in a soft kiss. When their mouths parted, she held onto her for a little longer as Sharni relaxed against her.

"See, this isn't so bad. Look at where we are," she whispered in her ear before letting go.

"I know." Sharni nodded and sighed. "It's just completely out of my comfort zone. This is so unlike my sister."

"Really? She seemed so happy every time we ran into them," Alex said as she began to carefully paddle them back to shore.

Sharni shrugged. "I guess I don't know her anymore. It's been a long time since we last connected. Our lives have taken us in opposite directions."

"Maybe this week was meant for you to reconnect."

*It seems like you're the only one I'm connecting with.* "Maybe," Sharni murmured as the kayak's nose slid into the sand. She stood and held onto Alex's hand as she climbed out. Alex got out behind her and pulled the kayak back up the beach to the rental hut. "I thought we might see them here," she said as she walked up with the paddles.

"We're not going in order, so who knows where they are. I figured it was easier and quicker to cluster things together."

"That makes sense. So, where are we off to now?"

"Somewhere that has green water."

"Excuse me, would you like me to take a picture for you?" a young woman asked.

Alex nodded, handing the woman her phone. Then, she stood behind Sharni and wrapped her arms around her. Sharni leaned back against her and grasped her hands. They both smiled towards the woman with the water and sunken city behind them. Then, they shifted slightly to look at each other before separating.

"Thank you," Alex said with a smile.

"Do you know where we can find secret green water and a pebble beach?" Sharni asked.

"Someplace that's in Epidavros," Alex added.

"Kalamaki Beach, perhaps?" the woman questioned, biting the corner of her mouth as she thought for a minute. "It's kind of a secret cove lined by trees and covered with pebbles just past Vagionia Beach, about ten minutes from here. The seaside village has restaurants, shops, and inns along the boardwalk and Vagionia Beach is just past that area. You take the narrow road between the olive trees and the coast that dead ends at the beach. From there, you walk down the beach until you come to a small cove. That's Kalamaki Beach. It's lined by trees and large rocks."

"Great. Thanks," they both said as they rushed through the sand towards the parking lot.

Sharni pulled the key fob from her pocket and handed it to Alex, who simply stared at her. "I'm tired of your bitching. Here, drive. I'll navigate."

"Thank God," Alex murmured, getting into the car. "Don't forget to send the picture and location. I texted the last ones. They went right through," she added as she quickly began looking up the beach the woman mentioned before starting the engine. "Did she say vagina beach?"

"What?" Sharni exclaimed.

"The beach the woman was talking about. I swore she said vagina," she replied as she searched her phone. "Vagionia Beach. I found it!"

"Close enough. Let's go to Vagina Beach!" Sharni laughed, inputting the address into her phone's GPS after the text was sent. She looked over, rolling her eyes at Alex, who easily maneuvered the car as if driving a stick shift were second nature.

Alex drove through the narrow streets, meandering with the traffic until something caught her eye off to the right. She quickly changed lanes and sped down a side road, coming to a stop against the curb.

"This isn't the beach," Sharni said, looking over at her.

"No, but that's a fountain. Come on!" She killed the engine and jumped out, grabbing Sharni's hand as they crossed the road to the small park. A handful of people were sitting on benches near a large fountain that was spraying water into the air. "Take off your shoes," she said as they walked up. Then, she turned to a young woman sitting nearby. "Do you speak English?"

"Yes," she answered with an American accent.

"Wonderful. Would you mind recording a quick video for us? We're competing in a scavenger hunt. It's a long story."

"Sure."

Alex handed her phone to the woman, then she grabbed Sharni's hand and pulled her into the cool, knee-deep water of the fountain. The various coins littering the bottom were slippery under her bare feet.

"What the hell?" Sharni protested.

Alex didn't have time to explain. What they were doing was no doubt illegal. She pulled Sharni against her and placed her hand softly on her cheek and the other around her lower back before kissing her like a lover. Alex's velvety tongue grazed Sharni's lower lip, inciting a soft moan as her lips parted, inviting Alex's tongue to meet her own. The sultry kiss lasted only a few seconds but garnered more than a few cheers from the bystanders in the area. When they parted, Sharni stared at her dumbfounded. Alex grabbed her hand, pulling the slightly confused woman out of the fountain. She grabbed her phone, kindly thanking the stranger as they threw their shoes back on.

"What the hell was that?" Sharni questioned, still feeling Alex's mouth on hers as they ran back across the road to the car.

"It's on the list."

"Huh?"

"Check the envelope," Alex replied, starting the car, and pulling out into the traffic and heading off in the direction the GPS was telling her to go.

Sharni opened the envelope and began reading down the list of quests. Cascade Your Love: have a spicy kiss in a fountain. "Wow," she muttered, shaking her head.

"You didn't believe me?" Alex asked, changing lanes, and downshifting to go around a turn.

"Yes, I did. I'm just surprised."

Alex nodded.

"Hey, on the way to Vagina Beach, look around for food. We can knock off the Nourish Your Love: feed each other something delicious and get something to eat," Sharni blurted as she texted the video to the number on the paper.

Alex looked over at her. "Didn't you eat breakfast?"

"Not a lot. My stomach was still angry. Besides, we've been at this for two hours already."

"Where is a New York hot dog cart when you need one?" Alex muttered.

"Wait, pull over. There's an ice cream shop!" Sharni squealed, nearly making Alex cause a pile up in the middle of the road.

"Holy shit," Alex huffed.

"Sorry, but you were about to zoom right past it!"

"Ice cream ... that's what you want to eat?"

"It says something delicious." Sharni shrugged.

"Uh huh," Alex mumbled as she pulled alongside the curb and turned the car off.

# Chapter 15

"English?" Alex asked apologetically when the woman behind the counter began speaking in Greek.

She nodded and smiled. "What would you like?" she asked in English with a heavy Greek accent.

"A small cone with coffee swirl, please," Alex answered, before turning to Sharni.

"I'll have a small cone with Madagascar vanilla and chocolate sprinkles," she said with a smile.

The woman nodded and quickly went to work making their treats.

"Are loukoumades donuts?" Alex questioned, looking at the honey coated pastry balls.

The woman nodded and smiled, then she pulled one from the shelf and handed it to Alex, gesturing for her to eat it.

Alex thanked her, then she held her phone out, taking a picture as Sharni leaned in and took a bite.

"Oh wow! That's yummy," Sharni exclaimed, licking the honey from her lips as Alex shoved the rest into her own mouth.

"That *is* really good!"

The woman handed their cones over to them and Alex paid the bill with the card they'd been using all day.

"You only took a picture of me. I'm pretty sure we need both of us," Sharni said as they exited the shop, each already eating her ice cream.

Alex put her phone in video mode and held it out as she grinned brightly at Sharni, showing her white teeth.

Sharni laughed. "So, I'm supposed to give you a bite of my ice cream?"

"I shared my donut!"

Sharni chuckled and shook her head as she held her cone to Alex's mouth.

Alex pressed record and took a bite, leaving ice cream remnants on the corner of her mouth. Sharni leaned in, kissing her, and cleaning up the mess on her mouth at the same time.

"Mmm, you taste like coffee," she murmured, pulling away.

Alex ended the video and began texting the picture and the video as they headed back to the car. Sharni stood on the passenger side, trying the locked handle several times.

"Are you going to open the doors?"

"Don't we need to buy something?"

"What?" Sharni questioned, crunching through her cone.

"The list. Isn't there something about a gift?"

"Uh ... yeah, I think so. Hold on," Sharni mumbled as she continued eating.

"So much for savoring your dessert," Alex laughed, watching her over the roof of the small car.

"It was melting!"

Alex rolled her eyes behind her sunglasses and continued casually licking the ice cream that was still above the cone.

Finished eating, Sharni pulled the list from her pocket. "Gift Your Love: buy a treasure or trinket for your love."

"Perfect," Alex said as she began crossing the road.

"Huh?" Sharni muttered, putting the paper back in her pocket before rushing to catch up with her. She looked around, unsure of where they were going, until she saw the souvenir shop down the block.

"Maybe we can find some kind of trinket for the bride and groom too," Alex mumbled between licks of ice cream.

"Are you going to eat that or make love to it?" Sharni asked with a raised brow.

Alex froze in place and locked eyes with her through their sunglasses. "Some things should never be rushed."

"Eating ice cream or making love?"

"Both," Alex said with a grin as she pushed her shades up on her head and walked into the store.

Sharni shook her head and followed.

Music was playing over the speakers. Alex held her cone in one hand and grabbed Sharni's hand with the other as she began moving her hips. Sharni laughed and allowed herself to be pulled in close to Alex, nearly grinding their hips together. Alex wiggled her brows and Sharni bent her head, taking a big bite of Alex's ice cream, down to the cone.

Alex let go of her and shrieked.

Sharni shrugged and winked before walking away, licking the coffee ice cream from her lips. She looked back over her shoulder and grinned at Alex, who was still rooted in place. "Come on, we're supposed to get each other a trinket."

Plus ONE

"What if I just leave you here as a gift for the owners instead?"

Sharni guffawed and made a beeline for a wall of magnets.

Alex headed the other way. She wasn't mad about Sharni eating her ice cream. In fact, it was quite the opposite. Sharni was a take-charge kind of person who wasn't used to being told no or having to wait on anything or anyone. If she wanted something, she took it. *You're acting, remember that. This is a paying job. If you can't get through this week without falling for her, you'll never make it as an actor,* she mentally chastised herself as she searched around, finally landing on a beautiful handmade bracelet with ceramic glossy beads in swirling shades of purple.

*

Sharni watched Alex from the opposite side of the store. She'd already picked out two magnets for Tracey, who's refrigerator stayed covered in them, and was still searching for the right thing to get Alex, when her eyes landed on a bracelet that had three small silver Aphrodite medallions with beautiful blue glossy beads in between each one.

"Are you ready?" Alex said, walking up behind her.

"Yeah," Sharni replied, hiding the bracelet under the magnets she was holding.

"I found this." Alex held up a statue of Asclepius with a serpent intwined staff. It was less than a foot tall and looked like white marble. "Remember, he's the god of medicine."

"Oh, that's right! My sister and Max will love it! Thank you."

"We need to get going. We're not far from Vagina Beach," Alex said as they made their way to the register and paid for their treasures and trinkets.

"The list says buy a trinket for your love. There's nothing about sharing a kiss or when to give it to them," Sharni said, reading from the paper.

"How about we exchange them when we get to the final destination? Then, if you want to kiss me, I might let you." Alex grinned and pulled her sunglasses back down over her eyes as they exited the store.

*

Alex brought the car to a stop along the curb next to a sign for Vagionia beach and cut the engine.

"This is the narrow road that woman was talking about. We're supposed to drive down it."

"I know," Alex said. "Live a little!"

Sharni raised a brow and followed as she got out of the car and walked over to the sign.

"We need a picture of Vagina Beach." Alex smiled, holding her phone out for a selfie.

Sharni laughed and wrapped her arms around Alex's waist, cuddling in close so they could get the sign in the background. After two pictures, one of which Sharni put her hand back behind them, trying to cover some of the letters so that it just said Vag Beach, they were back in the car and headed down the path with beautiful olive trees to their left and the gorgeous coastline to the right.

The road ended at a patch of rough ground half surrounded by olive trees and tall reeds. Alex cut the engine and looked around. A couple of campervans were parked a little further away and separated from each other. When she got out of the car, she walked around a bit, noticing the path through the reeds that obviously led down to the beach.

"This way," she called, waiting for Sharni to catch up to her.

"I really hope we don't get lost," Sharni muttered.

"I think we'll be fine. We're almost done."

"Thank God."

Alex chuckled and turned in time to see Sharni trip over something on the path to the beach. She reached out, grabbing her before she tumbled to the ground. Both women were wearing sunglasses, but Alex was sure she could feel Sharni staring back at her. Breath held in her chest, she nearly leaned in, pressing her lips to Sharni's, but a barking dog in the distance broke the stupor, bringing her crashing back to reality. She quickly let go of Sharni and backed away as she cleared her throat. "We're supposed to walk down the beach, I'm assuming this direction."

Sharni raised a brow and grinned. *Were you about to kiss me?*

"Are you coming?" Alex asked, waiting a few feet away.

"Uh ... yeah," Sharni mumbled, stepping onto the pebbly beach.

*

Both women ignored the people in the water, sitting in chairs, and enjoying picnics under the shade of the trees as they trudged on.

"Are you sure this is the way?" Sharni asked, wiping sweat from her brow. "We've been walking forever."

"It's been about ten minutes."

"I definitely didn't wear the shoes for this. I'd really like to know when my sister became all outdoorsy," Sharni grumbled.

"I think it's through these trees," Alex said, ignoring her rant.

The women turned a corner and found the secret cove on the other side of a makeshift path through the trees and reeds. A few couples were milling about on the pebbly bank.

"This is breathtaking," Sharni whispered, spinning around to take in the beautiful treelined cove, sparkling green water, and yellow lava rocks.

"Certainly, worth the walk," Alex added, taking a panoramic video on her phone. She stepped closer to Sharni and switched the phone to picture mode and snapped a few photos of her laughing and smiling as she took it all in.

"I wish I had my bathing suit on," Sharni said.

"I think we *are* supposed to get in the water."

"What?" Sharni pulled the list from her pocket. "Lavish your Love: have a long meaningful kiss in the secret green water and take a pebble for good luck."

"Told you."

"I'm not swimming in my clothes!"

Alex laughed. "It doesn't say swim. I'm sure we can just stand in it."

Sharni watched her walk up to a couple of young women sitting on the pebbly bank. She flashed a bright smile and spoke with them briefly before all three women walked over to where she was standing.

"This lovely French couple offered to take a video for us," Alex stated, handing one of them her phone before kicking off her shoes next to where Sharni had left hers.

Then, she grabbed Sharni's hand and tugged her towards the water. "Are you ready to do this?"

"As always," Sharni said softly as she stepped into the warm water. The pebbly bottom was a little slippery under her feet, causing her to grip Alex's hand tighter.

Once they were about calf deep in the water, Alex pushed her sunglasses up on her head, then she turned and did the same to Sharni before pulling her into her arms. They stood locked together and stared at each other for a few seconds.

"I told those ladies I was proposing to you, that's why we're in the water like this."

"Is this where I say yes, and you sweep me off my feet?" Sharni smiled.

"Sure." Alex grinned.

Sharni wrapped her arms around Alex's neck with one hand in the back of her hair while pressing her mouth to Alex's in a sensual kiss. Alex's arms enveloped Sharni, pulling their lower bodies fully together as their lips opened simultaneously, allowing their tongues to slide back and forth. The sound of clapping and cheering from the bank was lost on deaf ears as the two women continued kissing like lovers who had been apart far too long.

When they finally parted breathlessly, Alex bent down, picking Sharni up with one arm under her legs and the other around her back. Sharni kept her arms draped around Alex's neck, their lips finding each other once more as Alex carried her out of the water.

The women ended the video when Sharni was back on her feet and she and Alex were simply smiling at each other. One of them asked about the ring as she handed Alex her phone. She replied in French that it was back at the hotel. She didn't want to get nervous and drop it in the water. The two women laughed and congratulated them as Sharni and Alex pulled their sunglasses back down, slipped their shoes on, and walked away hand in hand, disappearing back through the path. Once they were on the other side, Alex let go of her hand.

"Welcome back to Vag Beach," Alex stated, sounding like a tour guide.

Sharni shook her head and laughed. "What were they saying when they gave you your phone?"

"They wanted to know where your ring was. I said I left it at the hotel, so I didn't drop it in the water."

Sharni smiled and shook her head. "Come on. We only have one more," she said, reaching for her hand.

Alex paused, bending to pick up a pebble and shove it in her pocket.

"A memory?" Sharni grinned, raising a brow.

Alex laughed. *I don't need a beach pebble to remind me what it's like to kiss you. I don't think I'll ever forget.* "I'm pretty sure I read we were supposed to bring a pebble back for good luck," she said, letting go of Sharni's hand so she could text the video. "I wonder who is getting all these back at the estate?"

Sharni stopped walking.

"What's wrong?" Alex questioned.

"I just realized these are probably being shared with my parents."

Alex nodded.

"They've never seen me kiss anyone or show PDA in general."

"Your sister walked up on us kissing in the olive grove."

"My sister, yes. But never my parents." Sharni sighed before breaking out into a soft chuckle. "They've certainly seen enough now."

"I'd say so."

"They're supposed to believe we're in love, so ..." She shrugged.

"We've sent some pretty damning evidence thus far." Alex smiled.

"Come on. I'm ready to get this over with," Sharni said, grabbing her hand once more as they continued down the beach.

*

Back in the car, Sharni stared out the window, taking in the scenery as they drove towards their final stop, some place with a medieval tower for them to declare their love from. Alex had searched around on her phone and found out there actually was a medieval castle about twenty minutes away and you could tour the remnants. This was it, the final quest.

"I wonder why we haven't seen the others since the very beginning," she muttered.

"Hopefully, they got lost."

"I doubt it," Sharni chuckled. "They're probably back at the estate eating lunch."

"That's not being served until two. I heard Max's grandmother talking about it. Apparently, lunch is a pretty big deal."

"Yeah, remember the spread we had for lunch yesterday?"

"That's right." Alex nodded.

Sharni's phone began ringing loudly, catching them both by surprise since no one had called either of them the entire time they'd been out on the crazy adventure.

"Hey!" Sharni answered excitedly.

"I haven't heard from you, so I figured I'd make sure you were still alive," Tracey said.

"I'm sorry. I meant to call. I arrived safe and sound."

"And the smoking hot model?"

"Yep."

"She's right beside you, isn't she?"

"Yep."

Tracey laughed. "How did your parents take it? You're still breathing, so it must not have been that bad."

"They're ignoring me."

"Are you serious?" Tracey huffed.

"Yep. My sister and Max have been great. His family is so kind."

"That's good. I bet your sister was floored."

"Actually, she reacted a lot like you."

"What's that supposed to mean?"

"Surprised, intrigued, maybe a little curious," Sharni said.

"Uh huh. So, have you had to kiss her yet?"

"Yep. Several times, to be exact."

"Get out! How was it?"

"Gentle, new, exciting, breathtaking, stimulating, with the possibility of becoming an addiction."

"Oh my god, I'm jealous and I'm straight!"

Sharni guffawed.

"If you sleep with her, I might have to take a bite of the forbidden fruit too!"

"That's definitely not happening."

"Uh huh. So, what've you been up to?"

"My sister's soon-to-be mother-in-law set everyone up on a romantic scavenger hunt through the nearby towns."

"What?"

"There are nine quests, and each has its own task to complete when you get there, and all of them end with a video or picture of a kiss."

"Ah, that explains all the kissing."

"Yep. And you have to send the evidence back to the parents as proof along the way."

"So, you're sending pictures and video of you and her making out to your parents?"

"Yep."

"Oh my God!" Tracey guffawed.

"So much fun," Sharni muttered.

Alex downshifted to go around a tight turn, causing Sharni to grab the door handle. "Sorry, that turn came up quickly," Alex said.

"Sure it did," Sharni muttered, eyeing her suspiciously.

"Was that her talking?"

"Uh huh."

"Even her voice is sexy."

Sharni laughed. "Girl, you need to get ..." Sharni paused, forgetting Alex was next to her. "You need to go out."

Tracey laughed. "I'm living vicariously through you."

"Trust me, it's not as exotic as it sounds."

"Listen to yourself. You might change your own mind."

"Not likely."

"Tell me you're not sharing the same bed?"

"You and I have done that."

"Girl, sharing a bed with me and sharing a bed with that sexy woman are very different, and you know it. Lesbian. Bi. Straight. It does not matter. Besides, you know I think everyone is a little queer. People are attracted to whoever gets their wheels turning at that moment, despite what's between their thighs."

Sharni guffawed.

"Is there anything else exciting planned for the week? I figured you'd be hanging by the pool this whole time."

"We're doing some family thing tomorrow and going to a dance class the day after."

"I bet she's a good dancer."

"That is correct."

"Oh, so you've danced with her," Tracey said in a chastising voice.

"Uh huh."

"Well, if you're not going to take advantage of that smoke show in your bed, have you seen any good-looking men?"

"Nope."

Tracey sighed, causing Sharni to chuckle.

"I think we're at our next stop," Sharni said.

"At least send me a pic! You've sent half a dozen to your parents, and I'm your best friend!" Tracey exclaimed as she hung up.

Sharni giggled and shook her head.

"Everything okay?"

"Yes. That was my best friend."

"Ah. I see. Let me guess, she knows about our arrangement."

"Yes."

Alex nodded.

"She wants me to send her one of the pictures we've taken today."

Alex raised a brow behind her sunglasses. "Does she know I'm a woman?"

"Oh yeah. She saw you on the side of a bus and is now smitten with you. And she's straight. Or maybe not, I guess. Hell, I don't know. She's never dated a woman as far as I know, and we've been friends for years. It's always been men. But I don't think she'd be opposed to it. You certainly caught her eye."

"What about you?"

"I thought we've had this conversation."

"Did I catch your eye?"

Sharni smiled. "Yeah, I guess. I don't think I would've been able to pull this off if you hadn't. Besides, have you seen yourself in that suit you were wearing the other night? I'd have to be blind to not notice you."

Alex grinned.

# Chapter 16

"This is it. The final one!" Alex said, pulling into a space in the municipal parking lot.

Sharni looked around at the small village as she got out of the car. "I'm confused. Where is the medieval castle?"

Alex pointed down the road. "That way."

Sharni nodded as they began walking.

"Did you send your friend a picture?" Alex asked nonchalantly as she studied the various buildings they were walking past. Some seemed to be built right on top of each other and the side of the hill.

"Yeah," Sharni answered, glancing at her. "You want to know which one I sent, don't you?"

Alex shrugged. "That's your business."

"Uh huh."

Stone ruins of the Byzantine castle came into view up on the top of the grassy hill as they grew closer. A couple of people were walking around the grounds, peering down at the village below. Alex grabbed Sharni's hand to balance them both as they made their way up the steep, narrow path along the rocky cliff. They both stopped halfway up to take pictures of what once was a cylindrical tower and remnants of the exterior walls jutting up from the green grass.

Sharni's phone chimed with a text message from Tracey. She laughed and shook her head while reading her best friend's response.

"Must be something good," Alex muttered as they reached the top of the hill.

"She had a lot to say about the picture."

"Oh, really?"

"Yep. So, what are we supposed to do up here?" Sharni asked, changing the subject.

"Besides kiss?" Alex grinned, taking in the rusty red roofs of the buildings in the village below.

"If I remember correctly, that wasn't on the list," Sharni said, pulling the paper from her pocket.

"That must be the church." Alex pointed. "I read that it was built in the 11$^{th}$ century and is still maintained to this day."

"Oh wow," Sharni muttered, looking up from the paper at the small stone building. "We have to go inside."

"Is that what it says?" Alex raised a brow.

"No, but how can we come all this way and not go in?"

Alex shrugged. "Maybe we'll get bonus points. Or go directly to Hell and not pass go."

"I didn't say we were kissing in there!" Sharni laughed. "Besides, Declare Your Love: atop the medieval castle, let those below hear the depths of your love; doesn't say anything about kissing."

"How are people supposed to hear our love?"

"Let's make a video saying how much we love each other for all to hear." Sharni shrugged.

"Sounds good to me."

Sharni put her phone in video mode and stepped closer to Alex, wrapping her arm around her neck before pressing play. "For anyone who wants to know, I am very much in love with Alex Mitchell!" she exclaimed with a big smile, spinning them in a slow circle in the center of the castle ruins.

"I am head over heels in love with Sharni Dinjavi! And I want everyone to know it!" Alex yelled, pulling her in tighter and lifting her off the ground.

Sharni looked like she was flying as they circled around once more. Forgetting she was filming or that no kiss was involved, she leaned down, pressing her mouth to Alex's. Alex stilled, wrapping her other arm around Sharni in a full embrace as she set her back on her feet. They searched each other's eyes slowly when their lips parted. Noticing her phone in her hand, Sharni quickly ended the video while taking a half step back to put a little space between them.

"I hear it's good luck to recite your vows inside," a man said, clearing his throat and nodding back over his shoulder to the ancient church that wasn't far behind them.

"Uh ... what?" Alex muttered, pulling her gaze from Sharni to look at him.

"Thank you," Sharni said as he walked away. Her eyes landed back on Alex. "That would certainly seal the deal."

"Yeah, no kidding," Alex replied, swallowing the lump in her throat.

"Come on. Let's at least go take a look inside." Sharni grabbed Alex's hand and tugged as she began walking towards the ancient church.

Alex let herself be led all the way inside the small stone building until they were standing together, side-by-side and holding hands in front of the altar. Greek graffiti was carved all around, but the crosses and paintings were still visible. A golden chalice was off to one side with a row of lit candles in front. Alex wasn't a religious person by any means, after being forced into it by her grandparents, but she felt the need to cross herself as she stood in front of this beautiful piece of history.

Sharni's family was Christian instead of Muslim or Hindu, which was why her grandparents had left their home country in the first place, immigrating with a large group of other Indian Tamil Christians. She'd grown up in the church but hadn't kept her religion for several years. Still, standing in that sacred space, she also crossed herself.

Neither felt the need to say anything at all. They simply held hands and let their souls take in all the energy buzzing around them. When another couple came in, Alex and Sharni nodded at each other and walked back outside.

"I'm glad our task wasn't declaring our love inside there," Sharni said.

"Yeah, me too. That would've been very real."

"And potentially bad luck."

"No kidding," Alex replied. "I don't need any bad Greek juju."

"Me neither," Sharni laughed. They took a quick picture of the two of them standing outside of the small stone building. "I guess we should exchange our gifts now."

"Oh, that's right!"

They each pulled a bracelet from their pocket, smiling and laughing as they exchanged their similar gifts.

"This is beautiful!" Sharni exclaimed, slipping it onto her wrist. "You remembered my favorite color," she added with a sweet smile.

"Of course." Alex smiled back as she slipped her bracelet on. "Is this Aphrodite?"

"Yes. She kind of reminds me of you."

Alex grinned and wrapped her arms around Sharni in a hug that brought their full bodies together. As they were pulling apart, Sharni kissed her lips softly.

"Thank you ... for everything. Coming here. Doing this ridiculous scavenger hunt. All of it," Sharni said, with her arms still loosely around Alex's shoulders.

"You're welcome." Alex smiled. *I'd wake up tomorrow and do it all over again.*

They snapped a quick picture of them wearing their bracelets and holding their arms up to show them off.

*

"Why does it feel like it's been all day?" Sharni sighed, looking out the window as the little car made its way through the winding streets. "It's only been four and a half hours," she added, sending the last text with the pictures and video from the castle ruins.

"Because we were traipsing all over the damn place doing crazy things. We're almost back to the estate ... finally."

"Do you think we'll be first?"

"I have no idea, but I hope there's food at the end of all this."

"Oh, look who's starving now." Sharni pinned her with a stare behind her sunglasses.

"Yes. It's lunch time!" Alex exclaimed.

They both laughed as they pulled through the gates. Suddenly, the yellow car was right behind them.

"Hurry! We have to get inside. We're the first ones back!" Sharni yelled.

Alex floored the gas and squealed to a stop outside as the yellow car did the same. She and Sharni jumped out and rushed to the door with Max and Neesa hot on their heels. The large, heavy wooden door swung open. Both sets of parents and Max's grandmother were all standing in the foyer to greet the winning couple as the four of them fought to get through the doorway. Alex and Sharni pushed through first with Neesa and Max tumbling inside with them.

"We won!" Sharni cheered, wrapping her arms around Alex's neck.

Her parents, Preet and Ganesh Dinjavi, turned around and walked away with appalling looks on their faces, a gesture that hadn't gone unnoticed by Max's grandmother.

"We were so close," Neesa said with a fake pout.

"All of you did wonderfully. Hopefully, you had fun, grew closer in love, learned more about each other, and took in a little history while you were at it," Max's mother said as she hugged everyone.

"It was so much fun. I haven't seen some of those places in many years," Max replied.

"I found it difficult not to stay and explore more of some places. This country is so beautiful," Alex added.

"Is this your first time in Greece?"

"I was in Mykonos a few years ago for a photo shoot, but only stayed long enough to work and experience a little of the nightlife before flying back to the States. I've wanted to return, but never found the time ... before now." She looked over at Sharni and smiled.

"Lunch is served," the chef called to the grandmother, who nodded at him.

"What about Leo?" Max asked as they began making their way to the dining room.

"They gave up a while ago," his father laughed, shaking his head. "You know your brother."

"Figures." Max smiled.

"He and Penny are having lunch in Athens. Then, he's dropping her off on his way back here," his mother said.

"Where are mom and dad?" Sharni whispered, looking at Neesa. "I didn't see them when we came in."

"We were kind of acting like a herd of elephants, so ..." Neesa shrugged. "Should I go find them?"

"Well, yeah. Otherwise, they're missing lunch and being rude."

"Excuse me while I go find our parents. I'm not sure they know lunch has been served," Neesa called to the room.

"I believe they're out on the terrace," Max's grandmother said. "I already sent the chef to inform them. Please, come sit." She waved her over with a smile.

Neesa turned back around and headed to her seat next to Max, with the two seats to her right open for her parents. He squeezed her hand and smiled at her as she sat down.

Alex was happy to be sitting adjacent to the grandmother, who was at the head of the table, and across from Max, instead of Sharni's parents, who looked down their noses every time they saw her. Sharni and her sister might not have seen them when they entered the house, but she did ... along with the repulsion on their faces. She felt bad for Sharni and knew all too well what it was like to be raised by people who didn't know you at all.

The Dinjavis walked into the dining room, taking their seats just as the food was being served.

129

"We're sorry. We were caught up in the beautiful view of the rolling hills," Preet said, flashing a smile that Sharni knew was fake.

She softly shook her head at her mother and opened the cloth napkin containing her silverware. The scavenger hunt drove her crazy, but she'd get up and do it all over again if it meant she didn't have to see her parents. Sharni loved her little sister and would do just about anything for her, but it was taking everything she had to be stuck in that house with her judgmental, prudish parents for a week. Knowing how uncomfortable they were around Alex, and the two of them together, made her glad she'd brought her along and showed up as a lesbian.

"We all enjoyed the pictures and videos you sent. It was interesting to see how each couple interpreted the quests. Of course, both of you completed everything, but you did it without going to a lot of the same places," the grandmother said. "Obviously, Max grew up here, but he hadn't seen some of those ruins since he was a boy. I'm curious as to how you and Sharni seemed to have gotten around so easily."

Alex laughed. "It wasn't easy at first. Have you seen her drive a manual transmission?"

Neesa guffawed. "Why in the world did you let her drive?!"

"I'm lucky to be alive," Alex giggled.

Sharni raised a brow and looked from Alex to her sister. "You're both so funny."

"Anyhow ..." Alex continued. "We actually relied on asking locals. Anytime someone took a video for us, we'd ask about our next destination. Everyone we spoke to was friendly and did their best to point us in the right direction, or at least give us something to go on. Google was a big help as well."

"I'm surprised you two found Kalamaki Beach. I was expecting Vagionia Beach, but you went all the way to the cove," Max's mother said. "And did I hear right in the video, was that a proposal?"

Sharni's mother dropped her fork onto her plate, causing it to clank loudly. She looked around apologetically and picked it back up.

"We needed a story for why we were standing in the water," Sharni replied with a smile as she glanced down the table at her mother.

"Speaking of stories ..." Max's father chimed in. "There's some old folklore about that medieval church you went into."

"Oh really?" Alex asked.

"You stood at the altar, you vowed your love for each other, and you exchanged gifts. Hundreds of years ago, the two of you would've been pronounced married."

"Wait a minute, you two went to an ancient church? I don't remember that being on the list," Neesa said as Sharni and Alex simply stared at each other.

"They went to the Byzantine castle ruins in Nea Epidaurus. The church that was inside the castle, presumably since it was built thousands of years ago, is still standing," Max's father answered.

"The castle grounds high up on the hill is where we did the declare your love thing, but we also exchanged the gifts there that we'd bought each other in the lavish your love, or whatever it was called. We couldn't pass up going into the stone church structure," Sharni replied.

"Wow, so you got engaged and married in the same day," Neesa teased with a smile.

Sharni laughed and shook her head.

"So, everyone saw the videos and pictures as we sent them?" Alex asked.

"Oh, yes. We were all in the theater room together. Each time we received something it went up on the big screen," the grandmother said. "After lunch, we should go back in there so you two can see what each other sent. It was quite fun."

"I'd love to!" Neesa squealed.

"Uh ... yeah. Sure." Sharni smiled while thinking back to all the videos of her and Alex making out. She knew she didn't need to see them again; they were engrained in her memory. But, if it meant making her parents squirm a little more, she'd sit through every minute of it.

"It looked like everyone had great fun. You will enjoy the videos," Sharni's mother said. "After lunch, Ganesh and I had planned to take a walk around the grounds."

Max's grandmother held up her wine glass. "I'd like to make a toast, congratulating the winning couple for their achievement today." She looked over at her daughter, Max's mother.

"The winners will receive a weekend on whichever Greek island you choose ... on us. We'll cover the flight, the hotel, and provisions. You just tell us when and where you want to go," Orphea said, smiling at Alex and Sharni.

"Wow," Alex mumbled in shock. "Thank you."

"Lucky ladies," Neesa said, smiling at them.

"Yes, thank you very much," Sharni added, just as surprised as Alex.

# Chapter 17

"I might need some ouzo to watch this," Sharni whispered, cuddling up beside Alex in the theater room. Neesa and Max were next to them, with Max's parents and grandmother behind them in the upper row. Sharni and Neesa's parents had come up with an excuse not to watch, but Sharni knew the truth. They didn't want to see her with Alex.

"Did I hear ouzo?" Max's grandmother said.

Alex laughed as the chef walked in with a tray of ouzo glasses, one for each of them.

"I was kidding," Sharni mumbled giddily.

"The best part of all the videos is the commentating from whoever was taking them," Max's mother said, starting his and Neesa's first video once everyone had a glass in their hand.

"Whatever stranger we could get to take it at the time," Neesa laughed.

"Aww," Sharni murmured, smiling over at her sister during some of the sweet moments as each of the videos played.

Everyone laughed at a few of the awkward selfie pictures.

"It's interesting we didn't see any pictures of you all together at the same place and same time," Max's father said.

"Well, we tried to follow them from the start, thinking at least Max would know his way around ... but, we had a minor issue with the car and lost everyone early on," Alex explained.

"The car? Why didn't you call?" he asked in surprise.

Alex grinned and Neesa started laughing as she said, "My sister can't drive a stick shift to save her life."

"Hey! I got us to where we needed to be," Sharni huffed with a smile.

"Yes, until I took over the driving before our transmission fell out," Alex added, causing everyone to laugh. Sharni playfully smacked her.

"Okay girls, here is the start of your adventure," Max's mother said, pressing play on Alex and Sharni's first video of them singing karaoke in the ancient theater.

"Oh, I know this song! I love Dirty Dancing!" Neesa exclaimed.

Alex began singing along and bobbing her head.

Sharni smiled brightly and shook her head.

"Not bad; definitely better than the other pair," a man's voice said just before you see Sharni and Alex share a brief kiss, then the video cut out, causing everyone to chuckle.

The next video started with Sharni and Alex standing in a fountain. A few cat call whistles were heard, along with a woman's voice saying, "oh my," as Sharni and Alex shared a very heated kiss while the water sprayed behind them.

"Whoa!" Neesa exclaimed. "Good thing you two were in the water; you might've caught on fire!"

Sharni grinned and shook her head. She caught sight of Alex next to her and paused, sharing a long gaze at each other as the next video started.

"Aww, how sweet," Neesa said, watching Alex take a bite of Sharni's ice cream cone, and Sharni kiss away the vanilla remnants at the corner of her mouth.

"I didn't realize you'd recorded all of that," Sharni whispered, watching the screen.

Alex reached over, squeezing her hand. Sharni opened her palm, taking Alex's hand in hers as the video of them at Kalamaki Beach began.

"The one on the left is proposing to the one on the right," the person videoing said. "Oh my God, she said yes!" the woman squealed as Sharni smiled and nodded before wrapping her arms around Alex's neck, tangling one hand in her short hair as their mouths came together in a passionate kiss. The woman videoing cheered like she was at a sports game as Alex swept Sharni off her feet, sharing another kiss with Sharni in her arms as she carried her out of the water.

"Is this real?" Neesa questioned excitedly, looking at her sister.

Sharni smiled and shook her head.

"I needed a reason for us to walk into the water and share a fiery kiss, so that's what I told the stranger who agreed to take the video," Alex said.

Neesa pouted.

"Well, now you have to top that when you do get engaged," Max's mother said.

Sharni and Alex both laughed nervously.

"We went to Vagionia, but never found Kalamaki," Max said. "How did you two find it?"

"We asked the locals." Alex grinned.

Plus ONE

He smiled and shook his head. He'd grown up in Epidavros and had been to different beaches many times over the years. Technically, he *was* a local.

"This is the last one," Max's father said as the video played with Alex and Sharni saying how much they loved each other. "You're right outside the church here. Did you go up to the altar?"

"Yes, right after this," they said in unison.

"It was magical," Sharni added.

"You exchanged your gifts here too, correct?"

"Outside," they both said, causing him to smile and laugh.

"Well, it's no wonder you two won. You got engaged *and* married!" Neesa teased.

"Not exactly," Sharni laughed, shaking her head.

"Your prize was a honeymoon," Max added with a giggle.

Alex rubbed her thumb over the back of Sharni's hand and smiled, knowing how uncomfortable Sharni had to be in that moment.

"Here are their pictures," Max's mother said, flipping through each of their rushed selfies and a few pictures they'd had strangers take.

"Wait, go back," Neesa said. "Was that at the Sunken City in a kayak?"

"Yeah," Sharni said, looking at the picture of her leaning back in Alex's arms with her head turned to the side for their kiss. "I don't know how Alex didn't drop her phone in the water."

"I damn near did because you almost dumped us over ... more than once!"

Sharni squeezed the hand she was holding as she laughed.

136

After the last picture, Max's mother turned the dimmed lights back up. "The goal of this was to have fun and see how much you love each other, which was proven many times over ... with both couples," she said, standing in front of the room. "Neesa, we're so happy to have you join our family. And Sharni and Alexei, we consider you family, too."

Sharni and Alex smiled, while Neesa got up and gave her a hug.

*

"I don't know about you, but I'm ready to relax. I feel like I ran a marathon," Sharni said as they walked out of the theater. "Do you want to go for a swim?"

"I need to return a few calls. I'll catch up with you in a bit." Alex smiled and winked at her before walking away.

"You are so in love. I'm very happy for you," Neesa said, standing next to her sister and wrapping her arm around her. "I can see you two getting married."

Sharni smiled at her sister. "So, what's next on the agenda for your big wedding week?" she asked, changing the subject.

"Tomorrow we're all spending the day together here at the house. They're big into bocce ball, so they've put together a family tournament."

Sharni nodded.

"I think mom and dad would rather milk a cow."

"What?" Neesa laughed.

"I'm serious."

"They *are* acting very standoffish."

"Neesa, this is your wedding week. If they want to act like prudes with their noses in the air, then oh well. I for one, am tired of them trying to run my life."

"You definitely sent them spinning out of orbit, showing up with a woman you're madly in love with. I thought their eyes were going to pop out of their heads when we arrived."

Sharni chuckled. "Can you imagine their faces watching those videos?"

"Oh God," Neesa giggled. "I didn't even think of that. No wonder they didn't want to watch again."

"I'm sure after the wedding and everyone heads home, back to their lives, I'll get a phone call telling me how much I embarrassed them and disgraced our family and so on."

"That's ridiculous."

"I'm not a doctor, Neesa. I'm also the oldest and unmarried. I do what I want, when I want, and with whomever I want. They hate everything about my life and constantly remind me of it."

"I'm sorry," Neesa said, pulling her sister into a full hug.

"It's not your fault. Come on, we're here to have fun and celebrate your wedding week. I'm headed to the pool to relax."

"Damn. I wish I could join you. Max and I are meeting with the officiant this afternoon. Maybe tomorrow."

"After bocce ball?" Sharni laughed and shook her head.

"I think we'll need more than the pool," Neesa chuckled.

"How's Greece?" a male voice asked with a French accent.

Alex adjusted the volume for the AirPods in her ears and kicked her feet up on the ottoman as she stared out the second-floor window at the rolling hills of the olive grove in the distance. "Quite different," she sighed.

"No wild parties this time?"

"Definitely not. I'm in the Peloponnese Region; the Greek countryside, to be exact."

"Sounds charming."

"Yeah ... something like that. Are you still in L.A.? I know you'd mentioned going to New York."

"Neither."

"Where are you?"

"Paris. My brother Franc rang me yesterday morning. Our uncle isn't well. He's the last one left of our parents' generation. I flew all night to get here."

"I'm sorry to hear that."

"Oh, don't be. He's a stubborn old mule. I'm only here to make sure his will is in good standing. He inherited our grandparents' summer chateau in Normandy. It's been in the family for multiple generations and survived two wars in its backyard. I need to make sure it doesn't fall into the hands of his half-witted children."

She laughed.

"Anyhow, I know we'd planned to touch base when you returned ..."

"Take all the time you need."

"No, it's not that. I'll be back in L.A. this weekend."

"Okay? Has something changed?"

"Yes and no."

"Jean-Pierre, you've been my agent for the past ten years. We both know Indigo is dumping me—"

"It may not be a breakup after all," he said.

"What?"

"Look at it as more of a realignment."

"What the hell does that mean?" she asked, frustration heavy in her voice.

"Nothing is concrete, but there's some merit to it. Indigo is adding a new brand to the house called Platinum, but you didn't hear this from me. It's still very closed door, hush-hush."

"What does this have to do with me and losing my contract?"

"That's just it. Are you ready to leave, or do you want to renegotiate as the face of Platinum?"

"Are you serious?"

"I wouldn't have called you otherwise."

"Wow," she muttered, slightly speechless. "What exactly is Platinum?"

"It's not just another part of the house of Indigo, it's a step up. And they're going to need a face to build the brand."

Alex watched a fluffy white cloud float by in the distance as she stood and began walking towards the terrace. "When will you know more?" she asked, noticing Max's brother Leo standing near the waist-high wall, peering down like a vulture at what she presumed to be Sharni, swimming in the pool ... alone.

"I imagine we're still a few weeks out. I could be wrong. I'll let you know as soon as I do."

She paused for a second, wondering how she should handle Leo and his prying eyes. The lines in this acting gig were so crossed, she wasn't sure what was an act and what was real anymore. "Jean-Pierre, if the deal is good, I'm in," she sighed before ending the call. *I'm done acting.* She slid her phone and AirPods into her pocket and walked out the French doors, onto the terrace.

*

Sharni stepped out onto the lanai, stretching her head and neck to the sky, allowing the sun to kiss her skin as she removed her linen beach cover, revealing the lavender colored one piece swimsuit that she wore underneath. The low V at the top and side cutouts showed quite a bit more flesh than a traditional one piece but was still modest compared to most of the swimsuits she owned. She unfolded her towel along one of the lounge chairs and placed her sunglasses down before walking over to the steps of the rectangle pool. Cool and refreshing turquoise blue water surrounded her as she descended, sinking down, and dunking her head as she swam off, completing a few relaxing laps along the length of the pool.

When she finally came to a stop, she rolled onto her back and floated in the middle of the water as if there wasn't a care in the world. It felt good to let go; forgetting all about everything around her, even if it was only for a few minutes. *What a crazy fucking day*, she thought as she watched a fluffy, cotton ball looking cloud drift past, bringing a slight breeze. *I wish Neesa had joined me. There's been so much time between us. I don't know if we'll ever catch up.* "She's going to be heartbroken when she finds out Alex and I broke up," she whispered to herself. "I'm beginning to think I will be too, and it's not even real," she added, thinking about the gorgeous woman she'd been kissing all day. *She's a good actor. She makes it so damn easy. But that's all it is ... an act. Don't fall for the character she's playing. It's going to be hard enough to let go when this is all over.*

Sharni blew out a long sigh and flipped over, swimming a few more casual laps to clear the thoughts from her head before she went down a mental rabbit hole she couldn't get out of.

\*

"It's rude to invade someone's privacy, ogling them like a beautiful piece of window art you'll never have," Alex said, walking up and sitting her hip against the stone low wall of the terrace, her back to the woman below.

Leo glanced at her and grinned like a cheshire cat. "It's not against the law to look at something as fine as that, but it should be."

"I had a feeling you were a little too friendly last night. Now, I know you were."

"You're not married to her. Besides, her sister's joining our family. Maybe she wants too as well." He smirked.

Alex laughed softly, shaking her head as she stood up; her right shoulder touching his. "You keep playing with fire and you're going to get burned," she muttered before walking away.

\*

Sharni swam over to the side of the pool. "I was wondering if I'd see you," she said, smiling at the gorgeous, androgynous woman walking towards her. "Did everything go okay with your call?"

"Yeah." Alex nodded and smiled as she squatted down. "You have the attention of Max's little brother. He's watching just over my right shoulder; up on the terrace."

"Figures," Sharni muttered.

"He thinks you're here for him and went as far as insinuating you'll marry him to join the family alongside your sister."

"Did you say something to him?"

"Yes. Would you rather I hadn't?" Alex questioned.

Sharni reached out, pushing Alex's sunglasses up, revealing her beautiful eyes. "I think we should show him just how wrong he is." She grinned and nodded towards the nearby steps and began walking towards them as Alex stood, reaching her hand out to Sharni for assistance when she stepped out of the pool with water running down her body, dripping to the ground.

Alex moved closer, placing her hands on the bare skin of her waist in the cutouts of the swimsuit.

"I'll get you all wet," Sharni whispered, looking into her eyes.

*You have no idea.* Alex swallowed the lump in her throat and pulled Sharni fully against her.

Sharni's arms snaked up around her neck, playing in her short hair as their mouths came together in a slow, seductive kiss. A whispered moan escaped her lips at the sensual feeling of Alex's soft hands on her skin and the warm body pressed against her.

Alex briefly thought about sliding her hands down to Sharni's ass, but that would lead to picking her up and laying her on her back right there on the poolside lounge chair. Instead, she deepened the kiss, parting Sharni's lips and sliding their velvety tongues together.

Neither woman knew how long their onlooker had been gone, but when the sultry kiss ended, they were completely alone. Alex took a step back and reached for Sharni's towel, handing it to her.

"Are you sure you don't need it?" Sharni smiled, seeing her full wet imprint along the front of Alex's clothing.

"I'll be fine." She grinned, catching her eyes before Sharni slid her sunglasses on. Alex pulled her shades back down from the top of her head as Sharni dried off and slipped the cover-up on over her swimsuit. "Do we have family plans tonight?"

"I have no idea." Sharni shrugged. "Why? I'm all for it if you have a better idea."

"Let's go to dinner. Somewhere ..."

"Away from here?" Sharni smiled.

"My thoughts exactly. Let's get out of here for a bit and take a breath. No rules. No tasks to perform. No fake display. Just you and me."

"Did you bring the suit I met you in?"

Alex grinned. "No. I left it for the cleaners."

Sharni bit the corner of her lip and nodded.

"But I did bring a similar one."

Sharni smiled brightly.

# Chapter 18

Alex looked out the window towards the driveway, sighing and shaking her head when she noticed the three Fiats they'd used in the scavenger hunt were gone. She couldn't go to Max and Neesa because they weren't back yet from their meeting with the officiant.

"Damn," she mumbled under her breath as she turned around.

"Anything I can help with?" Max's grandmother said.

Surprised, Alex searched all around, finally seeing her sitting in a chair across the room. Alex smiled and walked over. "Is this seat taken?"

The grandmother nodded for her to sit. "What has you so out of sorts?"

"I was hoping to take Sharni out tonight for a romantic dinner, just the two of us. However, the rented cars from this morning have already been returned. I'm afraid we have no transportation."

"That's certainly a dilemma."

Alex nodded. "You all have been wonderful. But I know she's looking forward to a little space to take a breath."

The grandmother pondered for a second. "The relationship between her and her parents can't be easy."

"So, you've noticed." Alex met her eyes.

"When you get to be my age, not much gets past you." The grandmother winked and smiled. "She's lucky to have you in her life."

"Thank you."

The grandmother stared into her eyes, then turned her head to look out the window. "You remind me so much of my son, Kostas. He was a romantic who led with his heart."

"Was?"

"Yes. He's no longer with us. But that's a story for another time," she sighed, standing up. "Come with me."

Alex nodded and followed along as the older woman led her through the house to the garage. A black Range Rover, belonging to Max's parents, was parked in the middle and the antique car was off to the side under a cover.

"Pull that cover back," the grandmother said.

Alex stepped over, pulling the dark gray cover off a pearl white vintage convertible. "Wow," she whispered.

"This was my husband's prized possession. Do you know what it is?"

"A Jaguar XK140, correct?" Alex said, peering down at the black leather interior.

The older woman smiled. "You know your cars."

"This one was pretty iconic." Alex smiled. "It's beautiful. I drive a Jaguar F-Type."

"Really?"

Alex nodded.

"My husband drove this when we were first married. His father purchased it new in 1956 and gifted it to my husband when he graduated college. He claimed the car was how he won me over," she chuckled. "Anyhow, he kept it all these years and had it fully restored with new everything and gave it to our son as a wedding gift."

"I see."

"After he died, my husband couldn't bear to drive it any longer. Then, my husband passed. So, here it sits. It's driven for maintenance once a month and kept in top shape. I couldn't bear to sell it. This car is a part of the Nikolaidis family and should remain that way through generations, just as my husband had planned."

Alex smiled and began pulling the cover back over the car.

"Don't you need a car for tonight?"

Alex paused and turned to face the older woman. "I could never ..."

Max's grandmother smiled endearingly. "You know how to drive. The car needs to be driven. You need a car for tonight. What could you possibly never?"

"Are you absolutely sure?"

"I wouldn't be offering if I wasn't."

"What about your daughter and grandsons?"

"What about them?"

"I don't want to ruffle any feathers," Alex said.

The older woman laughed. "The only feathers that seemed to be ruffled in this house are the Dinjavi's."

Alex smiled and nodded in agreement.

"Here," she said, handing Alex the key to the car. "The garage door opener is in the glove compartment. I know you'll be gentle and treat her like a lady, just as my husband did." She smiled almost nostalgically.

"Thank you," Alex muttered, but the woman was already gone. "Holy shit," she whispered, stowing the car cover off to the side. She ran her hand along the sleek metal and over the black leather interior before stepping back for another look at the exquisite roadster in showroom condition. She thought of going in search of the grandmother and giving back the key. Max's family had gone above and beyond to welcome them and treat them as family, and here they were, performing in a charade.

She shoved the key into her pocket and walked back into the house. Max's grandmother appeared from around the corner, handing her a piece of paper.

"The name and address of one of the best restaurants. Give them the name Nikolaidis," she said with a smile and walked away.

"Thank you, but ..." Alex said, realizing she was gone. She wanted to know more about the older woman and her family, and certainly why she felt so fond of Alex. But she knew better than to look a gift horse in the mouth. Instead, she hurried upstairs to get ready.

Sharni was in the shower, so Alex took her time sticking on the skin tone pasties that covered her nipples and spraying cologne on the pulse points of her neck and wrists before putting on her dark charcoal suit jacket and pants. She slipped black leather loafers on her feet and shoved her slim metal wallet into her pocket on her way out the door, without Sharni ever knowing she'd been in the room.

"You look ..." Neesa muttered in surprise, headed up the stairs as Alex was headed down. She took a long look at the way the tailored suit hugged Alex's body perfectly.

Alex's brow furrowed in question.

"Like a model," Neesa finished with a smile.

"Thanks ... I think," Alex laughed as she moved past her and headed through the quiet house towards the garage.

Once she was inside, Alex stared at the antique roadster, still in shock that she was about to take it for a drive. After a minute, she opened the door and slid into the seat. She reached into the glove box, pressing the button for the garage door before turning the key. A wicked grin spread across her face as the sportscar's engine turned over, rumbling to life. She let it idle for a minute, not knowing how long it had been since it was last driven. All the gauges were reading properly, and the fuel tank was three-quarters of the way full. She'd already programmed the address for the restaurant into the GPS on her phone, so she pushed the clutch in and shifted into first gear, rolling the car out of the garage with ease. She hit the button to lower the door as she drove around to the front of the house and cut the engine. She climbed back out, closed the door, and leaned against the side of the car as she waited for Sharni to come outside.

*

Sharni towel-dried her long curly locks, then applied eyeliner, a touch of eyeshadow, and lightly tinted lip gloss, which was the extent of her makeup collection, allowing her to rely mostly on her natural bronze complexion. She felt slightly giddy thinking about the dresses hanging in the closet that she'd brought with her. She knew she and Alex weren't *really* together, but it still felt thrilling getting dressed up to go out on a date. She'd brought a couple of sexy dresses in the slight chance she'd be able to get away from her family for a night out.

Walking out of the bathroom, Sharni immediately smelled the alluring scent of Alex's cologne, which hitched her excitement level up another couple of notches. She quickly went to the closet and chose a merlot colored, one shoulder midi dress with a slit up the side. She finished the outfit with black slingback heels and a pair of platinum bar earrings. Then, she checked the time on her phone before shoving it into her clutch purse and leaving the room with a few minutes to spare.

"Wow. You look great. Where are you off to?" Neesa asked, running into her in the hallway.

"Hot date," Sharni beamed.

"That must be why I ran into Alex also looking dressed to kill." Neesa smiled. "I'm pretty sure she wasn't wearing a shirt under her suit jacket," she added, mock fanning herself.

Sharni grinned like a cheshire cat. *I certainly hope not.*

Neesa leaned in, giving her sister a brief hug. "I miss seeing you so happy," she whispered.

\*

Alex's heart pounded in her chest like a bass drum when the front door of the estate opened, and Sharni stepped out. Wild dark curls bounced around her shoulders and her left thigh peeked through the slit in her dress as she walked, causing a throbbing deep inside Alex that she was completely unprepared for. *I could fall so damn hard for her. Why the hell did I agree to this?*

"Did you hear me?" Sharni questioned.

"Uh ... sorry." Alex cleared her throat and stood from her leaning position. "You're breathtaking," she whispered with a soft smile, holding her hand out.

"I said you clean up very nicely, but I already knew that." Sharni grinned, taking the offered hand as Alex led her around to the passenger side and opened the door.

"Do I even want to ask where you got this stunning car?"

"I stole this pile," Alex teased, closing her door once she was settled.

"What?" Sharni laughed. "Honestly, I feel like Cinderella."

"Since you mentioned it ... at midnight this car turns into a rusted-out VW bug; I turn into a wrinkled hairy old dude in a speedo; and you turn into your mother."

Sharni guffawed as Alex walked around to the driver's side and slid into the car. She was still wiping away tears of laughter as Alex started the engine and drove away, moving through the gears like a pro as the roadster rolled through the gates of the estate and continued down the road.

Alex reached over, turning the knob for the radio, which happened to be programmed to a foreign pop station. *Rose Colored Lenses* by Miley Cyrus was playing. She turned the volume up as Sharni lifted her arms over her head, letting them blow in the wind while singing along. She couldn't help smiling and singing with her.

"I'm pretty sure this is our song," Sharni said, looking over at Alex with a big smile.

Alex laughed and nodded.

"Where are we going?" Sharni asked, turning the radio down when the song ended.

"Do you like surprises?"

"No."

"Do you trust me?" Alex asked, changing gears as she slowed to take a turn.

"I barely know you."

"I've slept in your bed."

Sharni raised a brow behind her sunglasses. "In my bed, yes. Not with me."

"Touché." Alex grinned. "Hopefully, you're not allergic to seafood," she said, pulling into a parking space near the front of the restaurant.

Sharni slid her sunglasses into her clutch and waited as Alex walked around to open her door. A few onlookers watched the couple leave the car and walk inside the waterfront building.

"Table for Nikolaidis," Alex said to the host.

"Right this way," he replied with a smile, leading them to a candlelit table for two with a water view. He waited for the couple to be seated, then handed them two regular menus, plus a drink menu and a paper with the chef's specials listed. "Vasi is your waitress. She'll be with you soon."

"Okay, now this really feels like a fairytale," Sharni said, perusing the menu.

"Maybe it won't end," Alex mumbled without looking up.

Sharni closed her menu and peered at Alex, waiting to meet her eyes.

"Can you believe it's only been 72 hours since we met?"

"It feels like a lot longer. Especially after today," Alex replied, finally meeting her eyes.

"Hello, I'm Vasi. May I take your drink order?" the young waitress said, breaking their conversation and smiling at Alex.

Sharni ordered a glass of chardonnay and Alex did the same.

"Would you like an appetizer?" she asked, still smiling every time she looked in Alex's direction.

"No, we wouldn't," Sharni replied, cutting her eyes at the young woman.

"That was a little harsh."

"We're sitting here, obviously having a nice dinner together, and she's looking at you with googly eyes."

Alex raised a brow and grinned.

"What? Wait, are you interested in her?" Sharni questioned.

"God no. She's young and naïve. Good for her for obviously knowing what she likes, though." Alex grinned, setting her menu to the side.

Sharni shook her head.

Alex reached out, linking their fingers together on top of the table.

"What's that for?" Sharni asked, looking down at their joined hands.

"When she comes back over, she'll get the hint."

Sharni nodded. "You know what's crazy, I've never been a fan of PDA. I've always believed people should keep their business to themselves."

"Today must've driven you mad," Alex laughed.

"I was so far out of my comfort zone that I couldn't find the area code. I wanted to choke the life out of my sister for a bit," Sharni chuckled. "But by the end I was like, whatever. I'll never see these people again."

"Then, we had to watch all the videos with everyone," Alex laughed.

"Oh my God! I wanted to crawl into a hole. I know my parents saw everything. For once, I'm glad they're prudes and weren't in there with us." She smiled and shook her head. "In all my years, they've never seen me like this."

"You mean how you are with me?"

"Yes. I keep them further than arm's length because they're constantly trying to run my life. So, this is all very new," she said, rubbing her thumb against Alex's finger.

"To be honest, it's quite new for me too. I mean I've dated, but I've been too busy to ever have it turn into anything remotely close to this."

"I'm glad I chose you and not one of those weird guys who answered the ad."

"Would that have been better for you?"

"For my parents maybe, but not for me. I feel very comfortable around you," Sharni said softly, holding her eyes with a steady gaze until the waitress appeared with their drinks. They pulled their hands apart and made room for her to set the glasses down before giving their dinner order.

"She has impeccable timing," Sharni laughed, picking up her glass. "What should we drink to?"

"How about making the most of this adventurous week?"

"Sounds good," Sharni said, clinking her glass against Alex's and taking a sip as her eyes slid down to the smooth skin of her upper chest where the top of a calla lily tattoo peeked out. Parts of her collarbone tattoos were also visible at the edge of the jacket on either side. She quickly averted her gaze and took another long sip before Alex noticed.

\*

After dinner, Alex nodded towards the boardwalk along the marina. "Do you want to take a walk?"

"Sure." Sharni smiled, linking her arm through Alex's.

"I don't know why I'm here with you," Alex murmured.

"What do you mean?" Sharni questioned, looking into her eyes.

"You're incredibly beautiful, smart, funny ..."

"I've never found another personality that meshed with mine longer than a couple of months." Sharni turned her head, peering out at the inky water lapping against the side of the dock. "I work long hours; I like things a certain way; I don't have time to babysit or coddle someone."

"In other words, you're a grown woman who is adulting her way through life."

Sharni laughed. "Something like that. Unfortunately, it's kept me single. What about you? You're gorgeous, and don't tell me you don't know that."

"I've had my share of relationships, but they've all come because of my career, not me as a person. You've said it yourself; my face and body are plastered everywhere." She shrugged.

"I know on the plane you said you've always dated women. How did you know ..." Sharni murmured.

"That I was gay?"

Sharni nodded.

"I don't know. It just came naturally, I guess. I can remember being in high school and being so jealous of my friend's boyfriends. Not long after I signed with Indigo, they sent me to Italy for three weeks to train with a high fashion photographer. She was a little older than I am now. I remember the first time she kissed me. I thought my chest was going to burst open, my heart was beating so wildly." Alex smiled softly at the memory. "Anyway, I was sent there to learn how to, as my shoot manager says, 'make love to the camera,' and learned how to make love to her ... at the same time."

"Wow."

Alex smiled.

"Where is she now?"

"Married to a man. She left the fashion photography world when she married and began having children. I saw her in Milan about six years ago and barely recognized her."

"That's surprising."

"Not really. LGBT rights in Italy still have a long way to go, especially if you want to get married and have children. Heterosexual normalcy is currently the only way."

"How sad."

Alex nodded. "So, what about you?"

"What about me?"

"You dated a girl in college, right?"

"More like experimented with, but yes," Sharni said.

"What happened with that?"

"My parents were still running my life. If they'd found out, they would've gone mad." She shrugged. "I'm pretty sure the girl went back to dating guys. Hell, she may have never stopped. We were roommates and were only together in our room. We never saw each other outside of there. It only lasted a couple of months, anyhow."

"After you graduated and started your life you never thought about dating a woman?"

"No. Honestly, I buried that time of my life deep down. It recently bubbled to the surface like lava."

"When was that?"

"The night I met you."

Alex grinned.

"So ... what are we going to do about this island weekend trip we won?" Sharni said, changing the subject.

Alex shrugged. "Use it as a vacation for yourself or bring that best friend you keep texting."

"We won it together and worked our asses off doing so. I can't do that to you. I would be here without you, but I would never have done all of that today, if it wasn't for you." Sharni stopped walking, causing Alex to pause next to her as the sun slipped beneath the dark blue water lapping against the dock.

"It *would* be nice to come back," Alex said, smiling at her.

Sharni nodded.

"We should get back."

"Yeah," Sharni sighed. "I can only imagine what they have us doing tomorrow."

"Did you forget the itinerary for the week?"

"I purposely didn't remember it," Sharni said as they turned around and started back up the boardwalk.

"We're competing in a family bocce ball tournament."

"Oh, for fuck's sake." Sharni shook her head.

Alex laughed.

"Let me guess, you not only know how to play, but you're good at it."

"Nope. Never heard of it." Alex smiled.

Sharni chuckled and shook her head.

When they reached the car, Alex unlocked the passenger door and held it open. Once Sharni was seated, she closed the door and walked around to get in on the driver's side. Sharni grabbed her hand.

"Thank you."

"For what?"

"Being you."

Alex nodded.

# Chapter 19

The drive back to the estate was quiet. Alex pulled the car into the garage and cut the engine. They each got out and headed into the chef's kitchen from the side door. Sharni checked her phone, which had been tucked away in her clutch the entire time. She had a text from her sister saying they were in the basement, come down when she and Alex returned from dinner.

"My sister wants us to join them all in the basement."

"What do *you* want?" Alex questioned.

*Don't ask me that,* Sharni thought. "It wouldn't hurt to go say hi. I'm definitely not drinking any ouzo."

Alex grinned, remembering how Sharni had woken with a massive hangover. She held her hand out and Sharni took it, interlacing their fingers as they walked around to the staircase and headed down.

"Here they are," Neesa called as her sister entered the room. The group was gathered around the pool table.

"You two clean up nicely," Max said, holding up the bottle of ouzo. "Come have a drink."

"Oh, no thanks. We had wine with dinner," Sharni replied.

"I'll have a drink with you," Alex said, walking over to him.

Max smiled and poured a round for himself and Alex. "Leo? Neesa?" he questioned, still holding the bottle. His brother nodded and pulled his eyes from Sharni long enough to step over to the bar.

"What are we drinking to?" Max asked as he filled the third glass.

"Beautiful women," Leo said.

Alex grinned. "I can drink to that."

"Beautiful women it is." Max held his glass up. The other two clinked their glasses against his and then downed the clear liquor like professionals.

Sharni watched from the other side of the room, shaking her head.

"Alex certainly fits in," Neesa laughed.

"Yeah," Sharni mumbled.

"So, how was dinner? Where did you go?"

"I don't remember the name. It was a nice seafood place right on the water. We walked along the boardwalk afterwards."

"Sounds very romantic."

Sharni smiled.

"I've never seen you so happy. Love is love, and Alex is wonderful. Not to mention hot."

Sharni raised a brow at her sister. "How much have you had to drink?"

Neesa laughed. "You don't have to be a lesbian to notice a sexy woman."

Sharni shrugged and nodded in agreement. She'd certainly noticed all of Alex's sex appeal and she wasn't a lesbian ... or at least she didn't think she was. A two-month fling with a roommate in college certainly wasn't proof.

"Hey, you okay? You just went somewhere else."

"Yeah," Sharni cleared her throat. "I'm tired. It's been a long day."

"Tomorrow will be even longer. This family gets serious about bocce ball."

"Great," Sharni mumbled. She wanted to go up to bed. She didn't have to wait for Alex, and truthfully, she was scared to lie down next to her. "I'm going to call it a night," she said, stifling a yawn.

"Yeah, I'm right behind you. These boys can stay up all night emptying a bottle of ouzo, then get up and go about the day like nothing happened. I don't know how they do it."

"Me either. I wanted to die when I woke up this morning."

Neesa laughed. "Come on, I'll walk with you. Let me say goodnight to Max first."

Sharni nodded and stayed put.

"Aren't you going to say goodnight to Alex?"

"Oh ... yeah." Sharni shook her head and smiled as she walked across the room with her.

Leo stepped in front of Sharni. "You look gorgeous in that dress."

"Thanks," she replied with a smile and moved around him to Alex. "Hey," she said, grabbing her hand and pulling her away from the bar. "I'm headed up to bed, but I wanted to say I had a wonderful time tonight. Thank you."

Alex stared at her eyes, getting lost in the depth of the dark pools. Before she realized it, she was leaning in, pressing her mouth to Sharni's. The kiss was soft. Sharni pulled away before she let herself forget they were pretending. She put her hand on Alex's cheek and smiled, before turning and walking away with her sister. Alex watched her back until Sharni was out of sight. The center of her chest burned with agony over what she craved and couldn't have. *Damn it,* she sighed inwardly and turned back to the bar, sliding her empty glass to Max.

"If she were mine, she definitely wouldn't be going to bed alone," Leo muttered low enough for only Alex to hear.

She cut her eyes in his direction. "A woman like her will never be owned. Not by me. Not by you. Not by anyone. But you let yourself keep dreaming."

Max slid the full glass back to Alex who downed it in one long swallow.

Leo rolled his eyes. "I'm out. I'll see you in the morning."

"Care for a game?" Max asked, pointing to the pool table when his brother left.

"Sure, why not."

"We're probably going to wind up as in-laws at some point, so we're practically family." He smiled as he racked the balls.

"Don't put the cart before the horse," Alex replied as she chalked her cue stick.

"You're not thinking about marriage?"

"Maybe one day ... a long time from now," she said as she leaned down and smashed the white cue ball with her stick. It slammed into the triangle group, scattering the balls. A striped ball went into each of the side pockets.

He nodded. "I don't think I've ever known a model. That's more my brother's speed."

"I'm pretty sure I don't know any doctors," she replied, watching him easily sink a solid ball and miss his next shot.

He laughed. "I know we've talked about you traveling all over, but you didn't mention the fashion runway. I know that's what most people think about when they hear model."

"I've never done runway. I'm a print model. When you see an ad anywhere with a person in it, that's a print model. I've also been in commercials. I work for Indigo, so I pretty much model and advertise whatever they want," she said as she sunk two more balls.

"Wow. That's impressive, both your career and your pool skills. You're kicking my ass," he laughed.

She smiled. "You and Neesa have impressive careers. There needs to be more people like you both in the world."

"Thank you." He walked around the table searching for his next shot. "Neesa can't stop talking about how happy her sister looks. I know she loves her sister and used to be much closer to her. I assume she had no idea she was in a relationship with you."

"That would be correct."

"So, when you arrived here, that was your first time meeting their parents?"

"Meeting anyone in her family, actually." She could talk about herself all night. She was used to being in the spotlight, but she felt uncomfortable talking about Sharni and her family. "She holds her family at arm's length. I do the same."

"I'm not trying to get into your business, or hers. I'm speaking from my own experience with Mr. and Mrs. Dinjavi. They're not easy." He finally took a shot, sinking a single ball before missing his next one.

"You can say that again," Alex muttered.

"I hope this week brings Neesa and her sister closer. Leo can be a pain in the ass at times, but he's my little brother and I'd do anything for him. He's my best friend. I know Neesa misses that. What about you? Any siblings?"

"Nope. I understand what you're saying though. I guess every family is different. Each has their own reasons for why they're close, distant, or non-existent," she said as she sunk two more balls and missed her next shot. She was left with one stripe and the eight ball to end the game on her next turn. "What your family has is special. Never take that for granted."

He nodded. "That's what Neesa said to me the first time I brought her here to meet everyone."

Alex watched him search the table once more, looking for a shot to take. Part of her wanted to help him, but she also wondered if he was purposely missing to stall the game and keep their conversation going.

"So, what do you do for fun? When you're not traveling around and posing for pictures."

Alex raised a brow.

"Forgive me for being curious. I like you and want to get to know you. Like I said, we're basically family."

Alex nodded. "I live in West Hollywood, so I go to a lot of parties and mingle with people in the industry. But, if you're looking for something non-work related, I secretly like playing golf."

He quickly sank two balls and missed his next one. "I love golf. I wish I'd known. I would have saved time for us to get some holes in. My brother and I both play. Our baba tags along, but it was our pappou who taught us the game. He enjoyed playing golf."

"No one knows I like it. Not even Sharni. I sneak off and play when I need a break."

"Me too. I find it relaxing."

"So, where did this love of bocce ball come from? I heard it gets pretty competitive."

"You have no idea." He shook his head. "Baba grew up playing and introduced it to Mama when they were dating. It became a family sport when Leo and I were little. The whole family has been playing together for years. Do you know anything about the sport?"

"Nope."

"You are all in for a fun day, but be warned, we get pretty serious."

"Can't wait," she laughed and lined up her shot, easily sinking her last ball. She quickly repositioned and sunk the eight ball, ending the game.

"How did I know you'd beat me?" He smiled.

"I'm pretty sure you sandbagged." She grinned. "But it's been nice talking with you."

"You too." He patted her on the shoulder. "Shall we call it a night?"

"Yeah. It's been one of the longest days of my life."

He laughed and shook his head. "Wait until tomorrow."

# Chapter 20

Moonlight peeked through the slit in the curtains, streaming a path across the room and over Sharni's limp, sleeping form. The bedding had slid down, exposing part of her upper body, covered only by a silk, spaghetti strap top. Long, dark curls cascaded over the pillow behind her head. Alex's eyes moved from her slightly parted lips to the gentle rise and fall of her chest. She sighed softly and moved to the bathroom to peel out of her suit and take a cold shower.

When she returned to the bedroom in a wife-beater tank top and a thin pair of pajama shorts, Sharni had rolled over to face the other way. Alex got in between the sheets with catlike moves, careful not to wake the slumbering woman next to her. Thankfully, the king-sized bed allowed a good amount of space between them. Still, Alex faced the opposite direction, staring at the bathroom door until she finally fell asleep.

*

The sound of stirring in the hallway caused Alex's eyes to begin to open. Sunlight peered through the slit in the curtains and shone brightly on the bathroom door, but it was the warm body pressed against her back and arm casually draped over her midsection that caused her to come fully awake. *Not again,* she thought. The last thing she wanted was a repeat of yesterday morning. She casually stirred, inhaling a deep breath.

Sharni was lost in a dream when her eyes fluttered open. She moved to stretch in the sunlight and realized she was up against Alex's back. She stiffened, suddenly in a panic. Carefully, she removed her arm from her waist and inched back until their bodies were no longer pressed together. *She's like a goddamn magnet,* she thought, shaking her head as she gently climbed out of her side of the bed and padded to the bathroom to freshen up and get dressed for the day. She pushed aside thoughts of Alex and the body that kept drawing her in as she tried to figure out what to wear to play bocce ball.

A few minutes later, she walked back into the bedroom wearing a colorful boho beach skirt with a matching square-neck, cropped tank that left about two inches of space, allowing her bronze skin to break up the two pieces of material. She finished the look with a pair of tan sandals and allowed her natural curls to flow freely down her back.

Alex sat in bed with her knees pulled up under the covers and her arms folded over them, simply watching Sharni walk towards her. "You're beautiful," she said, tamping down the desire to get up and go to her.

Sharni smiled, turning to face her. "You're awake."

"It seems that way."

"I'll leave and let you get ready. I have no idea what time this thing starts, or even what it entails."

"From what Max told me last night, it gets pretty involved."

"Great," Sharni muttered, shaking her head. "You hung out with Max last night?"

"We shot a game of pool. I like him. He's genuine and loves your sister very much. He also thinks you and I are going to get married at some point."

Sharni's brows furrowed. "What gives him that idea?"

"He thinks we're deeply in love. He also said your sister is the happiest he's ever seen her because you're around."

"You sure talked about me a lot."

"Actually, we talked about a lot of things. Most of it was him asking questions and me answering."

"I see."

"I know none of this is real," Alex sighed as she got up out of the bed, forgetting she was only wearing a thin tank top and a pair of boxer-type sleeping shorts, with nothing under either one. "I'm simply playing the part I was hired to play. However, there are people here who do genuinely care about you and your happiness. You should let them into your life."

"That's not your decision, is it?" Sharni grumbled. She wasn't prepared for the way her body would react to seeing Alex get out of bed looking sexy and slightly disheveled from sleeping. Her core heated with a fire smoldering deep inside, reminding her what it felt like to be pressed against that warm body all night.

Alex put her hands up in defeat and turned to go into the bathroom. Sharni left the room without looking back. With the room to herself, Alex quickly freshened up and dressed in a light-grey linen V-neck shirt with drawstrings, dark blue khaki-style shorts, and dark blue canvas shoes. She too, had no idea what bocce ball was.

*

167

When Alex appeared in the dining room, everyone was just about finished with breakfast, making her and Sharni the opposite of yesterday morning. Sharni raked her eyes over the alluring woman standing in the doorway.

"Please tell me you're not hungover," Neesa chuckled.

"Oh, no. I went to bed a little late, so I slept in accidentally. I'm good to go." Alex smiled cheerfully and slid into the chair beside Sharni. The table was arranged similarly to the day before with an array of food. She added a little of this and a little of that to her plate and began eating.

"So, as I was saying," the grandmother continued, smiling in Alex's direction. She nodded her apology. "We will be playing with two teams. The bride and groom will be our captains. They'll choose players one at a time. Unfortunately, Mr. Dinjavi and I will both be sitting out today. However, we'll be cheering you on from the side, along with refereeing and measuring. So, that leaves two teams of four: the red team and the blue team. Here are the rules, we start with the pallino, a small white ball that is tossed to the other end. The teams then take turns tossing their balls underhand one at a time. The goal is to get as close as possible to the pallino. The team with the closest ball to the pallino wins the round. They get one point for that ball, plus one point for each additional ball that is closer than the other team's balls. You get two points for any ball that touches the pallino. We can measure if there are two very close balls. In the case of a measurement tie, the round will be a draw and there will be no score. Then, we gather the balls and start again. The team that throws the pallino also throws the first ball for the round. You have to win by two, and the first team to 10 points, or to go over and be ahead by two, wins the game." She smiled. "Neesa, pick your first player."

"Orphea," Neesa added, smiling at her soon to be mother-in-law.

"Baba," Max said, picking his father.

"Leo." Neesa smiled.

"Alex." Max grinned.

"Sharni," Neesa said, grinning back at him.

"Mrs. Dinjavi, you're with us," Max said, smiling at her.

"May the best team win," the grandmother added.

\*

Alex walked with Sharni as they followed everyone through the house to the covered patio looking out over the side lawn where an area of grass was cutout in the shape of a long rectangle and filled with sand that was raked smooth and flat.

"They really are serious about this," Alex mumbled.

"No kidding," Sharni replied in surprise.

"My husband built this when Max and Leo were small. We've kept it up over the years," the grandmother said, almost as if she'd heard them, but she'd been too far away. "We have two colored teams. To make it fun, we've given you each something to wear to distinguish you," she added. "Red team, you have your choice of boas or silly sunglasses. Blue team, you have your choice of silly sunglasses or straw fedoras."

Each member of the red team grabbed a red ball. Orphea and Neesa went for the boas, while Leo and Sharni took the sunglasses. Everyone on the blue team got a ball.

169

Max and Alex put on the straw fedoras and Preet and Thad chose the silly sunglasses.

Everyone put on their team ensemble and looked around at the others. Sharni pushed her red glasses up on her head and looked at her mother who had made a similar move with her blue sunglasses. Neesa and Orphea laughed as they wrapped their boas around their necks. Thad and Leo both had their silly sunglasses on their faces, one in red and the other in blue. The only two who looked like they were in their natural habitat were Max and Alex, strutting around in the straw fedoras. Alex was teaching him how to strike a model pose.

"Look at the two of them," Neesa laughed.

"Yeah, two peas in a pod," Sharni chuckled, shaking her head. Alex did look super cute in the hat.

"Is everyone ready?" the grandmother said, stepping out into the grass where the teams were gathered. "Red team won the coin toss and gets to go first. We will alternate each round after that." She walked over to the court to watch Leo toss the pallino.

Orphea, Max and Leo's mother, stepped up to throw the first red ball. It landed about a foot from the pallino.

"Let's go, Mama," Leo said, giving her a high five.

Thad, Max and Leo's father, took the first throw for the blue team. His ball went past the pallino but landed much closer than his wife's ball.

Leo had taken Sharni to the side, showing her how to hold the ball, swing her arm, and when to let go. Alex watched them out the corner of her eye as they laughed together. *This isn't real,* she told herself.

Meanwhile, Neesa tossed her ball, which landed about a foot and a half short of the pallino. Preet, Neesa and Sharni's mother, was next. Max had shown her how to hold and toss the ball, which helped, but it still landed at least two feet from the pallino. With it being his turn, Leo stepped away from Sharni and tossed his ball, which landed about eight inches from the pallino. The grandmother, who was watching like a hawk from the covered patio, cheered like a little kid as her family played their beloved game. Sharni hugged Leo and the rest of the red team gave each other high fives.

"You've got this, son," Thad said to Max as he stepped up to take his throw. His ball landed about four inches shy of touching the pallino.

"This is only the first round," Max said, smiling at Alex.

Sharni locked eyes with Alex as she got into position to throw her ball. Alex raised a brow and cocked her head to the side as if to say, show me what you've got. Sharni's ball landed almost a foot away from Leo's. She shrugged and threw her hands up.

Alex took her place at the line, casually checking the weight of the ball in her hand. She took a relaxed breath and tossed the ball. Everyone watched as the blue ball sailed towards the other end of the court, landing on the side where Max's ball was, but touching the pallino.

"Holy shit!" Max cheered, picking her up off the ground.

Alex laughed and threw her hands up when he set her back down. Thad gave her a high five and Preet clapped like she was being forced. Alex looked over her shoulder, winking and grinning at Sharni, who was smiling and shaking her head.

The grandmother walked out to the court with a pen and piece of paper. "Blue wins round one with two points for touching the pallino and one extra point for each ball that is closer than red, giving them four points." Everyone grabbed their balls and regrouped as she went back up to the patio. "Blue throws the pallino and the first ball," she added. "Isn't this fun?" she said, looking over at Mr. Dinjavi. "We used to play this for hours when our grandkids were small and continue to play at every family gathering." He simply smiled.

# Chapter 21

"Are we keeping the same lineup?" Thad asked, handing the pallino to Max for the start of round two.

"Sure, why not?" Max shrugged. "Alex, are you good with anchoring?"

She shrugged and nodded.

"You've played this before," Sharni whispered, sliding up next to her.

"I haven't and aren't you supposed to be over there with your team?" Alex replied.

"I see how it is ... game on," she said, turning and walking away.

"Game on!" Alex called to her back as Max tossed the pallino to the other end of the court to start the round. Then, he stepped aside so his father could throw the first ball. Again, he overshot the pallino, but only by a foot and cursed his bad luck. His wife, Orphea, went next. Her red ball dropped right against the pallino, causing the red team to cheer.

"It's still early, so you'd want to hit that red ball with your own, hoping to knock it away," Max said to Alex.

"So, it's a game of strategy?"

"Something like that. It's hard to do though. These balls tend to land and stop. There isn't much roll, if any at all."

"So, you'd want to literally hit her ball with yours, to move it."

"Right!"

"Got it."

Preet stepped up to the line.

"What you want to do is try and hit the red ball with yours to knock it away," Thad said to her. She nodded and tossed her ball. It landed on the opposite side of the pallino and a good foot and a half away.

Neesa went next. Her ball landed against Orphea's, securing it against the pallino.

Thad and Max shook their heads while Orphea and Leo cheered. Max walked to the line with his ball and gave it a toss. It landed on the opposite side of the pallino, about eight inches away from touching it.

Leo hesitated an extra second, then tossed his ball. It landed close to Neesa's. He wrapped his arm around Sharni's waist, talking to her about her next shot.

Alex saw them walking away together just as she tossed her ball. Both teams watched as it flew past the pallino, overshooting everyone and nearly landing outside of the court. "Fuck," she mumbled.

"It's alright. We'll get them the next round," Max said, patting her shoulder.

Sharni was last to go. Her ball was closer than last time, but still a good ten inches from the pallino.

"It's okay, we still won," Leo said, hugging her as his grandmother walked out to look at the court. "Red wins the round and gets two points for touching the pallino plus a point for each of the two balls closer than blue, giving them a total of four points. We are tied at four all. Red throws the pallino and takes the first toss."

When she went back to the patio, Sharni walked up behind Alex, running her hand down her back as she whispered, "You look a little flustered."

Alex spun around. "Maybe I let you have that one. I wouldn't want to beat you too badly. I do have compassion." She grinned and walked over to Max to talk strategy.

Sharni raised a brow and walked back to her team. "We're going to kick their asses," she said.

"Absolutely!" Neesa and Orphea agreed, giving a three-way high five. Leo put his arm around Sharni's shoulders as he reached in, adding his hand.

*

The red team gathered at the toss line. "Sharni, would you like to throw the pallino to start the third round?" Orphea asked, holding the little white ball.

"Uh ... sure," she muttered with a shy smile.

"It's easy, just toss it to the other end. Try to make sure it lands in the center," Leo said, smiling at her.

"Maybe you should do it," she replied, trying to hand it to him.

Alex watched them playing at the line, before grumbling and walking up to the patio to get a drink of water.

"Looks like you're having fun out there," the grandmother said to her.

"Yes." Alex smiled and nodded.

"Your first ball was spot on. You shanked the second one though."

"You saw that, huh," Alex sighed, still smiling.

"I see everything," the grandmother replied.

Alex met her eyes briefly before walking back out to the court. Neesa and Max were talking with her mother, who seemed to actually be enjoying herself for the first time the entire week. She decided to steer clear of that conversation. Preet Dinjavi had made it clear she didn't care for Alex on day one. Orphea had already tossed her ball, which landed at least eight inches from the pallino, and Thad was at the line, about to take his throw. Alex's eyes stopped when she saw Sharni off to the side with Leo behind her. He had one hand on her waist and the other holding her wrist as he manipulated her body, moving with her as they tossed a pretend ball. She clenched her jaw so tightly, she thought she might break a tooth.

Thad's ball landed about three inches from the pallino and on the opposite side of Orphea's ball. Neesa went next, her ball slipped from her hand and landed two feet from the pallino. She threw her hands up, smiling and shaking her head.

"Let's go, Preet!" Max cheered.

She smiled and tossed her ball. Surprisingly, it landed closer to the pallino than in the previous rounds, but still nowhere near close enough to score any points. "I tried," she said, smiling and shrugging.

Alex wondered if she was happy because Sharni and Alex weren't on the same team, so they were barely interacting, other than taunting each other. She also wondered why the hell she cared. These people meant nothing to her. This was a paying job. That was all. It was time she started remembering that.

Leo went next. His ball landed over by his father's, but slightly further away. He shook his head and sighed. Max stood at the line, concentrating on where he wanted to place his ball. He swung back and tossed it through the air.

The blue ball landed an inch from the pallino on the side where his father's ball was further out. He raised his fist in the air and smiled.

"You can do it," Leo said as Sharni stepped up to the line. She smiled at him and tossed the red ball. Everyone watched as it landed against the pallino. Leo picked her up and swung her around.

Alex ignored their celebration and with one quick movement, she tossed her blue ball through the air. It crashed into Sharni's red one on the other end of the court, knocking it away from the pallino as hers took its place. She turned around and simply shrugged at Sharni who looked dumbfounded.

"It's on now," Sharni muttered, pinning her with a stare.

"Blue team wins the round with one ball touching the pallino. Blue scores two points, plus two more for having two balls closer than red. Blue team has eight and red team has four. Blue throws the pallino and takes the first toss for the round," the grandmother said.

"No matter what, we have to win this next round," Leo and Orphea said. Neesa simply nodded.

"Damn right!" Sharni agreed, causing her sister to raise her brows in surprise.

*

Thad tossed the pallino to the other end of the court.

"This is it. Two points and we win!" Max said. "Come on, Baba."

Thad smiled at his son, then tossed his ball. It landed a foot from the pallino. "I'm off my game today," he muttered.

"It's okay. Alex and I got this," Max replied as Orphea took her shot, landing her ball two inches from the pallino on the opposite side. "Shit," he muttered.

"There's still time," Alex reassured as Preet tossed her ball. It landed right beside Thad's for her best throw yet. The rest of the blue team cheered for her while Neesa tossed her ball. It landed about eight inches from the pallino.

Max stepped up to the line and tossed his ball. Everyone watched it land about an inch from the pallino.

"Yes!" Alex cheered, hugging him.

"You've got this," Sharni said to Leo as he walked to the line with his ball. Both teams watched as his ball smashed into Max's, sending Max's ball away from the pallino and leaving his three inches away.

Alex spun the ball in her hand as she stood at the line. She tossed her ball a little harder than normal, hoping to hit the pallino square on, but she overshot it. "Damnit!" she growled.

Sharni was the last to go once more. Orphea's ball was the closest, followed by Leo's, so even if she had a bad throw, they'd get two points. But she aimed for more as she threw her ball towards the other end of the court. It landed right in front of the pallino. Leo ran down to see that it was touching and began cheering. Sharni jumped in the air as Neesa and Orphea jumped up and down with her.

The grandmother cheered along with them as she walked over to check the balls. "Red wins the round with two points for touching the pallino and two more points for having two balls closer. We're tied at eight!"

# Chapter 22

"It's not over yet," Sharni muttered with a grin, walking past Alex as everyone went to get the balls and go back up near the toss line.

"If you think so." Alex shrugged.

"Care to make a little wager?" Sharni said.

"I didn't know you were a betting woman."

"There's a lot you don't know about me," Sharni deadpanned.

Alex grinned. "You don't like to lose. I know that."

"It seems you don't either."

"Agreed." Alex nodded.

"Double or nothing?" Sharni said.

"As in?"

"I win ... I owe you nothing. You win, I owe you ten grand instead of five."

Alex stared at her for a second. "You're not actually serious."

"Want to find out?"

"Hey! Are you two playing, or what?" Neesa yelled over to them. Everyone was looking in their direction.

Alex realized she was holding the pallino and walked away, leaving Sharni alone to stare at her back. She tossed the little white ball to Neesa as she walked up to her team.

"Everything okay?" Max asked.

"Yep." She flashed a fake smile.

"Whoever gets this round wins it all. We have to put our heads together here," Thad said.

"I'm ready. Let's go!" Alex said.

Everyone watched as Neesa threw out the pallino. Orphea stepped up to the line with her ball and tossed it to the other end, missing the pallino by a little less than a foot. She walked away shaking her head.

"There's always next time," Thad said to her as he took her place.

She turned back towards her husband, faking an angry look until a smile crept in. "It's not over yet," she replied.

Thad's ball landed on the opposite side of his wife's, nearly equal distance from the pallino. Neesa went to the line after him. She looked back at Max, who was standing with Alex off to the side. She tossed her ball and overshot the pallino by about a foot. Throwing her hands in the air, she shook her head and stepped away as her mother moved up with her ball.

"I can't watch," Alex muttered.

"It's just a game," Max said.

Was it though? Had Sharni been serious? Could she literally be doing all of this for nothing? Would she really put all of that on a silly backyard game? What the hell am I doing here? Alex was lost in thought when Max bumped shoulders with her. She looked up to see Preet had landed her ball closer than ever before but was still further away than the other balls.

"It's down to you and me," he said, watching Leo get ready to throw his ball. A few rain drops began falling, but no one said anything.

Sharni stood off to the opposite side. "Come on, Leo. You've got this!" she yelled. When his ball landed closer than all the others, he and Sharni hugged and danced around.

The rain started falling a little harder as Max stood at the line. By the time his ball landed, overshooting the pallino, it had begun pouring. Alex and Sharni were last to duke it out for the win, but everyone began running to the covered patio. She watched as Leo grabbed Sharni's hand and tugged her along to where everyone was huddled out of the pouring rain shower. She shook her head and ran up to Sharni.

"I guess I win," she sneered, letting her anger get to her when she saw Sharni and Leo still holding hands. She pulled the straw fedora from her head and tossed it onto a nearby chair.

Unwilling to concede the win and unsure where this animosity was coming from, Sharni let go of Leo's hand and went out into the rain. She turned around with her arms up, taunting Alex.

Alex shook her head and walked out to her. Rain poured down, soaking them both. Calls from the patio to come back up out of the rain were unheard as the two women faced off next to the bocce ball court. Neither bothered to pick up a ball.

"What is your problem?" Sharni yelled.

"You!" Alex growled. "You're making me crazy! I know we're pretending, but you're flirting with him and it's fucking weird."

"You're wrong," Sharni grumbled, shaking her head.

"He's been after you since we got here. He even called you a thirst trap to my face!"

Everyone on the patio watched the display from the soaked women, but no one could hear the argument because of the pouring rain.

Sharni threw her hands up. "You have this all wrong!"

"I don't care anymore. If you want him, that's fine. We're not real. But wait until the week is over and I'm out of here. I'm fine with pretending to be together, but I'm not going to pretend to be getting cheated on!" Alex threw her arms up. She was soaked to the bone with water running into her eyes and dripping from her nose and chin as the rain continued pouring down.

Their clothing sagged from the weight of the water and Sharni's long locks were heavy and glued to her skin, but neither cared as they continued arguing.

"Alex, he's gay!" Sharni yelled.

"What?!" she snapped back in surprise.

"Neesa told me the first day. He's not out to his family and having us here ... together, and seeing how his family has welcomed us, has been great for him. He knows I know about him, and we've become friends. Gay guys are always flirty and touchy feely," Sharni explained hastily.

"What about Penny?"

"They've been best friends for years but have never been together. The family just assumes. That's why they ducked out on the scavenger hunt. They didn't want to spend the day kissing and pretending to be a couple."

"Oh, you mean like us?" Alex shook her head.

"I didn't want to at first, but in the end ... I was glad I did. I had fun. We had fun." She threw her hands up in frustration. "Alex, if I was interested in someone, I wouldn't be pretending to be in a relationship with you!"

Alex noticed everyone on the patio watching them like the prized fight was going down in the backyard. She quickly grabbed Sharni, pulling her close and kissing her with everything she had, pausing to lick the raindrop from her lips before sliding her tongue into her warm mouth.

Sharni kissed her back wildly, forgetting where they were and who was watching. They moved together, kissing passionately while sliding their hands along each other's body like two lovers who were seconds from stripping their clothes and taking things all the way.

Suddenly, Alex let go of her, throwing Sharni off guard, leaving her flustered and wanting more, which infuriated her.

"Are we finishing this fucking game?" Alex asked.

"I'm over it," Sharni said.

"And your bet?"

"We never agreed to it."

"Fine." Alex grabbed her hand and pulled her along as they walked back up to the patio. Everyone backed up, giving them some space, while Orphea handed them towels.

"Come inside and dry off before the two of you catch pneumonia," the grandmother said. "Lunch is probably ready."

"What about the game?" Leo asked.

"It's a draw," Sharni and Alex stated at the same time without looking at him.

Leo raised his brows to Max, who simply shrugged.

*

Alex went upstairs to continue drying off and change clothes. Sharni was headed up behind her when her sister pulled her aside. "Is everything okay?" Neesa asked.

Sharni nodded.

"The two of you sure made a spectacle of yourselves."

Sharni sighed. "That certainly wasn't planned."

"What happened?"

"Can we call it friendly competition and leave it at that?"

Neesa put her hand on her hip. Sharni might be the older sister, but she wasn't letting her get away without an explanation. "It looked like you two were about to strangle each other, then fuck."

"Neesa!" Sharni squeaked.

"I'm sorry, but ..."

Sharni finished toweling her hair and looked around. They were alone. "Alex thought something was going on with me and Leo."

"Oh my god," Neesa laughed. "Wait, you didn't say anything, did you?"

"Yes, of course! We've never argued like that before." Sharni wrapped the towel around herself and added, "His secret is safe. Alex would never out anyone."

"I guess that's when you two made up like a pair of horny teenagers on the verge of spontaneous combustion," Neesa said, crossing her arms.

Sharni grinned.

Neesa smiled. "I've never seen you like this. You two are obviously head over heels in love with each other."

"Yeah," Sharni mumbled. "I need to go get out of these wet clothes."

"I'd steer clear of mom and dad when you come back down. They weren't too happy about the display."

"Mom can go clutch her pearls for all I care," Sharni said, turning to go up the stairs.

Neesa laughed and shook her head.

# Chapter 23

Alex was dry and freshly dressed in a pair of khaki shorts and a light-pink button down with the sleeves rolled back to her elbows. The first few buttons were open, allowing parts of her collarbone and chest tattoos to peek out. "You look like a drowned rat," she said when Sharni walked into the room.

"I feel like one," she replied, stepping around her to go into the bathroom.

"Are we good?" Alex questioned, turning towards her.

"Why wouldn't we be?"

Alex sighed. "Things got a little crazy out—"

"The argument or the kiss?" Sharni said, cutting her off.

"I don't know ... both?"

"From my sister's point of view, it was hot. I'd stay away from my parents though," Sharni replied nonchalantly as she went into the bathroom with Alex following her.

"And you?"

"Alex ..." Sharni said softly as she turned around to meet her eyes. "I'm sorry for bringing you into all this and the position I've put you in." She reached out, placing her hand on Alex's cheek. "Today was a slap in the face. I knew I was using you; I mean I'm paying you to be here and pretend we're together, but I hadn't realized I was also

186

making you feel used. I'm insensitive. That's probably part of the reason I'm single." She moved to pull her hand away and Alex stopped it.

"That's not you. At least, not the you that I've gotten to know. I wouldn't be here if I didn't want to be, so you're not using me. It's a business deal. But I'd like to think we were at least becoming friends." She smiled. "I should've never called you out like a jealous lover. I had no right. You can be with or fall for whoever you want. I have no say in any of that. I'm sorry. I started all of it." She pulled Sharni's hand from her face and held it in her own. "The kiss ... I saw everyone watching us and panicked. We were both keyed up from the argument and obviously that drove us much further than we should've gone, especially in front of everyone. I'm sorry for that too."

"Never apologize for something we both did. I kissed you back just as fervently. And I should've realized how my friendship with Leo looked to you. So, don't apologize for something that's my fault."

Alex nodded. "It seems like we do a lot of this."

"What? Apologizing or having deep conversations?"

"Both," she chuckled.

Sharni grinned and shrugged.

Realizing she was still holding Sharni's hand; Alex kissed the back of it and let it go. "I'll leave so you can dry off and get changed."

"I was thinking of taking a hot bath. That clawfoot tub is too beautiful not to be used. Plus, I'm freezing!"

Alex smiled, mentally chastising herself for letting her brain wander astray with images of herself in the tub with Sharni. *This week needs to end before I lose control,* she thought.

Plus ONE

\*

No one was around downstairs. Alex meandered about for a little while, looking at various paintings on the walls before coming to a stop in front of the large windows in the tearoom. Water on the glass distorted the images in the distance as rain continued pouring down. Turning to walk away, her eyes landed on the beautiful piano. Assuming everyone was still in the house, despite being all alone as she'd wandered, she sat down anyway, sliding her fingers delicately over the keys.

Before she knew it, Alex was sitting on the bench playing *Creep* by Radiohead, a song she'd learned because she liked the way it sounded. Her fingers moved back and forth as she worked her way through the song with the words playing in her head. When the song ended, she went right into *Zombie* by the Cranberries, another song she loved because of the melody.

When she finally pulled her fingers from the keys, resting them on the top of her thighs, she heard clapping and pivoted to see Orphea standing nearby. "Sad songs," she said. "Am I wrong?"

"No." Alex shook her head. "Although, it depends on how you perceive it."

"Or how you play it ... which is beautifully, I might add."

"Thank you. It's been a few years. I'm rusty, but I can't seem to stay away from this thing," Alex replied, referring to the piano.

"My brother and father played it constantly." She smiled, reminiscing. "That gene skipped me, and apparently, my children."

Alex laughed.

\*

"Is that *Creep*?" Neesa whispered, walking up to her sister who was leaning against the wall outside of the tearoom.

Sharni nodded. She moved to say something when the piano started again with the song *Zombie*. Sharni smiled, remembering Alex mentioning her eclectic taste in music on the plane.

"Wow," Neesa whispered, shaking her head in awe. "Everything that woman does is sexy as hell."

Sharni raised a brow. "Are you sure you're the straight one?"

"I'm beginning to wonder," Neesa laughed. "She doesn't have a sister, does she?"

Sharni shook her head. "She's an only child. Why?"

"Just making sure."

"Uh huh," Sharni muttered.

"Does she play at home?" Neesa asked.

"The first time I ever heard it was here ... yesterday."

"You've been dating her for almost nine months and just now found out she plays the piano?"

"I knew she took lessons as a kid."

"If Max could do that, we'd never get any sleep. I'm pretty sure you're missing out on a few things," Neesa said.

"Piano or not, I know exactly how sexy Alex is. I can barely keep my hands off her," Sharni replied, suddenly sounding much louder. *Fuck*, she thought, realizing the piano had stopped.

\*

Orphea's brows shot up into her hairline and Alex froze. She was certain that was Sharni's voice and by the sound, it was close.

"Hello, ladies," Orphea said, stepping around the corner.

Alex got up and walked behind her. She grinned and shook her head when her eyes met Sharni's.

"We're sorry for interrupting," Neesa said. "We were just discussing how wonderfully you play."

Alex nodded.

"So, we heard." Orphea smiled, making Sharni want to crawl into a hole.

Alex moved closer and grabbed her hand, pulling her towards the tearoom. She let go and sat down on the bench once more, motioning for Sharni to follow. "What do you want to hear?" she asked.

"Surprise me," Sharni whispered, unable to let go of the gorgeous eyes holding hers.

Alex nodded and put her hands over the keys.

*

Orphea and Neesa had followed them into the room, but turned and walked back out, giving them privacy.

"Why didn't you get Max piano lessons?" Neesa asked.

"I did," Orphea laughed.

Neesa chuckled, knowing how untalented her fiancé was musically.

"Come on. Let's find your parents before they find them."

"Thanks. Sharni doesn't deserve the harsh treatment. They'll never let her be. She's the oldest, and to them, the biggest disappointment."

"She deserves just as much happiness as the rest of us, no matter who she loves," Orphea said, smiling softly at her.

Neesa briefly thought of Leo and how scared he was to come out, but she knew he would be welcomed with open, loving arms. She couldn't have picked a better family to marry into and silently wished the same for her sister.

\*

Alex began *A Whole New World* from Aladdin. It was the first song she performed on stage as a child. Once she got going, it came back like riding a bicycle. She felt like a kid again.

When she finished, Sharni grabbed her hand and leaned her head on her shoulder. "That was my favorite movie growing up. I wanted to be Princess Jasmine," she said softly.

Alex smiled. "It was my favorite too, but I wanted to be Aladdin," she laughed. "That was the first concert song I ever played. I must've been about eight, probably."

"Wow. I know why you didn't stick with it, but you're still very good."

"Thanks."

"Do you have a piano at home? My sister asked me, and I had to change the subject."

"Yeah, I heard," Alex chuckled. "No. Honestly, I haven't played in years. There's something about this piano that draws me in every time I walk by it."

"Maybe it's helping you replace the old memories with new ones."

Alex nodded. "Who knew you were philosophical?"

Sharni lifted her head and let go of her hand. "You bring it out of me, I guess." She grinned, looking at the eyes staring back at her when Alex turned.

"How was your bath?"

"Relaxing," Sharni sighed, remembering how good it felt to simply let go, even if it was only for a few minutes.

"Maybe I should've stayed." Alex grinned.

"You're funny," Sharni laughed, shaking her head.

"Come on. We missed lunch and your stomach sounds like a monster is trying to get out. It almost distracted me while I was playing," Alex said, standing and holding her hand to Sharni.

Sharni chuckled and playfully smacked her before taking her hand.

# Chapter 24

Sharni sat on a stool at the counter while Alex rummaged through the refrigerator and pantry. "I can't believe they ate without us," she muttered.

"Well, they probably thought we would be upstairs for a while ..." Alex trailed off as she began putting items on the counter. When Sharni didn't say anything, she paused and looked over at her. "What?"

"You think they thought we were up there having sex?"

Alex laughed and shrugged. "Why not?"

"My parents certainly don't think that way."

"Maybe not, but after what happened outside, I'm pretty sure everyone wanted to give us some space."

Sharni nodded in agreement. "I would've at least left us a plate or something."

Alex chuckled. "I'm not much of a cook, but I think I can piece some stuff together for a couple of stuffed pitas. Does that work for you?"

"Sure." Sharni watched her turn on the broiler oven and get to work, filling each pita. "I can cook, but I don't know anything about Greek food."

"I don't either, but I know this is meat and that's cheese."

Sharni shook her head and smiled.

Alex finished with the stuffing and put the pitas on a baking sheet that she slid into the oven.

"I didn't know you baked pitas."

"You don't. I put them in the broiler to heat them up, melt the cheese, and make them a little crispy." Alex shrugged, hoping her idea worked. "I'm starving and it's still pouring rain. So, it's this or we swim to a restaurant in town."

"No thanks. I'm done with the rain."

"My thoughts exactly," Alex said as she put on a mitt and pulled the pan from the oven. Using a spatula, she placed each pita onto a plate. Then she squirted a couple different sauces on the side of each plate to use for dipping, before handing one plate to Sharni and sitting down next to her with the other. "Lunch is served."

"It smells delicious!" Sharni said, brushing her long locks over her shoulder. Subconsciously, she looked around. They were still alone.

"Everything okay?" Alex asked, trying to take a bite without burning the skin from the roof of her mouth.

"Yeah," Sharni sighed. "I just expect my mother to appear at any moment, chastising me for eating with my hair down."

"What's her obsession with your hair? I've noticed her nagging you about it."

"We're Tamil and traditionally our culture is Hindu, not Muslim. The women wrap their hair up in a bun and use pins to secure it. It's almost never worn down, and certainly not when you're out and about or around people. However, our family is Christian, which is why our grandparents immigrated. The Christians were literally forced out of the country. Christian Tamils are nothing like European or Western Christians. We still follow a lot of Tamil traditions that are Hindu, so it's a mesh of the two. As kids our hair was always wrapped and pinned up. I think I told you both of our parents were born in Canada. Their mothers were pregnant when they immigrated, and that's as far as they got before the babies were born. They immigrated to the States when the children were still young. Eventually, those children grew up and married each other after becoming citizens, and later became our parents. My sister and I were born in Boston, which was where our family finally settled. We're American and live in America, but our mother and grandmothers will live and die by their traditions. Our father pretty much does whatever our mother tells him. In our culture, the women run the show."

Alex smiled.

"Neesa follows our culture, but not as strictly as our parents and grandparents. I'm sort of the black sheep."

"Yeah, I picked that up on day one," Alex laughed.

Sharni grinned. "So, you can see why I'm sick of hearing about my hair. If she tells me to put it up again, I may cut it as short as yours."

"No, don't do that. Your hair is gorgeous."

"Thanks." Sharni smiled. "What about you? Have you ever had long hair?"

"Yes. I told you I was adopted and raised by my grandparents. They are LDS. Talk about nutjobs. No offense to anyone who is LDS or religious in general, for that matter. It just isn't for me."

"I feel the same way. Everyone is entitled to their own beliefs and views on religion. So, what is LDS? I've never heard of it."

"The Church of Jesus Christ of Latter-Day Saints. They run the state of Utah, alongside the Mormons."

"Are they anything like traditional Christians?"

"Worse. So much worse. They literally control your entire life. You can only be friends with people who are in the church. You can only marry people who are in the church. They even live in LDS only neighborhoods! They have these ordinances they live by, which are barbaric. I hated every minute of it. I had to keep my hair past my shoulders and dress very plainly. You never draw attention to yourself, especially at the temple. As soon as I turned eighteen, I moved out of my grandparents' house and in with a friend who had also escaped a year earlier. I cut my hair off and worked a shit job as a bartender to pay for headshots. Once I had those, I sent them to multiple agencies and was denied, until Jean-Pierre Bardot, a very reputable French agent, contacted me. He was in L.A. and happened to see my photos. He arranged for me to fly out to him for an in-person meeting and to see if I had what it took. He knew Indigo was searching for a new vibe to take them in a new direction. He signed me that day and a week later, we were at Indigo headquarters, signing my contract. I never once went back to Utah, or to my grandparents whom I referred to as the wardens. I owe my career to Jean-Pierre. He has been my personal agent for ten years now."

"My parents drive me crazy, especially my mother, but I couldn't imagine not speaking to them."

"My grandparents took my mother from me. I was four when she died. They showed up, took me and a few of my possessions, and had everything else thrown away. I don't know how I managed it, but one of the things I kept was a picture of my mother holding me as a baby. I still have it to this day. I hid that like pirate treasure from the wardens."

"Oh my god. They just threw their daughter's life in the trash?"

"Yep. Then, they proceeded to try and mold me the same way they did her, but just like her, I ran like hell when the gate opened and never looked back."

Sharni shook her head. "What about your father?"

"I have no idea who he is. I was four, so I don't remember much of my mother, but she was fair-haired and fair-skinned. I must look more like him."

"What about your birth certificate?"

"The only one I have is from when my grandparents adopted me. They are listed as my parents."

"There must be an original at the vital statistics office in the state you were born in."

"You know, I haven't thought about that. He may not be on it, but it won't hurt to check into it when I get back. Thanks for the idea."

"You're welcome. With immigrant parents, I learned a lot about that years ago. They used to talk about what they went through to become citizens and how important it was to them."

Alex nodded.

"So, Jean-Pierre, he's the reason you speak French, am I right?" Sharni said, changing the subject.

"Yes. He's multi-lingual, and he was adamant that I learn French. I'm not fluent, but I speak enough to get by easily."

Sharni stood up, grabbing their empty plates. "I think you lied when you told me you can't cook," she said, walking to the sink to wash everything they had used.

"I'm not a chef," Alex laughed. "But I won't starve, either."

Sharni chuckled and continued washing the dishes.

"What do you think we'll be doing tonight?" Alex asked, as she got up, stepping around Sharni to dry the wet dishes and put them away before the chef returned to prepare dinner.

"I have no idea. Probably hanging out in the basement or whatever that room is with Max, Leo, and Neesa."

"Do you want me to do something else so you guys can double date?"

Sharni met her eyes and raised a brow. "You have jokes."

Alex smiled.

"Besides, haven't you and Max become best friends?"

"What?"

"You've been hanging out a lot."

Alex shrugged. "I like him. He's easy to talk to. His brother on the other hand ..."

"Leo's young and still trying to find himself. Give him a little slack. Don't you know any gay men?"

"Of course. I'm a model and I live in West Hollywood. I've just never had one taunt me about taking the woman I was with."

"He was probably teasing, and you took him seriously."

Alex shrugged.

"You know ..." Sharni dried her hands and turned her body towards Alex. "Even if he was a straight man, flirting with me and trying to get my attention, I still wouldn't look at him twice. Pretend or not, I'm here with you."

Alex smiled at the eyes looking back at her. Her gut tightened and her throat filled with saliva as she fought back the need to kiss her. *This isn't real*, she mentally chastised herself. "I could use a drink," she blurted.

"Me too, but I am not drinking that ouzo shit." Sharni shook her head.

Alex laughed. "I think it's fine once you get used to it. Just don't overdo it."

"Uh huh," Sharni muttered, following her out of the kitchen.

# Chapter 25

"There you are!" Neesa said, running into Sharni and Alex in the hallway. "The dresses have arrived. We're about to do the final fitting. Max and Leo are in the basement with their father, I think," she added, looking at Alex, who simply nodded.

"Better put your hair up," Alex teased, grinning at Sharni.

"Fuck you," Sharni laughed.

"Really?" Alex raised a brow.

"Get out of here," Sharni chuckled, shaking her head.

"You two are something else," Neesa giggled.

"Isn't that the truth," Sharni muttered.

"I can only imagine what tomorrow will be like with you two."

"What's tomorrow?" Sharni asked as she followed her sister towards the staircase.

"Dance lessons."

"We're probably going to kill each other," Sharni answered honestly.

"That or send the place up in flames," Neesa laughed.

"Why are you so enthralled with how hot my relationship is? Aren't you the one getting married?"

"Yes, but I'd bet money you'll be right behind me. I've never seen two people so made for each other."

"Who's made for each other? You and Max?" Preet asked as they entered the room.

"She was referring to me and Alex," Sharni replied, ignoring her mother's stare.

"Oh, I'd have to agree with that," Orphea said. "Speaking of Alex, where is she?"

"I sent her to the basement with the boys," Neesa answered.

"Poor thing," Orphea laughed, shaking her head.

Sharni paid no attention to them as they cackled on like old hens. She wanted to try on her dress, make sure it fit, and get the hell out of there before her mother's bitterness swallowed the room. She quickly unzipped the bag and removed the lilac colored, A-line dress, eyeing it up and down. It was a halter V-neck with a built-in bra. As she spun it around on the hanger, she noticed it was also backless. She slipped it on carefully and turned to look in the mirror. The dress was also asymmetrical, with the bottom stopping just at her knees in the front and was slightly longer in the back. The chiffon fabric was light and airy, flowing around her legs as she moved.

"What do you think?" Neesa asked, stepping over to her. "I wanted it to be something you'd wear again."

"I love it."

"Great." Neesa smiled, hugging her sister. "Mom hates it, just so you know," she whispered.

"She hates everything," Sharni mumbled.

"What's Alex wearing?"

"I assume a suit. We didn't really discuss it, past that," Sharni replied, taking the dress back off.

"Without a shirt?"

"That's what she usually does. Again, we didn't discuss it. Will that be a problem?"

"Not with me." Neesa smiled.

"Are you sure you're not a little bit lesbian?"

Neesa guffawed, grabbing the attention of their mother and Orphea, who were getting her dress ready to try on. "No. Not at all. But if I was, you'd have some competition."

"Uh huh," Sharni chuckled, putting her dress back in the bag.

"Are you going to appease our mother and wear your hair up?"

"Are you?" Sharni asked.

"Yes, but not because she wants me to. I think it's tradition for all brides to wear their hair up. I like it."

Sharni nodded. "I was thinking of wearing mine up, too. But not for her."

Neesa smiled. "I'm so glad you're here."

"Me too. I wouldn't miss my baby sister getting married."

"I haven't missed it have I?" the grandmother said, walking into the room. "Oh, my darling, that is exquisite," she added, looking at the dress Sharni was sliding back into the hanging bag.

"Mama, where were you? I looked everywhere," Orphea called from across the room.

"I had to take a call in your father's study."

"Is everything okay?" She stepped over to her mother with concern.

"All is fine. Now, let's see this bride in her gown." She smiled.

"Neesa, we're ready," Preet called. Orphea went back over to help her as Neesa slipped into her dress, making sure it fit one last time.

"That's beautiful, Neesa!" Sharni stated.

"She looks like a princess," Orphea added.

"You are going to be a gorgeous bride," the grandmother said.

"Quick, take it off before something happens to it," Preet demanded, ushering her back out of the stark white dress. Neesa rolled her eyes in her sister's direction and obliged their mother.

*

"Are you ready for the big day?" Alex asked, sitting on a barstool in the basement.

"As ready as I'll ever be, I guess," Max replied. He and his brother were playing pool while their father fiddled with the TV on the other side of the room.

"What about you, Leo? Do you think you'll get married one day?"

He looked at her and grinned. "Maybe. Sharni would fit right in with our family," he said.

"Max, come here," their father called. "I need you to turn the TV on or off when I tell you. I'm trying to fix the cable box."

Max handed his pool stick to Alex. "Here, take my place. It's almost over. Don't beat him too badly." He smiled.

She nodded and walked over to the table.

"I guess it's you versus me," Leo said, flashing another grin.

Alex leaned close, lowering her voice. "Listen, you little shit. I know the truth. If you don't stop baiting me, I'm going to sing like a canary."

He froze as his eyes grew to the point of looking like large white circles with a tiny brown dot in the middle of each one.

"I'm back," Max called, walking across the room. He cocked his head to the side as he looked at the same balls still on the table. "You two didn't finish it?"

"No, we were just talking, right?" Alex smiled at Leo and handed Max the pool stick.

"Who's shot is it?" Max asked his brother as Alex walked back to the bar.

"Alex, do you drink brandy?" Thad asked, stepping behind the counter.

"I've been known to partake." She nodded.

"I have an old bottle that belonged to my wife's father. He gave it to me a year or so before he passed, and I've been waiting for the right time."

"Baba, are you finally opening Pappou's bottle?" Max asked, stepping over to the bar with his brother after winning the game.

"I was thinking about it. How about a game of poker? That's more my speed," he said, smiling at Alex.

"I'm in," she replied.

"Do you think anyone upstairs would want to join us?" he asked, opening the old bottle. "This will need to breathe for a bit."

"I'm sure they would. I'll run up and ask." Alex slid off her stool and stood up.

"I'll go with you," Leo blurted.

She raised a brow but began walking anyhow. Once they were out of the room, Leo stopped her.

"Was the argument, or whatever it was, in the yard earlier because of me?"

Alex sighed and crossed her arms.

"I'm sorry. I never meant to cause any trouble. I don't know how to be me around my family. Straight guys always flirt with pretty women. Sharni was very happy and in love with you, another woman, so I figured flirting with her would be safe. She wouldn't be interested, and it would be all in good fun pretending to be straight."

"Only straight guys who are assholes flirt with women who are unavailable. They do it for the thrill of trying to steal her away. It's a dick move," she stated.

"I never thought about it from your viewpoint. I'm sorry, Alex. None of that was my intention. You two are great together. Honestly, I hope to have a love like that someday. Seeing how my family is with the two of you ... well ..."

"Leo, you have a loving, accepting, happy family. I'm sure they will welcome you with open arms. You're very lucky."

"Thank you. I hope so. I'm planning on telling them after the wedding."

Alex nodded. "Come on, we need to find the rest of the group."

*

Alex and Leo had checked just about every room of the large estate when Neesa and Sharni walked out of a room, followed by Orphea and the grandmother.

"Baba's opening Pappou's bottle of brandy. We're about to drink it and play poker," Leo said.

Sharni looked at Alex, who simply smiled at her.

"Count us all in," the grandmother said with a smile.

"What about your parents?" Leo asked, looking at Sharni, then Neesa.

Both women shook their heads. "They won't come down," Neesa said, "but I'll go ask them."

The grandmother made brief eye contact with Alex before shaking her own head.

*

"Levi always brought out the brandy for special occasions," the grandmother stated with a smile. They were seated around the table, each with a stack of poker chips, giddily anticipating the start of the game. "Thad, this bottle belongs to you, so the toast is yours," she added, lifting her glass.

"Forty-eight hours from now, our oldest son will become a married man. I dreamed of this day since he was a little boy, knowing how proud I'd be of him, even back then," Thad said. "First, raise your glass up for those who can't be with us, Leviticus and Konstantine, we miss you dearly." Everyone lifted their glass. "Now, raise your glass up to the bride and groom, Maximos and Neesa, may you have all the happiness in the world." Everyone raised them again. "Finally, raise your glass up to family. May Nikolaidis, Papadakis, and Dinjavi always be one." All the glasses came together above the center of the table before everyone took a long swallow of the mahogany-colored liquid.

Neesa and Sharni looked at each other and cringed from the strong alcohol. Meanwhile, the rest of the group took a second sip and began discussing the flavors. Some got hints of vanilla and others picked up on maple and cinnamon.

"This must be an acquired taste," Neesa mumbled, setting her glass down.

"One which we did not acquire," Sharni chuckled.

"We also have ouzo," Thad said, smiling at the two of them.

"No!" Sharni exclaimed, causing everyone to laugh.

"How about a martini? I thought I saw gin earlier," Alex said, getting up from her seat.

"Yes, please," Neesa replied thankfully.

"I like it dirty," Sharni said, winking at her.

Alex grinned and shook her head as she walked over to the bar. She grabbed two martini glasses and the bottle of gin. Then, she searched around for the dry vermouth, which she found near the jar of olives. She made both drinks with equal parts, garnishing one with a twist of lemon peel before pouring a bit of olive brine from the jar into the second glass and finishing it off with a toothpick that had three olives on it.

"Who knew we'd had a bartender here all week," Max said.

"Hardly," Alex replied as she handed the glasses to the two women. "I worked under the table as a bartender for a ratty joint when I was eighteen."

"Isn't that illegal?" Neesa asked.

"Yep. I lied on my application." She smiled. "I only worked there until I signed my modeling contract about six months later."

"Well, you've still got it," Sharni said, sipping her drink.

"I agree," Neesa added, clinking her glass to her sister's.

"Those are hand-picked olives from right here on our land. Aren't they delicious?" Orphea said.

"Yes," Sharni agreed, nodding her head with a smile.

"Anyone else before I sit down?" Alex asked.

"I might hit you up for one tomorrow. It's been a while since I've had a good martini," Orphea replied.

When everyone else stayed quiet, the grandmother yelled, "Come on, let's play cards!"

They all looked to the end of the table where she was poised and ready to school them at Texas Hold'Em.

\*

One by one, players left the game as they ran out of chips, until Alex and the grandmother were the only ones still at the table. Leo went to call Penny. Max went with his father to check everything outside, since the rain had finally stopped, and clean up the bocce ball game. Orphea went to speak with the chef who was busy prepping for dinner. Neesa and Sharni were the only two left behind to watch the game play out.

"I wonder if Alex should concede. I mean, she's my fiancé's grandmother," Neesa whispered, sipping her second martini.

"I want her," Sharni mumbled.

"What?" Neesa leaned closer.

Sharni set her glass down, realizing she'd had enough alcohol. "I said, let them play. They're having fun."

"That's true. Alex fits in really well with this family. You both do. They've welcomed you with open arms."

Sharni nodded. "They'll welcome Leo, too."

"I'm sorry our mother is such a bitch to you. Dad just goes along with whatever she says and does."

"Thanks." She smiled and wrapped her arm over her sister's shoulders from the side. "I don't lose sleep over the two of them. Life's too damn short."

"I agree."

"Besides, we're here for you. I'm so proud of you, Neesa. You're going to be a beautiful bride, and Max is going to make a great husband. It won't be long, and we'll be gathered again to welcome a little one."

"Oh, hell no!" Neesa exclaimed, causing the two women at the table to look over at them.

"Sorry." Neesa smiled sheepishly before cutting her eyes to her sister. "We want children, yes. But we're still young and want to open our own practice and hopefully do more work with Doctors Without Borders first."

Sharni nodded.

"What about you? Do you and Alex want kids?"

Sharni nearly fell off the arm of the couch she was leaning against. "Damn," she grumbled, straightening herself back out.

Neesa giggled like a teenager. "Are you drunk?"

"No. Of course not." *Maybe a little,* she thought to herself.

"Alright, Alexei. Time to see what you're made of," the grandmother said, pushing all her chips to the center of the table.

Neesa and Sharni watched in suspense. "Why does she call her Alexei?" Neesa questioned.

Sharni shrugged. "It's Greek for Alex," she replied, holding her breath as Alex pushed her chips to the middle.

"What have you got, kid?" the grandmother asked.

Alex looked at the five cards on the table: the jack of spades, the queen of diamonds, the seven of hearts, the queen of clubs, and the five of diamonds. Then, she peeked at the two cards in her hand: the jack of clubs and the jack of diamonds. "Full house. Queens and jacks," she said, placing her cards on the table face up.

Sharni's breath hitched, causing her to gasp slightly.

"Uh oh," Neesa whispered.

"That's a great hand. A winning hand ... at most tables." The grandmother grinned. "But not this one. Four queens," she said, flipping her two cards over.

"Ah! You got me," Alex replied, smiling brightly.

"You were close," she replied, standing and hugging Alex before strutting towards the door like a boss. "She's special. Don't let go of her," she whispered, patting Sharni on the arm as she passed by her.

Sharni nodded, looking back at Alex and Neesa cleaning up the table.

# Chapter 26

Dinner was strained for the Dinjavis while everyone else enjoyed talking about the poker game. The rain had stopped hours ago, but the ground was still wet and squishy.

"Max and I walked around outside. It's soft, but there's no more rain in the forecast until late next week. The heat will soak up the water in the morning, leaving it dry and firm by the time the tent company arrives later in the day," Thad said.

"That's good. I was worried we'd have an issue," Orphea replied.

"The wedding will be outside facing the rolling hills and olive groves. The reception will be in an air-conditioned tent on the other side of the property," Neesa said, looking at her sister.

Sharni nodded. "How many guests?"

"Fifty. We didn't want anything too big. It's both our families, of course, plus our friends and colleagues from Doctors Without Borders, and family friends," Max answered.

"In lieu of gifts, we asked everyone to make a donation to DWB in our names," Neesa added. "I won't be changing my last name because it would be a nightmare with my medical license. But it's fine. When we have children down the road, they'll have the Papadakis surname like Max."

"I hope that's not too long of a road," the grandmother said, smiling at them.

"Yiayia," Max started, but she held her hand up at him.

"I know. I know," she continued. "Your careers and charitable duties come first. I'm very proud of you both for what you do and what you've accomplished, especially at such a young age. The world needs more people like you in it."

Orphea smiled at her son and soon-to-be daughter-in-law before turning to Sharni and Alex. "So, what about the two of you? Will we hear wedding bells soon? Hopefully, you're not on the same long road they're on," she laughed.

Alex looked like a cartoon character who ate a bird as she swallowed a lump in her throat. Sharni simply smiled and shrugged.

"That's not happening," Preet muttered.

"Why not?" Orphea asked. "They're two people in love. Marriage is generally the next step."

"We won't be a part of it, and we won't pay for it," Preet stated matter-of-factly.

"It's a good thing we both do well then," Alex said, smiling and winking at Sharni. "However, there's no proposal and no wedding planned. We're here for Neesa and Max's beautiful love story and wedding. I for one, would love to hear how you got engaged."

Sharni grabbed her hand, squeezing a silent thank you. Alex rubbed her thumb over the back of Sharni's hand in reassurance.

"It probably wasn't as romantic as most people," Max replied, referring to their engagement. "I'd bought the ring after a few months of dating. I had a feeling Neesa was the one, and I knew I wanted to get married. We were on a trip with DWB in Tanzania and part of the group was headed out to Kilimanjaro for the day. We decided to tag along. I'd brought the ring with me in case I got up the courage to ask her." He looked at Neesa.

"I was busy watching an elephant walking with her baby about twenty yards away through the window of the safari truck, when it suddenly came to a stop. Smoke billowed from the engine as it sputtered and shut off. We were a group of doctors from all over the world. If there was a medical emergency, we'd use a tent as a makeshift ER and save a life, but none of us knew a damn thing about cars. Everyone stared at each other and the wild animals not too far away. Before anyone could say anything, the driver jumped out, popped the hood, said a bunch of words I wasn't familiar with in Swahili, then slammed it closed and got back in. He turned the key and the truck groaned back to life. Once again, we were headed down the road."

"Oh my god," Sharni laughed.

"Yeah, it was something. Anyhow, once we got to our destination, it was beautiful. Of course, no one went to the top, but we did hike up a good way. I was perched on a rock, watching the animals in the distance, when Max stepped in front of me, blocking my view. At first, I wondered what he was doing. This was my space. There were plenty of other rocks and spots to sit and look out."

"I knew it was now or never," he said. "I pulled the ring from my pocket, bent down on one knee, and asked her to spend the rest of her life going on adventures with me."

"Of course, I said yes!" Neesa smiled. "We have a picture of us, taken by one of the other doctors. I'm sitting on the rock and he's kneeling in front of me."

Sharni wiped a tear from her cheek as she smiled at her sister.

Thad and Orphea talked about how they got engaged. The grandmother told her story of meeting and falling in love with her late husband and how he proposed. The Dinjavi's marriage was basically arranged by their two close families, so they didn't have a story to tell, other than saying it was a happy arrangement.

*

As soon as dinner was over, everyone left the room, scattering about the house. Sharni bumped shoulders with Alex as they walked into the parlor and sat down on the couch side by side. "It's half over. We just have Thursday and Friday to get through, then hop back on a plane Saturday. Where will you go from here?"

"Probably L.A. to re-sign my contract. Then, Monaco and Dubai from there, more than likely. Jean-Pierre said Indigo is hitting the ground running with the campaign for this new line and those shoots are already on the books."

"Wow. You really are a world traveler."

"According to my passport, yes. But I haven't seen enough of anywhere to say I've really been there. Does that make sense?"

Sharni nodded. "When will you be back in L.A.?"

Alex shrugged. "I'm usually in and out of the exotic locations quickly, then back home or New York City for fittings and to shoot in the studio. It all depends on the ad and how it's supposed to look. It may be a new line of suits, so they'll shoot me in five different colors, in five different places. Those pictures will go in five different magazines or whatever. I can travel for three months straight, then be home for three or four with nothing happening."

"What a whirlwind schedule."

"Yeah, but I'm used to it," Alex said. "Unfortunately, it's also what keeps me single. Who wants to wait while I travel all around?"

"I'm the opposite. I usually wind up with someone who has to be attached to me twenty-four/seven. I'm super busy with my job. It's not easy to get a start-up off the ground and grow it enough to sell it off to the highest bidder. It takes a lot of dedication and long hours. I choose to be single, so I don't have to deal with the neediness of a relationship."

Alex nodded. "Sounds like we're made for each other," she laughed.

Sharni smiled. "It's probably why it's been so easy. We understand each other."

"Until Leo appeared."

"He hasn't been so flirty. Did you say something to him?"

"Nothing really."

Sharni raised a brow.

"He tried goading me earlier today. I told him I knew his secret and if he didn't stop, I'd sing like a canary."

"Alex!" Sharni shrieked.

"Calm down. We had a talk. He apologized and explained everything to me. He didn't realize what it looked like from my point of view. We're good now."

Sharni smiled and shook her head.

"He has no idea how good he has it. I wish I had a supportive, loving, kind family," Alex muttered.

"Me too."

"We'll always have each other. Even when this is over, I'll always be there for you." Alex put her arm around Sharni's shoulders.

"I feel the same way," Sharni murmured, looking at her eyes before leaning in and laying her head on her shoulder.

*

When they finally retired for the night, Alex realized they hadn't gone to bed at the same time all week. Sharni had wound up in bed before her and was fast asleep by the time she joined her. Feeling slightly awkward, she sat down on the chair in the corner. "I'll let you get ready for bed first. I'm going to take a shower."

"You should try that tub. I nearly fell asleep in there," Sharni replied, walking past her and into the bathroom.

"Maybe if you were in it with me," Alex mumbled to herself.

Sharni poked her head out. "Did you say something?"

"Nope."

She nodded and closed the door.

Alex picked up her phone and sent a quick text to her agent. *I'm ready to hit the ground running. Have you heard from Indigo?*

*Yes. We're re-signing this week. I assume you'll be back in L.A. by Monday.*

She sent a thumbs up and kissing face emoji. *How are things in Paris?*

*Total shitshow.*

She started to reply, but the little dots popped up, indicating he was sending another message.

*Are you going to tell me who you're with? It's not like you to sneak off to Greece for a week.*

*Nope and not what you think,* she replied, sighing as she set her phone on the small table.

"It's all yours," Sharni said, stepping out of the bathroom in a black satin spaghetti strap top and matching shorts that barely covered anything.

Alex averted her eyes as she stood and walked towards the bathroom, needing a cold shower now more than ever. "Yeah. Fine. I was just texting with my agent."

"Everything okay?"

"Yep. He was curious about who I was with."

"Oh."

"I don't travel unless it's for work."

"Really?"

Alex nodded, glancing at her before she closed the door. Sharni was already snuggled under the covers. Two and a half more days," she whispered to herself as she turned on the shower and began undressing.

# Chapter 27

Alex awoke the next morning with Sharni once again cuddled up to her back with her arm draped over her mid-section. She was literally on the edge of her side of the bed, facing away from Sharni and she managed to seek her out during the night anyhow. She sighed inwardly. Pretending she didn't want to run her hands over Sharni's beautiful body was becoming less and less of an act. She couldn't help being attracted to her. Sharni was breathtaking, smart, funny, sincere ... and so much more. Kissing her like a lover and sharing a bed with her was like soaking a tree in gasoline and leaving it in the woods. It would only take one spark to burn down the entire forest.

Her stomach was growling, and she needed coffee. Careful not to wake the sleeping woman, Alex lifted Sharni's arm and slid off the bed as delicate as a mouse while placing her arm back down. As soon as she was clear, she quickly exchanged her tank top and sleep shorts for a crème-colored, linen henley shirt and khaki shorts, and slipped her feet into dark brown boat shoes before going quietly out the door. She left the top buttons undone on her shirt and pushed the sleeves back to her elbows as she made her way down the stairs.

The family was gathered around the table having breakfast. Alex wasn't interested in being around everyone. She snuck into the kitchen for a cup of coffee and stole a banana on her way out. She made her way outside and around to the pool deck, carrying her banana and casually sipping her coffee. Once she had settled on one of the loungers, she put the coffee on the table and peeled back the sides of the banana. The sun had risen nearly an hour before, casting everything in soft orange glow as far as the eye could see. This trip to Greece had been nothing like her previous. The island of Mykonos was beyond comparison to the Peloponnese countryside. She wasn't sure which she liked better. In a way, she kind of preferred both: the stunning beaches and nightlife and the tranquil serenity.

"Hey, you," Sharni said softly.

Alex looked up at the woman standing next to her in a short, pink sundress. A matching hair kerchief held her long, wild curls back, and white sandals donned her feet. She smiled and slid over, allowing Sharni to occupy the lounger with her. "Did you have breakfast?"

"No. I went looking for you."

Alex peeled her banana a little further and offered her a bite, along with her coffee mug.

Sharni chewed the fruit and sipped from the mug, allowing the black coffee to soothe her. "Are you sure we're not a real couple?" she laughed.

Alex smiled and shook her head. "I'm so confused, I'm scratching my watch and winding my ass."

Sharni guffawed, nearly spilling the coffee as she handed it back to her.

"Well, aren't you two just the cutest," Neesa said, walking towards them. "I was wondering why I didn't see you at breakfast."

Sharni raised the banana and took another bite before offering it to Alex, who in turn took a bite after sipping from her mug. Neesa laughed and sat down nearby. "It's so pretty here. I wish we could stay," she sighed.

"Where will you go after the wedding?" Alex asked.

"We have an apartment in Athens and another in Boston. We'll go back to the States after the honeymoon and regroup with DWB in Thailand. But it'll probably be a while before we're back here at the estate."

Alex nodded.

"I don't know if I'd ever leave, if I owned this," Sharni said.

"I was thinking the same thing," Alex replied.

"The whole family owns it technically. They're all shareholders in the business that is run by this estate. Max's grandmother is the head of everything, and his mother runs a lot of the day-to-day stuff. His father is an attorney. Leo is a little like you, Sharni. He started in law school, then left to go do his own thing."

"Oh, really? What does he do?" she asked.

"Marketing and sales for one of the big hotel chains. Max thinks he's going to take over the family business after their mother one day."

Sharni and Alex nodded.

"So, are you two ready to learn how to dance?" she asked with a huge smile. "Max is so nervous. I'm pretty sure he has two left feet."

"Alex has had dance lessons," Sharni said.

"Cool! Maybe you can help teach all of us."

"It's been a minute." Alex smiled.

"Piano had been a minute too. Look how quickly that came back to you," Sharni said, grinning at her. She watched Alex eat the last bite of the banana she was holding, causing her lips to part, and suddenly wanted to taste her mouth.

"You're a wonderful piano player, by the way," Neesa added, pulling Sharni's brain from the fog that had encompassed it.

"Thanks." Alex smiled, sipping her coffee.

"Anyway, I came to tell you we have a car service taking us to the studio. We're leaving after lunch. Leo and Penny should be here soon. They're riding with us. We're all going out for dinner and more dancing afterward, before everyone splits for the night."

"Sounds good." Sharni nodded. "I woke up with a few voicemails that I need to go answer before it gets any later in L.A.," she added, moving to get up.

"Do you want any more of this?" Alex asked, holding up her mug.

"Nah, I took enough of your breakfast." She grinned.

Alex smiled and shook her head, watching her walk away. "She makes me crazy."

"Yeah, but you love her," Neesa said with a smile.

"Uh huh," Alex muttered, swallowing the last sip of her coffee.

*

Sharni was glad to get away without kissing Alex. She wasn't sure what would happen if their lips met. She needed to go get control of herself. She also needed to return Tracey's call. She scrolled through the favorites in her phone and tapped her name as she headed up the stairs.

"It's almost midnight," a groggily voice answered as Sharni went into her and Alex's shared room.

"Sorry," she replied, closing the door. "I saw you called and was just now able to get free. I'll call you back later. I keep forgetting the time difference."

"You might as well talk now. I'm up," Tracey said, sitting up against her headboard.

"I'm in over my head."

"What do you mean? How are things going with that gorgeous piece of arm candy?"

"Fine."

"I feel like you're leaving a lot out of that sentence," Tracey laughed.

"Yeah," Sharni sighed. "The wedding's tomorrow, so we'll be flying back on Saturday ... and parting ways from there."

"You sound sad about that."

"Maybe I am. Hell, I don't know."

"First, you didn't want to go. Now, you don't want to leave."

"It's beautiful here. Plus, I'm really enjoying spending time with my sister again. Her fiancé's family is amazing. My parents hate me and Alex. I'm pretty sure they loathe seeing us together."

"That's a lot."

"Yep," Sharni sighed. "Alex is wonderful though. We've gotten so in step; it's starting to feel more real than fake. We were actually laughing about that earlier."

"Hmm."

"What?"

"Nothing. You sound happy. Honestly, happier than you've been in a long time."

"Maybe it's the fresh air."

"Or that sexy woman sharing your bed."

Sharni laughed. "On that note, I'll let you go get some sleep. You're starting to sound delirious."

Tracey giggled. "It's one a.m., so you're not wrong."

"Bye," Sharni chuckled, shaking her head. She got up from the bed and opened the door just as Alex was walking in.

"I'm sorry," Alex said in surprise. "I thought you went somewhere else."

"It's fine. I'm off the phone. I was just talking to Tracey."

Alex nodded. "How are things in L.A.?"

"I don't know. All she did was ask about you. I think she's borderline obsessed," Sharni laughed.

"I'll have to meet her when I get back from Dubai."

"She'd die."

Alex grinned. "I know we said we'd always be there for each other. I'm assuming you want to stay in touch. I guess I didn't think about that."

"Of course. I mean, I usually don't keep in contact with my exes, but I can make an exception for you." Sharni smiled.

"Oh, really?" Alex raised a brow.

"Do you?"

"What? Keep in touch with my exes?"

Sharni nodded.

"You'd have to be in a relationship to call someone your ex, so ... no. But I do occasionally run into women I've dated. We generally move in the same circles." She locked eyes with Sharni. "This fake relationship has been the most real relationship I've ever had."

"You're quite good at it."

"It somehow comes naturally with you. I can't explain it." Alex smiled.

"I know what you mean. It feels easy and unforced. That's actually how a relationship should be," Sharni said, speaking from experience. "So ... what does one wear to dance lessons?" she asked, changing the subject.

"Something comfortable and either loose-fitting or stretchy. You need to be able to move around freely."

"Like a dress?"

"Dress, skirt, pants ... whatever makes you feel sexy. To me, dancing is sensual."

Sharni raised a brow and grinned.

"What?"

"Are we dirty dancing or wedding dancing?"

"Dancing is only dirty if you perceive it that way. A simple slow dance can be clean and classic, or it can be sultry and seductive."

Sharni nodded; her brain went to the clothes she had hanging in the closet. *Sexy,* she thought, mentally flipping through her dresses.

# Chapter 28

Alex stood at the bottom of the stairs, leaning against the rail as she waited for everyone. She'd dressed in black slacks, a dark purple, slim-fitting dress shirt with the top three buttons open, and the black leather oxford dress shoes she'd brought to wear to the wedding.

"Max and Neesa are liable to be late to their own wedding," Orphea said, walking up to her.

Alex smiled and shoved her hands into her pants pockets.

"Here they come," Orphea stated, hearing footsteps and laughter on the stairs.

Sharni appeared first, wearing a black bodycon mini dress with a cowl neckline, spaghetti straps, and a lace-up back. Black strappy heels were on her feet and platinum and diamond bar earrings dangled from her ears, matching the bracelet on her wrist. She'd added a little eyeliner and shimmering lip gloss to her otherwise flawless complexion.

"Wow," Alex muttered, stepping up to grab her hand and walk her down the last few stairs. "You look—"

"Sexy?" Sharni said, cutting her off as she looked at her with a raised brow and sly grin.

"Breath-taking," Alex finished, still holding her hand.

Sharni's grin curled into a full smile before they both turned to see Max and Neesa coming down the stairs.

He was dressed similarly to Alex, but his shirt was red, which matched Neesa's red and black patterned midi dress.

"You all look ready to go out dancing," Orphea said, snapping a quick photo of the group. "The car service is here. Leo and Penny are already outside. Everyone, have fun, and you two enjoy your last night being single!"

"Thank you," Neesa said, hugging her.

"Don't worry about your parents. We're all going out to dinner."

Sharni looked at Neesa and raised her brows. Neesa held in the chuckle trying to escape her smile.

*

"Here we are," the driver announced, pulling up along the curb. Alex got out and held her hand for Sharni, then Penny. The other three got out of the other side.

"Are we really dancing for three hours?" Leo asked as they made their way inside the building.

"We'll stay for as long as it takes," Max replied, giving him a stern look.

"Welcome to Florakis Dance. I'm Basil Florakis and this is my wife, Cora. We are three-time national ballroom champions who are retired from competition and living our best life now as instructors." They were older, probably over fifty, but very trim and fit. She had light brown hair twisted up in a tight bun and he had salt and pepper hair slicked back in a thin ponytail. Both wore professional dance attire.

"Who do we have here?" Cora asked.

"I'm Max and this is my fiancée, Neesa. That's my brother Leo and his girlfriend Penny, and this is Neesa's sister Sharni and her girlfriend Alex."

"Great, so you're the bride and groom. I take it best man and maid of honor?" she asked, pointing to Leo and Sharni.

"Correct," Neesa replied.

"Wonderful. So, we have you booked for three hours. Our notes state you'd like to learn a waltz to use as your first dance, but you'd also like to learn some fun dancing for the reception as well, yes?"

"Whatever you can teach us." Max smiled.

"Has anyone had dance lessons?" Basil asked.

"Alex is formally trained," Sharni blurted.

"Really? Competition or ..." Cora looked at her.

"I competed in ballroom as a kid. It's probably been fifteen years since I stopped," Alex stated.

"It's like riding a bike. It'll come back." Cora winked and smiled.

"Okay, we're going to start with the waltz," Basil said. "You're dancing at your wedding, not the competition floor. We're going to teach you seven basic steps to make you look timeless and elegant, but not overly complicated so that you both feel very comfortable. This is what it will look like." He grabbed Cora's hand and moved to the center of the room. They moved through the seven steps flawlessly around the dance floor before stopping.

"That's beautiful," Neesa said.

Sharni smiled at her sister.

"First, we start with the basic box step. Leaders with me, followers with Cora." Basil lined up Max, Leo, and Alex on one side of the room and Cora took Neesa, Sharni, and Penny to the other. "You've had professional training, so this should come natural." He began moving his feet and the others followed along, as he counted from one to six. Once they had it down, everyone met back in the middle to discuss the frame and how the partners moved through the box as a couple.

Alex moved slowly, leading Sharni through the six count box steps. Leo and Penny struggled at first, but finally got it. Max and Neesa took a few times, but also got the steps down easily. They all continued dancing the box over and over until Basil stopped them.

"Okay, now we're going to progress those steps to move around the floor. The waltz moves in a counterclockwise direction on the outside of the floor." He partnered with Cora to show them, before pairing off again to teach the lead and follow steps.

"You have the box down. Now, we're going to progress instead of box," Basil said, showing them the new six count. He then lined them up and had them go through it side by side until he felt they were ready. "Okay, let's pair up again. Remember to always be offset of your partner, looking over his or her shoulder, and leave a little space between the two of you. Once you get more comfortable with the steps and the movement, you can try closing the gap a little."

Alex held Sharni's right hand with her left and placed her other hand just past her arm pit, curling it around to her back. They moved together slowly through the steps. If Sharni messed up, Alex simply started over.

"This looks so much easier when other people do it," Sharni whispered.

Alex smiled. "You're doing really well."

"Next, we're going to do a left turning box," Basil said, gathering everyone again. He and Cora showed them how it should look. Then, they paired off once more.

When everyone had the steps down, a simple underarm turn was added to finish the steps, then they began dancing around the room to music. Cora and Basil worked with the bride and groom, making sure they were comfortable with the movement and flow of the dance.

After about ten minutes of waltzing around the room, Cora and Basil stopped everyone. "There are a few more moves we can teach you, but it's up to you and your comfort level," he said.

Max and Neesa looked at each other. "I think we have enough. It's only two minutes by ourselves, then they join us for the rest of the song. It doesn't need to be intricate, just look nice," Neesa said.

"Wait. What?" Sharni questioned.

"You and Leo are our wedding party, so you'll join us in our dance. That's why you're here learning this with your partners," Neesa replied. "At first, Mom wanted you and Leo to dance together, but I changed it. I like this better anyhow."

Sharni nodded.

"It'll be fine," Alex whispered, checking her watch. They'd already been there over an hour.

"Wonderful. Let's move on to some reception dancing." Basil smiled. "You've already learned the basic box step, so we're going to build off that with the American Rumba and add hip rocking with cross-body leads." He grabbed Cora's hand and walked her to the middle of the dance floor as the music started. They fell easily into the quick and slow, sultry moves of the sexy dance.

"Can you do that?" Sharni whispered, looking at Alex, who nodded.

"You can do it too, just relax your hips and feel the music."

"Sexy," Neesa said, watching the pair in the middle of the room.

"Okay," Basil called, stepping away from Cora. "Leaders with me."

Cora took the followers to the other side of the floor and began showing them the steps along with the hip movements. "You move through the basic box like this, but when you do so, you're doing two quick side steps followed by two slow steps, rotating your hips in a figure eight as you do so."

Alex had kept up with some of her dances by going to the nightclubs, so she was very familiar with this rumba. Max and Leo struggled at first but began getting the movements once they loosened their hips.

Once the women on the other side of the room had the steps, Basil and Cora showed them how to incorporate the under-arm turn, similar to the way they'd done it with the waltz, plus cross-body leads to turn and change direction.

Everyone paired off and began dancing the rumba to music. Alex kept a firm frame and easily led Sharni around, moving closer and closer until their lower bodies were nearly connected.

Feeling Alex's hips rotating with hers caused Sharni to forget her movement and step on Alex's foot. Alex smiled and started again, this time keeping Sharni close to her from the first step. Their bodies moved as one with their hips rolling together while dancing around the floor.

"Feel the music," Alex whispered.

Sharni heard the music, but all she could feel was Alex's body against her, until she put space between them and led Sharni through an under-arm turn. Two quick movements and they were glued together once more, swaying their hips in a connected figure eight. Once again, Alex created space and moved into a cross-body lead that sent them into a side-step left, then a side-step right, before moving back into the box.

"Wow!" Neesa said as she watched them dance. Neither Alex nor Sharni had realized they were the only two still dancing, until the music stopped.

"You two definitely have it down. You must be used to dancing together," Cora stated.

Alex shook her head no.

"This is the first time I've ever done this dance," Sharni said. "I guess I have a good leader," she added, smiling at Alex.

"This concludes our three-hour session," Basil announced. "It's been our pleasure instructing you. Congratulations on your wedding. We wish you all the best."

"Thank you," Max and Neesa replied together.

\*

The sun was still an hour from setting when they stepped out onto the sidewalk. Sharni casually linked her fingers with Alex's as they walked towards the waiting vehicle. Alex opened the door and held her hand out for Sharni to enter, then Neesa. She climbed in behind them, while the others got in on the opposite side.

"Where are we going now?" Sharni asked.

"Dinner," Max replied. "Then, dancing."

"Great. More dancing," Leo laughed.

"This is like a combined bachelor/bachelorette, sort of," Neesa said. "We wanted one last night of fun before we tie the knot, and what better way to do it than with all of you." She smiled. "Plus, some of us need to keep practicing our dancing," she added, winking at her sister.

"It's hard to believe this time tomorrow, you'll be a married man," Leo stated, looking at his brother.

"Yeah." He nodded, looking at Neesa.

"Wow, I didn't think about it like that. Holy shit. You'll be a married woman tomorrow," Sharni said.

"Yep." Neesa looked back at Max, and they shared a smile.

\*

Dinner went by quickly and before they knew it, they were back in the vehicle headed to the dance club. "What kind of place is this?" Alex asked.

"It's called Club International. They have a big, full bar and a bunch of high-top tables surrounding a large dance floor. The music is supposed to be a mix of fast and slow-tempo rock, pop, and Latin, with dancers of all levels. It was recommended by the dance studio, actually."

Alex nodded.

"We're going to have a blast!" Penny exclaimed. "I came here about a year and a half ago for my friend's birthday." She looked at Leo and said, "Angelina."

"Oh, yeah. I remember that night," he replied.

"It's probably like the clubs that I've been to at home," Alex muttered to Sharni.

"Do you go a lot?"

Alex shook her head. "I used to."

The vehicle came to a stop outside of a building that looked like a warehouse. Club International was written in neon above the wide double doors. A line was already forming against the wall for entry to the upscale nightclub. Everyone exited the vehicle and Max gave his name to the bouncer, who let them right in.

"Do we know someone?" Neesa asked, wondering how they skipped the line.

"If you reserve a table and pay the cover in advance, you get priority entrance," he said, smiling at her before giving his name to the guy inside. They were shown to a pair of high-top round tables pushed together with six stools scattered around, near the edge of the dance floor.

A slinky blonde walked up, stopping very close to Alex. "I'm Lina, and I'll be handling your table tonight. If there's anything you want ..." She eyed Alex up and down. "Or need from the bar, let me know."

"We're celebrating. My sister-in-law and her fiancé are getting married tomorrow," Alex said, grabbing Sharni's hand.

"Wow. Congratulations! We have Dom Perignon. It's perfect for a celebration."

"I'm sure we'll be drinking champagne tomorrow," Max said.

Everyone nodded in agreement and gave their drink order. Alex unbuttoned the cuffs of her shirt and rolled them back to her elbows as she looked around the large room. Couples and groups occupied various tables surrounding the large dance space in the center, which was quickly filling with people.

"Let's put our new moves to the test," Penny said, pulling Leo off his stool. Neesa and Max followed, leaving Sharni and Alex alone when the drinks arrived.

Alex took a few long sips of her bourbon, feeling the smooth liquor go all the way to her core. Sharni swallowed more than half of her martini and grabbed Alex's hand. "Come on, Hollywood. Show me what you can do."

Alex grinned and raised a brow but allowed Sharni to pull her through the crowd to the dance floor. The other two couples were nearby, fumbling through the rumba steps they'd learned. *You asked for it*, Alex thought, pulling Sharni against her. She bent her backwards with their bodies connected at the waist, then brought her back up before spinning her around and pulling her in once more as they went into the rumba steps, rolling their hips together. Sharni wasn't a hundred percent sure she remembered the steps, but it didn't matter. Alex was pressed tightly against her, leading her body through every movement.

Neither woman paid attention to the couples around them who were grinding, twerking, gyrating, and doing other various forms of dancing. Alex let go of Sharni's upper back and grabbed her hand. Now holding both of her hands, she put some space between them as they moved through the steps, looking eye to eye. Alex raised her hands, lifting them above their heads as their bodies closed the gap once more before separating. Alex let go of one hand and spun Sharni around before bringing her back in again.

*I have no idea what I'm doing, but God don't let it stop,* Sharni thought. Her chest heaved and hot blood raced through her veins as she looked into Alex's eyes.

As the song changed, Alex put Sharni's arms around her neck and ran her hands down her back, all without missing a step in their dance or losing eye contact. The offset dancing position allowed Alex to slide her leg between Sharni's naturally as she moved through the steps, but with their bodies so close, it was much more erotic.

One of Sharni's hands went into her hair while the other slid down to the open buttons of her shirt, resting on her chest with part of her fingers under the material. She was playing with fire, and she knew it. Alex grinned and grabbed her hands. She spun Sharni around and slid up behind her, rolling their hips with her crotch against

Sharni's ass, before spinning her back out to dance the box steps once more.

Sharni's face was beaming when they finally made their way back to the table to finish their drinks. She couldn't remember the last time she'd felt so free-spirited.

"I thought you two were going to burn a hole in the floor," Neesa said, smiling.

"Right!" Penny added, clinking her glass to Neesa's.

"Oh, please. There were people doing all kinds of crazy things out there," Sharni replied.

"I wasn't sure you'd noticed anyone else," Leo interjected.

"Was she supposed to?" Alex questioned. "When someone is dancing with you and you're the lead, their eyes, their body ... everything should be concentrated on you. When you move, they move. When you breathe, they breathe. Being in sync with each other is what makes the dance happen. It could be the waltz, the rumba, or the country two-step, as long as you connect. That's what makes your partner know when and what you're about to do. You can dance with a stranger if you're a good leader."

"When did you say you quit dancing?" Max asked.

Alex laughed. "Competitive ballroom? About fifteen years ago. In the local clubs? A year, maybe less." She shrugged. "You do know we were doing the same rumba dance you all learned today."

"That definitely did not look like the same dance," Neesa muttered, shaking her head.

"It's the same basic box steps. Once you have that down, you can go in and out of the box with other moves. When you're comfortable with your footing and your partner, you can move in close."

"Apparently, I should've paid more attention in class today," Penny muttered.

"If you two dance like that tomorrow, our mother will have a stroke right on the spot," Neesa replied with a chuckle.

"Maybe that's the point," Sharni added. "Besides, dancing is only dirty if you perceive it that way." She winked at Alex.

"Are we going to sit here and talk about dancing or are we going to dance?" Leo said, getting up from the table.

The waitress came over for another round, but Max waved her off as he held his hand out to Neesa.

Alex locked eyes with Sharni. "Have you seen enough?" She grinned.

Sharni chuckled and held her hand out.

Once they were back on the dance floor, Leo came up to them. "I'm going to put you to the test," he said, looking at Alex. "You dance with Penny; I'll dance with Sharni."

"What?" Alex stated, confused.

"If you're a good leader, you can dance with anyone. Let's see it."

Alex wanted to smack him, but she'd prove her point, as long as it was okay with Sharni ... as well as Penny, of course. She looked at Sharni who simply smiled and shrugged as she took Leo's hand. "I guess that leaves us," Alex said, smiling at Penny.

"I'll warn you, I'm not as good a dancer as Sharni," she replied.

"Don't sell yourself short. Come on. Let's show them how it's done. Just follow my lead; feel the push and pull." Alex grabbed her hand and moved to the middle of the floor. They immediately went into the traditional hold and began the box steps.

Penny kept up with Alex, remembering the steps and trusting her. She'd never danced with a woman before, but it didn't seem to be any different, other than she knew what she was doing. Alex spun her, then pulled her in close as their hips rolled together.

Sharni watched the pair next to her as she danced with Leo. He wasn't a bad dancer, but he wasn't a leader like Alex. Still, she managed to have fun and kept him from stepping on her toes. Her smile quickly faded, and her chest began to burn when she saw Alex pull Penny close. Jealousy wasn't a feeling she was familiar with, but something was taking over her body and she didn't like it.

Alex spun Penny and slid in behind her, rolling their hips together before spinning her again and changing direction. Both women were smiling and seemed to be having fun. The faster music allowed for more open box steps and a lot of playful hip action, which Alex loved. She led with confidence and Penny followed along easily.

"She really loves you," Leo said, breaking Sharni's concentration.

"Huh?"

"She's dancing with Penny, perfectly I might add, but her eyes are on you."

Sharni turned her head and immediately locked eyes with Alex. They were both dancing with other people, but somehow still together. Sharni's heart raced and her knees weakened watching Alex roll her hips with Penny's while her leg was between her thighs. She had no idea if Alex had purposely pulled Penny closer, raising the temperature of their dance, but it was driving Sharni mad to see her with someone else.

The song had changed and in turn, Alex had adjusted the tempo of their dance, slowing it down to accentuate the sultry moves of the rumba as she brought their hips together for the quick steps and slow rolls. She spun Penny left, then right before bringing her back in once more.

Penny finally understood the magic of the rumba when her body flushed, and it wasn't from the heat in the room. She swallowed the lump in her throat and followed the hips against hers and the hand on her back, guiding her. She felt like a mix of Cinderella at the ball and Baby in the movie *Dirty Dancing*, with all eyes on her, but she was sure no one was watching.

When the song ended, everyone headed for the table.

"I bow to you. Goddess of all Dancing Gods," Leo said, curtseying in front of Alex, which made her smile and shake her head.

"If a broomstick could lead like her, I'd dance with it," Penny added, causing everyone to laugh. Sharni nodded in agreement.

"Are we ready to go? Or are we still dancing?" Max asked. "Because some of us are getting married tomorrow and need their beauty sleep."

Neesa smiled and lightly smacked him on the arm. "Let's get out of here. I don't want my groom looking disheveled with bags under his eyes like a binge drinker who slept on the floor all night."

Max chuckled and waved for their waitress so he could get the bill.

"Here, let me get it," Alex said, but Max shook his head.

"It looks like Baba paid for our tab," he muttered, looking at the piece of paper.

"How did he do that?" Leo questioned.

"They knew we were coming here. He probably called and gave his card number over the phone."

"That was nice of him," Neesa said.

"Right. We should've ordered that bottle of Dom," Leo added as they headed toward the door.

Sharni grabbed ahold of Alex's hand, so she didn't lose her in the crowd, which had tripled since they'd arrived.

"Did you have fun?" Alex asked once they were outside.

"Yeah." She smiled. "I actually didn't want to quit dancing."

"With Leo?" Alex teased.

Sharni raised a brow. "Your jokes are back."

Alex spun her and caught Sharni with their bodies together. One of Sharni's hands was pressed against the top of Alex's chest and the other was behind her neck. "I'll dance with you whenever and wherever. All you have to do is ask," she whispered before kissing her lips softly. When they parted, the others were watching, and Penny was whistling.

Sharni and Alex both smiled and shook their heads as they walked over to the group who was waiting for the car service at the curb.

# Chapter 29

Once they arrived back at the estate, after dropping Penny and Leo at her apartment in town, the two couples walked inside. Max and Neesa had planned to keep things traditional and spend the night in separate rooms. They shared one last hug and kiss before parting ways.

"I don't know if I could do it," Sharni muttered, pulling off her shoes once she and Alex were in their room.

"What? Sleep alone the night before?"

"Get married," she stated.

"It's not for everyone," Alex replied, removing her own shoes.

"What about you?"

"Do I want to get married?" Bright light caught Alex's eye, coming in from the bathroom window. She hadn't realized it was a full moon until now. She stared at it for a second while she thought about her answer. "I used to say never. I wasn't interested in settling down ... at all. I think life changes a little every day." She began undoing the rest of the buttons on her shirt as she continued talking. "I think it was Aerosmith who said, 'Life's a journey, not a destination.' If I met the right person and fell in love, who knows what that journey would be like. Therefore, I can't say never."

Sharni's mind raced through thousands of words, but her brain couldn't quite put them into sentences as she

240

watched her loosen one button after another. So, she simply nodded.

"Put on something comfortable, shoes are optional," Alex said, turning around and rummaging through her clothes.

"Should I ask why?"

"Nope," she called over her shoulder.

Sharni shrugged and headed reluctantly towards the bathroom. She began untying her dress when she remembered she needed clothes to change into. She pulled the door back open to find Alex sitting in the chair in a pair of khaki shorts and a light blue linen button-down with short sleeves. She was barefooted with her legs crossed at her ankles. Sharni stared, slightly disappointed, having hoped to maybe catch her in the middle of dressing. "What are you, Houdini?"

Alex raised a brow and cocked her head to the side like a dog.

"How did you change so quickly?"

Alex shrugged.

Sharni shook her head and looked through her clothes, opting for a pair of small black shorts and a tight white tank top before heading back into the bathroom. When she emerged again a few minutes later, Alex was leaning against the dresser with her phone in her hand. She smiled and shoved it into her pocket.

"Where are we going?" Sharni asked when she pulled the door open.

Alex held her finger up to her mouth and stepped out into the hall, barefooted. Sharni looked down at her own bare feet, wishing she'd put on a pair of shoes, but Alex grabbed her hand and tugged her towards the stairs.

The massive house was eerily quiet as they made their way through to a side door that opened onto the large deck surrounding the rectangular pool. Light from the full moon illuminated the grounds, casting everything in a soft white glow. Sharni stood rooted in place, gazing up at the stars as Alex walked over to the chaise lounges and grabbed one of the small tables between them. She placed it in an open area of the deck on the opposite side of the pool and waved for Sharni to join her as she removed her phone from her pocket.

"Dance with me," she said, pressing the play button on her phone and holding out her hand.

"What? Out here, like this?" Sharni questioned, looking down at her bare feet.

"There's no one around to judge you. No one to impress. No reason to pretend. It's just you and me." Alex smiled.

Sharni grabbed her hand and stepped in front of her. Alex got into position, keeping their hands together while placing her other hand under Sharni's armpit, curving around to her back. The music was soft and slow, so Alex led her through the rumba steps slower than usual, keeping with the rhythm. Their hips rolled together seductively with every step. Alex led Sharni through a gentle spin in one direction, then once more the opposite way, bringing them back together even closer than before. Sharni avoided looking towards her eyes. Instead, she concentrated on the hands and body leading her, and the leg that kept sliding between her thighs.

A few songs later, Sharni's heart pounded in her chest. She was on fire. The smell of Alex's cologne; the touch of her body; the seductive sway of her hips. Sharni couldn't take much more. *This isn't supposed to be real, but*

*God, I want her.* She turned her head slightly, immediately connecting with Alex's eyes in the glimmering moonlight. Their dancing came to an abrupt stop and suddenly, instead of being offset, they were face to face.

Alex took the hand she was holding and placed it on her chest above her breasts and under the open buttons of her shirt. Sharni's fingers spread out over her skin and moved up to her collarbone and along the side of her neck before sliding back down. She ran her left hand along Alex's shoulder to her chest and under her shirt where the other one rested. The feeling of Sharni's touch caused Alex to close her eyes. When she opened them, Sharni was inches away. Dark eyes full of desire stared back at her. Alex hesitated and Sharni closed the distance, pressing her mouth softly to Alex's while gently teasing her tongue between the parted lips. As the kiss deepened, Alex ran her hands under the back of Sharni's tank top, placing flat palms against her silky-smooth skin.

Sharni felt like her body was on fire and Alex was the water it craved. She slid her hands down Alex's chest, pausing to loosen each button. When she reached the bottom, she ran her hands back up Alex's soft skin, lingering slowly as her palms slid over small breasts, before pushing the shirt off her shoulders. Alex ran her hands up Sharni's sides, sliding her tank top with them, causing her breasts to bounce slightly when they were freed.

Alex pulled her lips away gently, catching the gaze in Sharni's eyes before lifting her shirt the rest of the way. It fell to the floor beside them as she allowed her own shirt to slip down her arms. She raked her eyes over the dark bronze skin of Sharni's bare torso.

Sharni reached out, tracing the tattoos on Alex's abdomen and sides with her fingers. She remembered how erotic they were in the ad on the side of the bus, peeking out from Alex's sports bra and underwear, but seeing them in person ... touching them, sent her own body into overdrive. Alex was unlike anyone she'd ever been with. The idea of making love with her both excited and scared Sharni. She ran her hands back up the front of Alex's body, cupping her small breasts, tracing the tattoos along both sides of her collarbone, then over her shoulders and up into the back of her short hair as she brought their bodies fully together. Feeling Alex's bare breasts pressed against hers made her slightly weak in the knees.

Alex put her hands on Sharni's waist, before running them gently up her sides and around her back, under her long wavy hair. She locked questioning eyes onto Sharni, with deep, dark pools staring back at her. "Are you sure about this?" she whispered.

"I've never wanted anything more in my life," Sharni murmured huskily.

"Out here?"

"I don't care where we are," Sharni said, crushing their lips together in a fiery kiss.

Alex grazed Sharni's velvety tongue with her own and bit her lower lip gently as she walked her backwards towards one of the wide cushioned loungers along the side of the pool. They broke the kiss long enough to slide their shorts down. Sharni raised a brow at Alex's bare, shaved crotch.

"I told you to put on something comfortable." Alex shrugged.

Sharni smiled and slid her lacy panties down her thighs, revealing herself to be just as hairless. She kicked the garment to the side with her foot and pulled Alex down on top of her as she lay back on the soft cushion. Alex kissed her gently before pulling away to run her mouth over Sharni's jaw and down her neck, tracing a path all the way to her perky breasts. She glanced back up at Sharni's eyes before taking a dark, peaked nipple between her lips. Sharni bit her lower lip between her teeth when Alex's warm, wet tongue grazed her nipple. One of her hands was in Alex's hair and the other on her shoulder as she moved back and forth between her breasts, licking and sucking one while kneading the other.

Alex gradually moved lower, tracing a path with her mouth down to the top of Sharni's thighs where the scent of arousal permeated her senses before continuing all the way back up to her lips, kissing her like a starving lover feeding from her mouth. Sharni pushed Alex to her back, breaking the kiss as she moved on top of her and sat back to straddle her hips. She stared down at Alex's eyes as she ran her hands over her chest, kneading her small breasts and flicking her nipples with her thumbs. Alex sat up, wrapping one arm around Sharni's waist while her other hand slipped between her wet thighs. Sharni brought her arms up around Alex's neck, pressing their lips together once more as Alex's fingers slipped delicately over her throbbing center. She continued making leisurely passes back and forth, teasing her entrance each time, until she slid two fingers inside of her. Sharni gasped against her mouth and began slowly moving her hips up and down. Alex kept her hand still, letting her set the pace until she felt her growing closer to release.

Careful not to fall off the chair, Alex rolled Sharni to her back, removing her fingers as she slid her body down, tracing an agonizing path once again over Sharni's body with her mouth until she settled between her legs. Sharni moaned and bit her lower lip to keep from crying out as

Alex's tongue stroked up and down between her wet folds, brushing her clit delicately with every pass. Alex ran her hands over Sharni's stomach, feeling the muscles contract against her palms.

Sharni sat up on one elbow, running her free hand through Alex's hair as she watched her intently. The full moon illuminated the night in a blue tint similar to cool lighting, but all Sharni focused on was Alex's eyes staring back at her. She felt like she was buzzing with electricity from head to toe with her senses on overload and her body in overdrive. Alex stalled her tongue and lifted her mouth. She kept her eyes locked onto Sharni's as she kissed her way back up her body, slipping her hand between her thighs as their lips came together in a breathless kiss.

Tasting herself on Alex's mouth sent her over the edge. She opened her mouth and her legs to her, kissing Alex passionately while writhing against the fingers sliding back and forth over her clit. She gripped her short hair with one hand and wrapped the other around her back, holding on as wave after wave rolled through her trembling body. She'd never felt anything so intense in her life.

Alex placed soft kisses along her neck and collarbone as she pulled her hand free and moved to Sharni's side to give her some space to catch her breath. "You're beautiful in the moonlight," she whispered when Sharni lulled her head to the side and met her eyes.

Sharni smiled and ran her hand over Alex's chest and up along the side of her cheek as she leaned in, kissing her once more. Slowly, she pushed Alex to her back and dragged her hand down the center of her body. Alex moaned against Sharni's mouth and jerked her hips as Sharni's fingers slid through her wet folds in teasing strokes. Alex's senses were already heightened from touching her, it wouldn't take much for Sharni to give her the release she craved, but Sharni kept her caress light and languid, taking her time before pulling her lips away from the kiss to glide them down Alex's body, replacing her hand with her mouth.

Alex moaned and writhed under Sharni. The feeling of her tongue tracing her clit in delicately slow circles was driving her mad. She reached down, running her hand through the long dark curls spread over Sharni's bare back as the waves of orgasm hit her. Alex's entire body shuddered as she threw her head back, reveling in the twinkling stars above her before pulling her eyes back down, locking onto Sharni's gaze as she began gradually kissing her way back up. Alex rolled Sharni slightly, so they were lying on their sides, somewhat tangled together as their lips met in a sultry kiss. Tasting herself on Sharni's tongue made Alex hungry for her all over again. She ran her hand over Sharni's breasts and down to her thighs, pausing for her legs to part before gliding her fingers through her wet folds.

Sharni grazed her hand along Alex's stomach, inching further as she adjusted her position, giving Sharni room to slide her fingers gently through the wetness awaiting her. No words were spoken as they traded intoxicating kisses and sensual touches until they came together, panting and watching each other's eyes as a tidal wave of euphoria washed over them.

When they finally caught their breath and peeled themselves apart, Sharni brushed her palm over Alex's cheek before sitting up and swinging her shaky legs to the side. Alex ran her hand up Sharni's bare back, under her long wavy curls, before also sitting up.

"You've done this before," she murmured.

Sharni looked back at her. "I told you my roommate and I experimented in college."

"Define experimenting." Alex smiled.

Sharni grinned and shook her head.

Alex stood on wobbly legs and began walking towards the pool, completely nude.

"What are you doing?" Sharni questioned.

"Rinsing off," she said, trying not to squeal as she moved further into the cool water.

Sharni shrugged and did the same, careful to hold her hair up so it wouldn't get wet. "Oh my god! It's cold!"

"I'll warm you up," Alex said, moving towards her.

Sharni smiled and backed away. "We need to go back inside and get some sleep. Who knows what time it is."

Alex agreed and followed her back out of the water. Sharni stood beside the pool with her arms wrapped around herself while Alex went up under the covered patio to the cabinet in the corner and pulled out two oversized towels. She handed one to Sharni, who was shivering like a wet dog, and dried herself with the other. Once they were redressed, Alex grabbed her phone from the table, noticing it was almost three in the morning.

"The door's locked," Sharni said as Alex walked up behind her.

"What?" Alex muttered.

"It's locked!"

Alex gave her an odd look, then tried the knob herself. It turned, but the deadbolt was latched. "What the hell?"

Sharni threw her hands up.

"Come on. There's more than one door," Alex said, grabbing her hand and walking barefoot around the house to check the side door, then the garage and basement, and finally the front door. All the deadbolts were locked. "Son of a bitch."

"That's an understatement," Sharni muttered.

"What about the reception tent?"

Sharni shrugged and followed her back around the house. Unfortunately, the zippered entrance was padlocked. "Damnit!"

"We have to knock," Alex said.

"And wake up the entire house? No way. I am not dealing with the wrath of my parents. They already think I'm an embarrassment," Sharni grumbled.

Alex began leading the way back to the pool deck.

"Let me see your phone." Thankfully, Sharni had her sister's number memorized, but it simply went to voicemail each time she called it. "Motherfucker!" she spat.

"I guess we're stuck out here," Alex sighed.

"Why did you even come out here? I should've stayed inside."

Alex met her eyes. "I thought it would be nice to dance in the moonlight. I certainly hadn't planned for everything that happened, much less getting locked out. I'm sorry."

"It's not your fault," Sharni sighed, shaking her head. "What a fucking mess."

Alex walked away, leaving her with her own thoughts as she searched around for something to ward off the chill of the night air that was starting to set in, especially after being in the cold pool. She went back to the cabinet up on the patio and pulled out two more of the oversized pool towels. "We'll have to make do with these," she said, coming back over to the wide lounge chairs.

Sharni watched her avoid the one they were on earlier as she moved to the clean one next to it. "Are we supposed to just go to sleep out here?"

Alex shrugged. "Nothing is going to get us. There are no wild animals roaming around. If we cuddle together and use these," she said, holding up the towels. "We'll be warm and yes, hopefully, we'll fall asleep." She sat down on the chair and stretched out on her side with the towel over her like a blanket. It wasn't large by any means, but it fully covered her. "It's kind of like camping." Alex smiled.

Sharni laughed and shook her head. "Move over. I want that side."

"Yes, ma'am," Alex chuckled as Sharni lay down behind her and cuddled up against her like she'd done every night in the bed and pulled the towel over her. "You know, I can be the big spoon," Alex murmured.

"Nope," Sharni said, placing a kiss behind her ear.

Alex grabbed the arm that was over her waist and pulled it up along her chest, bringing them even closer together as she closed her eyes.

# Chapter 30

"Good morning!"

Alex pried her eyes open in the sunlight to see Max standing a few feet away, sipping a cup of coffee. She immediately came fully awake as Sharni stirred and slowly woke beside her.

"Did you two spend the night out here?"

"Not by choice," Sharni grumbled, stretching as she sat up. Her body ached in good places, reminding her of what they'd done, but also in other places reminding her she was not a teenager anymore.

"We came out to take a walk in the moonlight and the door locked behind us," Alex stated as she stood and stretched. She held her hand out to Sharni and pulled her to her feet.

"The deadbolts automatically lock at midnight. It keeps the place safe and locked up because none of us live here daily. So, if someone leaves and maybe forgets to lock the door, the place locks itself. There's a key hidden in one of the plants on the side patio."

"That would've been good to know up front," Sharni muttered.

"Look who I found passed out in a pool chair," Max announced when they all entered the house. Everyone was finishing breakfast and getting up from the table.

"What?" Neesa said. "You two slept outside? I figured you were upstairs asleep."

"I tried calling you a hundred times!" Sharni stated.

"You did? It never rang. I had my phone set to send all non-family calls to voicemail. It should've gone through."

"My phone was in here. I was calling on Alex's. No wonder you didn't answer!" Sharni shook her head. She was hungry and tired.

"Why didn't you guys knock on the door?" Orphea asked.

"By the time we realized we were locked out, it was late. We didn't want to wake the entire house," Alex replied.

"You poor things," the grandmother said. "It's a good thing the wolves didn't get you."

"Excuse me?" Sharni exclaimed, looking at Alex. "You said there was nothing out there to get us." Everyone began laughing, except for Sharni and Neesa's parents who stayed silent.

"How was I to know there were wolves here?" Alex shrugged. "Is that real?" she questioned, looking at the grandmother.

"Oh, we see one or two a year," she laughed. "But, never on the pool deck."

"They're usually way off in the distance," Max said.

Alex sighed and shook her head as everyone continued to laugh at their expense.

"I'm going to take a long, hot shower," Sharni muttered, walking away.

Alex turned to follow her but walked over to the grandmother instead. "Are there security cameras outside?"

She nodded and watched Alex's eyes grow as round as saucers.

"I'll delete the footage without looking at it," she said.

"Thank you," Alex whispered kindly. She walked by the table and snatched a banana on her way out of the room.

\*

Sharni was already out of the shower and dressed casually in shorts and a loose-fitting button-down shirt when Alex walked into the room with a mouthful of banana. "Where did you get that?" she asked, looking up from towel-drying her hair.

"The table. Here, you can have the other half," Alex said, setting it on the sink counter. "I really need coffee."

"Me too, but I needed a shower more." She watched in the mirror as Alex stretched her sore muscles. Then, she put away the towel and grabbed the remainder of the banana before leaving the bathroom. Once she heard the water running, she grabbed her phone and called her best friend.

"Hey, stranger. Is it the big day?"

"Yeah. The wedding is this evening," Sharni said. "It's not the middle of the night there, is it?"

"No, almost eleven," Tracey replied.

"I keep forgetting you're ten hours behind me."

"You sound tired. How are things going?"

"I *am* tired. I spent the night in a pool chair."

"What?"

"Yep. Alex and I got locked out and had to sleep on the pool deck."

"Wait, back up. What were you doing outside?"

"It's a long story."

"I have time."

Sharni laughed. "I don't. Alex is in the shower. She'll be out in a minute."

"Well, give me the important details. Were you in this chair together?"

"Yes."

"And were you clothed?"

"Not the entire time," Sharni mumbled.

"You slept with her!" Tracey exclaimed.

"On a lounge chair," Sharni chuckled.

"Oh my god!"

"Best night of my life," Sharni muttered. She quickly cut Tracey off when she heard the shower stop. "I gotta go. I'll be home in a couple days and tell you all about it." She ended the call and left the room.

\*

Alex took her time getting dressed, choosing a pair of dark khaki shorts and a baby blue, henley-style linen shirt. The four buttons at the top of the shirt were open, creating a wide V, and the sleeves were rolled back to her elbows. She slipped her feet into a pair of dark brown casual loafers and left the room.

When she got downstairs, she realized everyone was busy with wedding preparations. She had no idea where Sharni was, but when Thad asked her to help him and Leo with the set up for the reception and the ceremony, she quickly obliged. Everything was in the middle of being delivered, so the crews had no idea where to put what. She and Leo began arranging tables and chairs around the dance floor in the tent as they were brought in, while Thad worked outside on the ceremony area, lining up the chairs with the aisle runner down the middle and making sure the arch was centered.

Once everything in the tent was set up, Alex walked outside in time to see the florist unloading a van full of flowers. She and Leo quickly stepped to the side to stay out of the way.

"The champagne fountain will be here any minute. Leo, figure out how that works and get the glasses on the table," Thad said. "Alex, do you mind helping him?"

"No, not at all."

"I thought Mama was dealing with the fountain," Leo replied.

"There was an issue with some of the guests checking into the hotel. She had to go up there."

"I'm eloping," he muttered.

Alex laughed. "Me too."

"You don't think Sharni would want all this chaos?" he asked as they went around the house to look for the delivery truck.

Alex shrugged. She honestly had no idea what type of wedding Sharni would want; she wasn't even sure she wanted to get married for that matter. "She's less traditional, so something less ceremonial for sure," she answered from her gut.

*

"It's your wedding day. You don't have to do everything our mother asks of you," Sharni said.

"I promised to keep some of our cultural traditions," Neesa replied. "What were you and Alex doing out on the pool deck all night?"

Sharni raised a brow and grinned. "You don't want to know."

"You didn't!" Neesa chuckled.

"Didn't what?" their mother questioned, eyeing Sharni suspiciously.

"Nothing," she muttered.

Since Neesa wasn't wearing a traditional saree, the three of them gathered around the wedding gown and recited a blessing for a happy marriage full of prosperity and fertility. Then, their mother called Max into the room, along with their father. She walked over to the table where a small, wooden trinket box sat, adorned with carvings, that looked to be a hundred years old. The inside was lined with silk and cradled a small glass vial.

"This anointment oil has been in my family for five generations," Preet said, removing the bottle. "Every marriage from my great-grandmother's to now has been blessed with it." She opened the lid and put a dab onto her finger before tracing a cross on Neesa's forehead, and then Max's. After that, she traced the circle of both their wedding rings with it, as well as the palms of their hands. "May our ancestors and our God bless you both with good health, unite you as one in marriage, and bless that unity with happiness, faithfulness, love, and understanding. May you never forget your God is watching," she continued, placing their palms together. Everyone in the room held hands as she recited a prayer in Tamil. When she finished, she closed the vial and stored it back in the box. "Your grandparents and great-grandparents are with us in spirit. I can feel it," she muttered, holding her hand over the small antique box. "This is a union they are very proud of."

Sharni rolled her eyes but gave her sister a big smile. Today was her day, so she'd go along with whatever she wanted, including playing a nice happy Tamil girl for their mother.

"Let us leave them. I'm sure they have a lot to do," Ganesh said, looking at Max.

"Lunch is being served in a couple hours. Yiayia assured me it's light and simple, just enough to hold us over until the reception later," Max added before leaving the room with the girls' father.

Once they were gone, the women began preparing to put their hair up. Sharni wasn't exactly thrilled about wearing her hair in a tight bun, but this was another tradition Neesa had allowed, meaning all three of them would have their hair up. The girls started with their mother since it was customary for the mother of the bride to go first. After that, it would be Sharni's turn, leaving the bride for last.

"Don't bridal parties usually drink champagne while getting ready?" Sharni said, holding the pins while her sister did most of the work.

"The party is after the wedding ceremony," their mother chided. "You must take your vows with the utmost purity."

Neesa shrugged at her sister, who rolled her eyes.

Sharni thought back to the night before. *There was certainly nothing pure about that.*

"Hello!" Neesa said, holding out her hand, impatiently waiting for a pin.

Sharni grinned sheepishly.

"What is going on?" Preet demanded.

"Everything is fine. We're almost finished," Neesa reassured while furrowing her brow at her sister.

*

"It looks like a water fountain. How hard can it be?" Leo mumbled as he and Alex studied the gold, antique-looking, three-tiered champagne fountain in the center of the table.

"The directions are in Greek, so ..." Alex shrugged.

Leo read over the paper. "It says we pour the liquid into the bottom, then turn it on."

"That's it?" she laughed.

"Yep."

"Simple enough." She grabbed the cord and ran it towards the back of the table to the extension cord awaiting it. After that, they both turned to the crates full of glasses and began unpacking them.

"Is there a rhyme or reason to this?" Leo asked, setting the glasses onto the table two at a time.

"I assume we just surround the fountain with them like this," she replied, arranging the glasses. "Feel free to create your own design."

Leo shook his head. "I might be gay, but I'm not the decorating and designing type," he muttered low enough for only her to hear.

"I'm a lesbian, so don't look at me. We play softball and build things."

"You do those?"

"Hell no," she laughed.

They were both guffawing like hyenas when Max walked into the tent.

"It's nice to see you two bonding," he said, checking out the table.

Leo and Alex simply shrugged at him.

"What's that smell?" Leo blurted, wrinkling his nose.

"Anointment oil," Max replied nonchalantly as he started helping arrange the glasses around the fountain. He looked up to find them both staring at him like he'd sprouted a horn. "Neesa's family did a marriage ritual to bless our union." He smiled at Alex. "You'll do it too when it's your turn."

"Somehow, I don't see that happening," she muttered, going back to the glasses.

"Getting married or following their customs?"

"Both."

"You and Sharni have only been together eight or nine months, right? You'll start to get the itch soon."

She nodded and thought, *More like eight hours; and I wouldn't call it dating.*

"You can't wash it off?" Leo questioned, changing the subject.

"I didn't ask," Max said, causing them all to laugh.

"You're going to get married smelling like donkey sweat," Leo chuckled.

"He's not wrong," Alex added, wrinkling her nose.

"Don't tell Neesa. If she notices it's gone, I'll tell her it must've worn off."

Alex and Leo both nodded in agreement.

"Alex, thank you so much for helping with all of this. You're a guest, but this week, you've really become part of the family."

"I'm happy to help." She smiled. Once Max snuck off, she turned to Leo. "What about you? Do you want to get married one day?"

"I'd have to find someone first. But yeah. Maybe. Seeing how happy my brother is and watching this all come together, it seems like a fairytale more than reality."

"Why is that?"

"Yes, Greece just legalized same-sex marriage, but we're lightyears behind with acceptance."

"The States aren't a walk in the park, trust me," she sighed. "I've traveled all over the world and the one thing I've learned is, life is different everywhere. Be you and live your life. Don't wait for anyone to *accept* you. At the end of the day, it is your life, no one else's. Take me for example. I'm pretty sure Sharni's parents hate my guts, and they don't even know me. But I couldn't care less."

"Sharni said something along those same lines."

"About her parents?"

"No, the other stuff."

"She did?"

He nodded. "I've heard lesbians start to become each other after a while."

Alex tilted her head like a dog.

"They dress alike, finish each other's sentences, some even begin to look alike."

She laughed. "Where are you getting your information from? And if you say TikTok, I'm going to strangle you."

He chuckled. "Podcasts, mostly."

She shook her head.

"Hey, you two. The fountain and glasses are beautiful," Orphea said. "Also, look who I found," she added as Penny entered the tent behind her. "I finally got everything situated at the hotel. It looks like all the guests have arrived. We have four taxi vans set to head this way about forty-five minutes before the ceremony starts. That'll give them time to get here and sit down."

Leo and Alex chuckled. Penny simply stood with her brows raised.

"You two go on. Penny and I can do this. All we have left to do is put down the tablecloths and add the centerpieces and battery-operated candles to each table. The caterers will set up their area over there, and the DJ will be in the back."

"Let me know if you need anything else," Alex said before leaving the tent. She went around the side of the house and ran into Sharni headed towards her on the pool deck. She was wearing a short-sleeve, button-down top and khaki shorts, but her hair was twisted up into a tight bun with gold leaves pinning it in place. "You look different."

"Don't get used to it. I rarely wear my hair up, and never like this."

"You're breathtaking either way."

Sharni raised a brow. "This coming from the model who's plastered in pictures all over the world in her underwear."

"Exactly. That gives me some authority on beauty." Alex grinned.

Sharni smiled and shook her head.

"Anyway, I was wondering where you were. I haven't seen you since—"

"We were locked out here?" Sharni said, cutting her off. She smiled and looked at the lounge chair before turning her attention to the eyes staring back at her.

"Yes."

"About that ... and last night ..."

"I'm not sorry."

"I'm not either," Sharni sighed.

Alex stepped closer, grabbing her hand. "Nothing about last night was fake."

"I agree. This week has been a whirlwind charade. But last night was very, very real." Sharni smiled softly and reached up, caressing Alex's cheek before letting her hand fall back down.

"It's crazy to think this time last week, we hadn't even met yet," Alex said, grabbing her other hand as it fell.

"Yeah," Sharni chuckled. "Look at us now." She squeezed the hands holding hers. "You know, I think this is the first business deal I've ever brokered and subsequently broken."

"If it's any consolation, I think my acting days are over. I much prefer modeling."

They both laughed.

# Chapter
# 31

Everyone was gathered around the dining table, making small plates of finger foods, when Alex and Sharni walked in holding hands, laughing, and smiling at each other like teenagers.

"You two look happy," Neesa said, grinning at her sister.

Sharni rolled her eyes.

"Everything outside is beautiful and ready to go. Thank you, Alex and Penny, for all your help," Orphea stated.

"Today we become a family. I couldn't be prouder of my children and my grandchildren, and I am so happy to welcome the Dinjavis into our home, into our lives, and into our hearts," the grandmother said from the head of the table. "That includes you, Alexei," she added, smiling at her.

Alex returned the smile and nodded.

"We are happy to see Neesa and Max come together as one and join our two families," Ganesh stated.

Neesa smiled lovingly at her father. "I just want to say a quick thank you to both our families for all that you've done to bring this day together. And to my sister, and Alex, for coming early to spend this crazy week with us. I can't wait to do this all over again with the two of you."

"I second what she said," Max added, making everyone laugh.

"They're not getting married," Preet said.

"What was that?" Orphea asked, unable to hear her mutter from the other end of the table.

Sharni's mother stood up and tossed her napkin down. "You have shamed yourself, embarrassed our family, and ruined your sister's wedding week," she spat, looking directly at Sharni.

"Mom, that's enough!" Neesa exclaimed.

"No, Neesa. You must know the truth. Your sister and this woman have been deceiving everyone all week. This is an arrangement. They're not together. It's all fake!"

"Do you really want to do this? Here ... now? On Neesa's wedding day? How vicious are you!" Sharni growled.

"Me? You're the one who came here with that woman, pretending to be together and rubbing it in all our faces. You disgust me!"

"You can't stand the fact that I won't let you control my life. You belittle me every chance you get. I'm not a doctor, so I'm not successful. I moved across the country to hurt you. I'm over thirty and not married, which disgraces you. I don't wear my hair up, bathe in ancient oil, and say prayers for my Tamil ancestors, so I shun my culture. I am in a relationship with another woman, so I am an embarrassment to the family. Whether it is real or fake, doesn't matter. Do you see my point? I can't do anything right with you, and I'm sick of it! And for the record, her name is Alex. At least give her that decency. She's had to put up with your snide comments and rudeness all week. And thankfully for her, I've been able to avoid you and your pettiness and enjoy my sister's wedding week."

"Enough! You should both leave!" Preet demanded.

Max's grandmother stood up. "This is my family home, and I will not tolerate any more of this. Today is Neesa and Max's day. Mrs. Dinjavi, today was not the day for this. Who is with who, what is real and what is fake, none of that matters. Today should be a day full of kindness, happiness, and joy." She held up her glass of ouzo and nodded for everyone else to do the same. "Today, we celebrate love and family. Today, we honor Neesa and Max. May they be happy, healthy, and fruitful. Oompa!"

Everyone lifted their glass and drank down the liquor with her.

"Lunch is over. We all have a wedding to prepare for. Guests will be arriving in a couple hours."

Sharni looked at her sister. The wet tears on her face said it all. She didn't bother looking for her parents, who left quickly when everyone scattered like roaches. "I'm so sorry," she said, sitting down next to her and wrapping her arm over her shoulders. "I never meant for any of this to happen."

"Why is mom saying your relationship with Alex is fake?"

Sharni sighed. "It started that way, but it's become so much more."

"Why now? Why her?"

"You know how hard she is on me. If I'd shown up without someone, I would've never heard the end of it. When I met Alex, I knew it had to be her. I'd be safe. She'd get along well with everyone. And mom would be so busy avoiding me because of her disgust, I wouldn't have to deal with her. I know it was wrong. I'm sorry. This was your week. This is your wedding day."

"Have you slept with her?"

"Define sleep. We've been sharing the same bed all week."

"Sex, Sharni! Have you had sex with her?"

"Yes." Sharni furrowed her brow. "What does that have to do with anything?"

"Are you a lesbian?"

Sharni grumbled and sighed audibly. "I guess so. I don't know."

"What about men? Do you date men?"

"Neesa, I haven't dated anyone in a long time. I'm too busy and most people are too needy. Yes, I was dating men. I had a girlfriend, if you even want to call it that, in college. I knew mom and dad would disown me, so I moved on from that after I graduated. They already belittled me enough as it was for not being a doctor."

"How come I never knew?"

"You and I haven't been close in years. We grew apart a long time ago."

"I hate that," Neesa sniffled. "I've enjoyed this week so much, mostly because I got to spend it with you."

"Me too. I've missed you so much, Neesa."

"I've missed you too."

They hugged each other tightly.

"Come on. You have a wedding to get ready for." Sharni smiled, pulling back to look at her little sister. "I'm so proud of you."

Neither of them knew Max's grandmother was standing in the doorway, when they got up and left the room.

\*

"Today is my wedding day. I'm not tolerating anymore from the two of you. I want you to apologize and hug it out, or I'm not putting this dress on," Neesa stated, standing in the room with her sister and mother.

"Neesa, I will not—" her mother started.

"Nope." She crossed her arms over her chest. "We are a family. You are mother and daughter. I don't understand this animosity. If you want to snatch each other bald tomorrow, go for it. But today, you're going to act like you care about me."

"We do care," Sharni said, eyeing her mother. "I'm sorry."

"Me too," her mother replied, turning her head.

Neesa rolled her eyes.

"Oh, for fuck's sake," Sharni muttered and walked over, hugging her mother very quickly. "You're going to be a great parent," she said, moving back across the room.

"Thank you." Neesa smiled. "Now, we have work to do."

*

"I'm sorry for everything. This is your day. I wish you nothing but happiness," Alex said, hugging Max.

"I don't even know what's going on."

"It's a long story," she sighed. "One that shouldn't have played out today."

"Preet and Ganesh can be rough around the edges. They were a little callous with me at first, but once they got to know me, things smoothed out."

"That's because they dote on Neesa. Sharni is the black sheep. In their eyes, she does everything wrong. They're quite hard on her."

"That's no way to treat your kids."

"I agree. I grew up with a shitty situation myself. I think that's what drew Sharni and I even closer."

"Was it all fake?" he asked.

"We never meant to deceive anyone. Sharni just wanted to show up happy and in love so she wouldn't have to deal with her parents all week. She knew they would avoid me at all costs, making things easier for her. She never expected it to blow up like this. But to answer your question, no, not all of it. I'm having a hard time deciphering what was and wasn't, myself." She smiled. "Anyhow, I won't keep you. I just wanted to say I was sorry and wish you the best of luck with everything."

"Thanks," he said as she turned and walked away.

# Chapter 32

Sharni and her mother finished helping Neesa into her wedding gown, along with most of the additional pieces that went with it, saving the veil for after the bride applied her own light make-up, and her uncomfortable heels for the minute before she was set to walk down the aisle.

"You look beautiful," Sharni said, smiling at her little sister.

"And you're stunning," Neesa added, taking in the maid of honor dress Sharni was wearing. "Just make sure Alex doesn't rip it taking it off you," she whispered.

"Neesa!" Sharni exclaimed.

"What's wrong?" their mother questioned, rushing over to them. She'd also changed into her dress, along with a traditional Tamil sash.

"Nothing. Neesa has jokes," Sharni muttered.

"The ceremony isn't starting for another thirty minutes. I'm going to go check on your father."

As soon as she was out of the room, Sharni looked at her sister and shook her head. "I should probably go find Alex."

Neesa nodded and smiled.

Sharni walked down the hall towards the bedroom she and Alex had been sharing and was surprised to see it empty when she walked inside. She checked a few other rooms, then walked down the stairs. After searching all around the first floor, she went down to the basement and found Leo and Penny. "Have either of you seen Alex?"

"Yeah, she left with the first shuttle," he said.

"What?"

"I tried to stop her, but she said it was for the best."

"I don't understand. Where did she go?" She furrowed her brow.

"The hotel, I assume. She had a suitcase with her."

Sharni turned and quickly rushed back to the main floor, then up the stairs. She was barely in Neesa's room when tears began falling down her cheeks.

"What's wrong!" Neesa exclaimed, rushing over to her.

"Alex is gone."

"What do you mean she's gone? Where did she go?"

"She left! Leo said she went to the hotel with her suitcase." Sharni shook her head. "We didn't talk after everything blew up with Mom at lunch. Come to think of it, I never saw her again. She probably hates me."

"Is this what you want? Is *she* who you want?"

"Yes," Sharni murmured. "I'm in love with her, Neesa. It's crazy, and I can't explain it. It just happened."

"I'm so happy you finally found love." Neesa smiled, hugging her.

"Yeah, well ... I also lost it."

"Go after her."

"What? You're getting married in thirty minutes. I'm not going to miss my sister's wedding."

"I love you, but I don't care if you're here. Go after her, Sharni. Do it now, or you'll regret it forever. If you really love her, you have to go."

"I love you," Sharni said, wiping away the last of her tears before hugging her sister. "Okay," she muttered, taking a deep breath as she headed out of the room in search of keys to a vehicle and the name of the hotel. She checked room after room, until she opened the door to what appeared to be a home office. Max's grandmother was sitting behind the desk. She looked up as Sharni apologized quickly and began shutting the door.

"Wait. Come in, sit down," the grandmother called, getting up from the desk. "Is everything okay?" she questioned, walking over to the brown leather sofa in front of the fireplace.

Sharni tried to hide it when she sat down, but her face was still slightly wet, and her eyes were red from crying. "Alex left," she sighed. "I'm trying to go after her, but I can't. There's no one here with keys or a car."

"Can I ask you something?" She softly put her hand on Sharni's.

Sharni nodded.

"Do you love her?"

Sharni swallowed the lump that grew in her throat and nodded.

"I'm very sorry about the way your parents have acted this week. No child deserves hostility because of the person he or she loves. A parent must be free to let their child choose love, accept that love, and understand what it will cost them if they do not," she sighed, shaking her head.

"Thank you. You and your family have been so kind."

The grandmother smiled. "You said she left."

"Leo told me she went to the hotel. I don't even know where that is." Sharni shrugged and stared at the fireplace. She hadn't noticed the grandmother getting up, until she returned with her hand out.

"Go get her," she said, dangling the key to the antique Jaguar.

"Oh, I can't take your car." Sharni shook her head.

"Alexei should be here. Go get her."

"I don't know what hotel or where it is."

The grandmother handed her a piece of paper. "That's the name of it. It's about twenty-five or thirty minutes from here. Head towards the coast."

"Thank you," Sharni said, wrapping her in a hug.

\*

Sharni had no idea how to drive the old roadster. She remembered how sexy Alex had looked behind the wheel. "Damnit. Okay. I can do this," she muttered, kicking off her heels and pushing in the clutch barefooted. She turned the key and the car sputtered to life. She revved the engine a couple times, then moved the shifter around until she found reverse and popped the clutch, causing the car to lurch out of the garage. She smashed the brakes, worked the non-power-steering wheel until it was turned in the right direction, and jammed the shifter around once more. Finding first gear, she let off the clutch and stalled the car. "Motherfucker!" she spat, turning the key to restart the engine. Once she finally got it going again, she sped off down the long winding driveway and out onto the main road, viciously grinding the gears the entire time. With the top down, her hair began coming loose from the bun, blowing dark, curly tendrils around her face as she raced through the streets like Cruella De Ville.

Exactly seventeen minutes later, the roadster careened to a stop outside of the hotel. Sharni jumped out like a madwoman, fumbling around to get her heels on. A man in a hotel uniform rushed over with his mouth steadily going. She didn't understand a single word he was saying, so she shrugged and kept walking towards the door.

"No park here!" he finally said in broken English.

"Then, write me a fucking ticket!" she yelled, sprinting inside the hotel when the double doors opened.

\*

Alex stood in line at the counter with her suitcase next to her. She wasn't really looking for a room, but no one could tell her how to get to the airport. At least she was out of that house. She hated running out on Sharni, but with her out of the picture, the wedding could go on smoothly without all the animosity. It was over. She'd gotten Sharni through the week as planned. Now, she needed to get back to L.A., repack, and head to Monaco and then Dubai for the first photo shoot of the new campaign. Her agent had sent an email during the night informing her the new contract would be ready for her to sign on Monday, as long as none of the provisions had changed. Everything was done digitally now, as opposed to when she'd first started ten years earlier and had to meet in person to sign paper documents.

She tried to keep her focus on work: signing the new contract; jet-setting around the world for shoots and parties; countless hours in the local studio. Anything to keep her mind off ... "Sharni?" she muttered, certain she'd just heard a familiar voice. Alex turned towards the door, gasping when she saw Sharni standing in the middle of the busy hotel lobby looking disheveled and windblown in her maid of honor dress with her hair half in the bun and half out.

"Next?" the woman at the counter called.

Alex felt like her feet were glued to the floor when Sharni's eyes landed on hers.

"Don't do this," Sharni said, rushing over to her. "Please, don't go. I know this is crazy. I've never done anything impulsive in my life, but I'm doing it now." Sharni paused, taking a deep breath. "I know we've only known each other for a week, but somewhere along the way I fell in love with you." She searched the caramel eyes staring back at her.

"I don't know how to do this. How to be in a relationship," Alex said, staring into her dark eyes and shaking her head.

"You've been doing it all week." Sharni smiled. "And you're really good at it."

A grin spread across Alex's face as she reached out, cupping Sharni's cheek with her hand.

"I love you, Alex," Sharni whispered, reveling in her touch.

"I love you, too," she said, leaning forward, claiming Sharni's mouth in a heated kiss.

Everyone in the room began clapping and cheering, despite half of them not speaking English. When they parted, someone asked about her dress and Sharni looked down.

"The wedding!" she exclaimed, as if she'd forgotten. Shaking her head, she said, "Neesa was the one who told me to go after you."

"You can't miss her wedding. She's your only sister." Alex grabbed her suitcase. "How did you get here?"

"I drove," Sharni said as they rushed out of the hotel holding hands.

Alex was surprised to see that she'd driven the Jag since they'd learned early on Sharni couldn't drive a manual transmission. However, she was more shocked to see a tow truck backed up to the antique car. She rushed over to him, pulling a wad of euros from her pocket and pointing at the car. She didn't speak Greek, but fortunately he understood enough English to get what she was saying to him. He took the offered money and stuffed it into his own pocket before waving them off. "Oh, thank God," she mumbled, holding her hand out to Sharni. "Give me the keys."

"You have to get dressed. You can't go to the wedding in jeans and a t-shirt."

"Who's going to drive?"

"I will," Sharni said, running around to the driver's side of the car. She opened the door and got in, removing her shoes before starting the engine. "Come on!"

Alex wasn't religious at all, but she crossed herself and got in. The car lurched forward as Sharni popped the clutch and peeled out.

The GPS called out turn by turn directions as Sharni grinded the gears and careened through the streets. Alex was thankful she didn't get motion sickness from being slung around as she replaced her jeans with black slacks and her t-shirt with a white button down. "Pull over!"

"What? Why?"

"Just do it," Alex stated, slipping her feet into black, leather loafers. As soon as the car came to a stop, she jumped out and ran around to the other side. "Move over!"

"I can drive!"

"I'm pretty sure you left the transmission two miles back that way. Let me drive, please."

Sharni grumbled under her breath and hiked her dress up to crawl over the gearshift and into the other seat.

Alex tossed her luggage into the small trunk and got into the driver's seat.

"I'm surprised you're wearing a shirt," Sharni said as Alex easily maneuvered the car like a well-oiled machine.

"If it gets hot, I can take the suit jacket off," she replied, turning down the main road that would take them to the estate.

"I wouldn't have an issue with you taking it off." Sharni grinned.

Alex smiled and shook her head. She turned onto the long drive that serpentined back towards the mansion. "Do we have any idea what we're coming in on?"

Sharni shrugged. "Neesa told me to go after you, and Max's grandmother insisted that I go get you and take this car."

"Really?"

Sharni nodded. "They all love you."

"I love *you*," Alex said, meeting her eyes as she brought the car to a stop and killed the engine.

"I love you too, and I don't give a shit what anyone thinks about it. Come on. The reception should be going."

Alex got out and grabbed her jacket from the trunk. She slid it on and tucked her shirt in. "What about your hair?"

Sharni looked at her reflection. "Fuck it," she laughed, grabbing her hand. Together, they walked around the house towards the reception tent, but realized everyone was still seated for the ceremony. Alex led them through the side door where Neesa was waiting with her and Sharni's father.

"Finally!" Neesa said.

"Were you waiting for us?"

"Of course. I wasn't getting married without my sister and maid of honor by my side," Neesa said. "Alex, you better be worth it," she teased with a big smile.

"Sharni, I hope you know what you're doing."

"Dad, I'm a grown adult. This is my life. Take it or leave it." She shrugged, squeezing Alex's hand.

"Your mother is not going to be happy," their father said as Alex walked out the door to go sneak a seat in the back row. Both Max and Leo gave her a thumbs up from the altar, causing multiple people to turn around, including Sharni's mother, as well as Max and Leo's mother and grandmother.

Preet spun her head back around so quickly, it could've twisted off. The other two women gave small waves in her direction. Alex nodded and smiled at everyone just as the music started.

Sharni walked down the aisle first, holding a small bouquet of flowers. With her hair completely out of the bun, her curls flowed wildly around her back and shoulders. Her darker complexion contrasted nicely against the light, lilac color of the chiffon dress. She didn't see Alex until she got to the front and turned around to face the small crowd. That's when their eyes met. Alex touched her fingers to her lips briefly, almost like blowing her a kiss, and Sharni smiled brightly at her.

The doors to the house opened once more and the crowd rose to their feet. Neesa and her father appeared at the end of the aisle and began walking slowly up the center. Sharni reached up, dabbing away a tear as she watched her little sister. She was happy and proud of her, but a little sad knowing if she ever did get married, her father wouldn't be walking her down the aisle and her mother wouldn't be crying in the front row.

# Chapter 33

The ceremony was over quickly, and the bride and groom headed back up the aisle together, followed by Sharni and Leo. When they reached the last rows, Sharni reached out, running her hand up Alex's arm and over her shoulder when they walked by. Max's parents were next in the line coming up the aisle. Orphea smiled and patted Alex's shoulder as they passed her. Sharni's parents kept their eyes straight ahead, avoiding her at all costs. When Max and Leo's grandmother got to her, she stopped and held her arm out to Alex.

"Come on," she said.

Alex smiled and got up. The grandmother linked arms with her, and they followed the rest of the family over to where the photographer was taking photos while the rest of the guests went to the reception tent.

"I'm glad Sharni brought you back. You deserve to be here." She smiled, patting Alex's arm with her other hand.

"Thank you. Although, I'm pretty sure the Jaguar is going to need a new transmission."

The grandmother guffawed. She and Alex stood off to the side watching the photographer pose the bride and groom, then he added the maid of honor and best man. After that, he added the bride's and groom's parents, followed by just the bride and her family and then the groom and his family.

"Come on," the grandmother said when she was called over.

"I'm good here," Alex replied.

"You're family. I insist."

Alex nodded and smiled. She kept the grandmother's arm linked through hers as they joined the others. The photographer took a couple shots of just the groom and the family, then everyone all together.

"What was that about?" Sharni asked, walking over and grabbing her hand when they'd finished.

Alex shrugged. "Max's grandmother practically demanded."

Sharni smiled. "She's really taken a liking to you."

Alex nodded. "I think we bonded over the piano."

Sharni laughed.

"You're so beautiful," Alex whispered, changing the subject when she reached up and brushed the hair from her face as the wind blew. Then, she cupped her cheek and leaned in, kissing her softly. Neither of them realized the photographer had finished and was now shooting pictures of them, caught in a tender moment.

When Alex and Sharni parted, the family was walking into the reception tent. The two of them quickly caught up and walked in behind Max's parents, saving the bride and groom to be announced last. Sharni and Alex were seated at the table with Leo, Penny, the grandmother and Max and Leo's parents. Sharni and Neesa's parents were seated with friends who had come to the wedding.

"I'm so glad we're sitting here," Sharni mumbled.

"You *were* sitting over there," Orphea said, nodding towards Sharni's parents and their friends. "We made a little adjustment to the place settings."

Alex smiled, wondering if that was before the lunch argument or after. She watched the bride and groom get called to the buffet line, which was an array of Greek and Indian food. Their table was called next, followed by Sharni's parents' table. The rest of the room was called by number after that.

\*

Once everyone finished eating and the toasts took place, the DJ called the bride and groom to the dance floor. A soft, romantic song started playing and Max and Neesa began waltzing around the floor with all eyes on them. With about thirty seconds left in the song Leo and Penny, along with Alex and Sharni, joined them on the dance floor.

Sharni was glad she remembered the steps they'd learned in the class, but Alex led her around as if her feet were off the ground. The song ended all too quickly and everyone hugged each other before heading back to their tables. Alex held her chair as Sharni sat down.

"Aren't you chivalrous," Orphea teased.

"That's my middle name," Alex replied nonchalantly as she sat down.

"No, it's not," Sharni laughed. "Her middle name is Nicole."

"So, Alex Nicole," Orphea stated.

She nodded.

"Neesa wants me to go meet her work friends," Sharni said, getting back up.

"Have fun," Alex replied, watching her walk away. She was glad she wasn't being dragged around the room for introductions.

"Darling, I think it's our turn to show these young ducks how it's done," Thad said, holding his hand out to his wife. She shook her head and chuckled but let him lead her to the dance floor. Leo and Penny were also back out there dancing, leaving Alex and the grandmother at the table.

"Shall we dance?" Alex asked, finishing the last of the champagne in her glass and standing with her hand out.

The older woman stared at her for a second with a smile across her face. "I'd love to," she finally said, getting up from the chair.

"Can you waltz?" Alex questioned.

"I've been waltzing since before you were born," she replied.

Alex smiled as she stepped into position and began leading her around. The song was more upbeat, so the dance was quicker. They both smiled and laughed, having a great time moving around the floor with the other pairs. When the song ended, Max stepped into Alex's place to dance with his grandmother, and she went in search of Sharni.

"She went to refill her glass," Neesa said, seeing Alex looking around the room. "Come on, it's our turn to dance."

Alex obliged and followed her to the dance floor without looking towards the champagne fountain in the corner.

"So, when are you going to ask my sister to marry you?" Neesa questioned as they moved around the floor.

Caught off guard, Alex nearly stepped on her foot by accident. "We literally just started dating ... today."

"You're more than dating. The two of you are in love."

Alex stayed silent.

"I know you were pretending to be together this week, but you can't fake love. There is so much passion between the two of you. I saw it right from the start."

"Aren't you a pediatrician?"

"Yes, why do you ask?"

"Because you sound more like a psychologist," Alex said.

Neesa laughed and shrugged.

*

"You're Neesa's sister, yes?" a deep male voice asked.

Sharni turned to see a man standing next to her, also refilling his glass as champagne flowed from the spouts of the fountain. She nodded.

"She only mentioned she had a sister who lived in California. She never said how beautiful you were." He smiled. "I'm sorry, Tom Diachenko," he added, holding his hand out. "I work with Max and Neesa at Doctors Without Borders. Perhaps I should've started with that."

"Probably," she replied, shaking his hand. "If you'll excuse me, I need to go find my girlfriend. It was nice meeting you." Sharni turned and walked away before he could say anything else. He watched her with his head twisted sideways like a dog trying to understand a human.

*

"May I cut in?" Sharni said. "I met your friend, Tom," she added, looking at her sister.

"He's a general surgeon. Super nice guy."

"He hit on me."

Neesa laughed. "Can you blame him?" she said, looking at Alex who just smiled and shook her head.

"I need to go steal my husband from his grandmother. Husband ... that's a word I have to get used to," Neesa muttered, kissing them both on the cheek.

"I saw you dancing with Max's grandmother," Sharni said, stepping into the dance space her sister had just occupied. "She really likes you."

Alex smiled, pulling her closer as the music slowed down. Sharni wrapped her arms around Alex's neck with one of her hands playing with the back of her short hair as they swayed together. Alex reached up, grabbing Sharni's hands as she stepped back. She spun her and slid up behind her with their bodies pressed together. They swayed side to side with her crotch pressed against Sharni's ass. Alex pressed her lips to the side of Sharni's neck just below her ear and Sharni leaned her head back, laying it against Alex's shoulder.

As the slow song neared its end, Sharni spun around in Alex's arms with their bodies against each other. Her hands landed on Alex's shoulders, grazing both sides of her neck. "I love you," she whispered, looking into the eyes staring back at her.

"Show me," Alex murmured.

Sharni leaned in, claiming her lips in a sultry kiss that enticed a few whistles and cat calls from the wedding guests. Both women had sort of forgotten where they were and what they were doing. They backed away from each other, smiling and holding hands as they left the dance floor.

"This display needs to end. There's no need to continue faking this vulgarity. You're embarrassing yourself and shaming this family," Sharni's mother said, walking up to the two of them.

"You did that this morning in your attempt to humiliate your own child," Sharni replied, shaking her head. "No matter what you think you know, I am very much in love with Alex, and I am very happy with my life. This is who I am."

"Mrs. Dinjavi, I've been nothing but respectful to your family this entire week. I came here under false pretenses, that is true. But there was no animosity intended. Sharni needed a date for the week, and I obliged. It was as simple as that. Neither of us planned on falling in love; truthfully, we were just hoping we'd get along. It turned out to be the craziest and happiest week of my life." Alex smiled at Sharni. "She's your daughter. I don't understand why you can't be happy for her. I haven't seen my mother since she died when I was four years old. I'd give anything to have her see me now. Your daughter is right here in front of you and all you can do is put her down every chance you get. You're ashamed of her, well ... shame on you. You're not a parent. You remind me of the tyrants who raised me by bullying and belittling me after my mother passed, and she was their only child. I haven't spoken to them since the day I turned eighteen and moved out, ten years ago. They are nasty, bitter people who only have themselves."

Sharni squeezed her hand and wiped a tear from her own cheek.

"Think about your actions and your words before you push your oldest daughter away for the rest of your life.

You have no idea how painful that feels," Alex finished. She turned to walk away and noticed all of Max's family standing there listening, along with him and Neesa, and Neesa's father. What she didn't see was Max's mother and grandmother wiping tears from their cheeks.

"It's time for the bride and groom to cut the cake," the DJ said, bringing everyone back to the wedding. Neesa and Max headed to the cake table with his family following. Sharni and Alex went outside to get some air, leaving Preet and Ganesh alone.

\*

"I'm sorry," Sharni said, wrapping her arms around Alex.

"What for? You didn't do anything wrong. I should be saying that to you. I never meant to go so far with your mother. I just couldn't take it anymore."

"Is that why you left? So, she and I would work things out?"

"I figured if I was out of the picture, she would have no reason to keep putting you down. I know how hard it is to not have a mother ... or family at all for that matter. It's not easy. I don't want that for you."

"Alex, my mother has been treating me like this for years. Having you here with me this week might've been the height of it, but it certainly wasn't the start. You have nothing to be sorry for. She deserved to hear everything you said to her. Whether she takes it to heart or not is up to her. One thing I do know is I love you and we have each other. Also, I'm pretty sure we've been adopted by the Nikolaidis/Papadakis family." She smiled.

Alex laughed and kissed her softly. She sighed when they parted. "Is this thing over soon?" she whispered, kissing her lips again.

"Why? Do you have a hot date?" Sharni teased.

"Yes, as a matter of fact I do, and I can't wait to be naked with her ... in a real bed."

Sharni grinned. "The pool chairs are on the other side of the house."

"Don't tempt me," Alex muttered. "Come on, I want a piece of cake."

\*

The tent was full of laughter and happiness when Sharni and Alex walked back inside. Most of the guests were holding glasses of ouzo and encircling the bride and groom, who were dancing in the center as the circle spun left, then right.

"Oompa!" everyone yelled and drank from their glasses, then spun the opposite way and did it again.

"We missed something," Sharni muttered. She looked over at Alex who was busy with her mouth full of cake.

"Do you want a bite?"

"Thanks for waiting until it was almost gone to ask," Sharni laughed, shaking her head no.

"Alexei! Sharni! Come join us!" the grandmother yelled, seeing them standing by the cake table.

Alex put the plate on the table and washed the rest of the cake down with a long sip of champagne before grabbing Sharni's hand and joining the circle. Neither of them paid attention to the Dinjavi family, who were seated at their dinner table with their friends.

Sharni held her glass and tossed the liquid over her shoulder when everyone yelled Oompa and toasted once again. Alex caught a glimpse of her action and burst out laughing. When the glasses were finally empty, the circle broke, and the guests dispersed so the bride could get ready to toss the bouquet.

Alex stood off to the side, but Neesa made her sister get in the group of unmarried women. She had no idea where anyone was because once she turned her back to them, they all moved around. Neesa counted to three, then tossed the arrangement over her head. It hit the roof of the tent and landed in the hands of one of her doctor friends. Everyone cheered and clapped. Sharni blew out a sigh of relief and smiled at her sister before looking over at Alex, who was grinning and shaking her head.

"Hey, will you two help me with something?" Leo asked when Sharni walked over to where he was standing near Alex.

"Sure," they replied.

He waved for Neesa and Max to come over as everyone went back to dancing on the wooden floor.

"What's up?" Max questioned.

"Hold on." Leo walked away, returning with their parents and grandmother, as well as Penny.

"Is everything okay?" Orphea asked.

"Yes. I know today is your day, Max ... and Neesa. Everyone is so happy. I feel I need to be honest with all of you. Penny and I are not together. She's my best friend, don't get me wrong. But we're not in a relationship. I'm gay."

"It's about time," Orphea said.

Everyone smiled.

"What?" Leo muttered, confused.

"Honey, we've known for quite some time," the grandmother added.

"You have? All of you?" He looked at his father, who nodded.

"Why didn't any of you tell me!"

"This is your journey. We had to let you go through it," Orphea replied.

"How come I'm the only one who didn't know this?" Max questioned, slightly surprised.

"We've been busy traveling and wedding planning," Neesa said.

"Wait. You knew?"

She nodded.

"I love you, little brother. I don't care who you love, as long as you're happy," Max said, hugging him. The rest of the family began hugging him as well.

"I have to say thank you to Alex and Sharni. If they weren't here this week, I don't know if I would've ever told you."

Alex and Sharni hugged him.

"So, are you dating anyone?" Orphea asked.

He shook his head.

"Well, when you do, we'd all love to meet him," Thad said.

"It's about that time," the DJ called, slowing the music.

"That's our cue," Max said to Neesa.

"Are you leaving ... already?" Sharni pouted.

Neesa hugged her. "I love you. I'm so glad you've been here all week."

"Me too. I love you, little sis."

"After everything settles back down, I'm going to come visit. I want to hang out with the celebrities."

"That's all Alex. I don't know anyone," Sharni replied with a smile.

"I got you covered." Alex winked.

Neesa pulled her into a hug. Then, she hugged Max's family while he hugged Sharni and Alex. "Okay, we need to get out of here before I start crying. It's my wedding day, damnit."

Everyone laughed.

Max and Neesa went around saying goodbye to their guests, as well as her and Sharni's parents, before rushing into the house to change clothes, grab their luggage, and meet the car service waiting to take them to the hotel for the night. They were set to fly to Tuscany in the morning.

Once the SUV pulled away, Sharni grabbed Alex's hand. "I can't believe my little sister is married."

"I can't believe we survived the week," Alex mumbled as the shuttle buses arrived to take the guests back to the hotel. They said goodbye to a few of Neesa and Max's friends whom they'd met during the night and were turning to head back to the tent when Sharni caught sight of her parents getting into one of the vans with their luggage in tow.

"You've got to be kidding me," she spat, shaking her head.

"Come on," Alex said softly, wrapping her arm around her.

# Chapter 34

"Everyone has left the building," Thad said when Sharni and Alex walked into the tent. He was shutting off the champagne fountain. The caterers and DJ were busy packing up, and the rest of Max's family was turning off the centerpiece candles and making sure nothing was left behind by the guests.

"Where should we start?" Sharni asked.

"Start what?" Orphea questioned, turning around to face her.

"Cleaning up."

Thad laughed. "The crew will be here first thing in the morning to clean up and dismantle everything. Go on in the house. There's leftover cake in the refrigerator."

"We'll be out of here first thing in the morning," Alex said.

"There's no need to rush off. We've enjoyed having you both here," the grandmother replied. "I saw your parents leaving with the guests," she added, looking at Sharni. "You are family to us. You'll always be welcome here."

"Thank you. I'm sorry they ran out without offering to help. Did they at least thank you for everything?"

"No thanks were needed. We did this for Max and Neesa. Not them," Orphea stated.

"Hey! One bottle didn't get opened," Thad called, holding up a champagne bottle that was at the bottom of the cooler on ice. "We might as well finish the lot!" he added, bringing it over to a nearby table, along with some glasses.

"Oh, I don't think so," Sharni said, shaking her head.

"Come on. It's still early. What else are you going to do?"

Sharni and Alex looked at each other briefly.

"Leave them alone. Don't you remember being young and in love?" Orphea said, furrowing her brows at him. "Have a good night, ladies."

"At least you have a bedroom this time," the grandmother added, causing Alex to laugh.

Sharni smiled thinly and grabbed her hand. "What was that about?" she mumbled when they were outside of the tent. "Do they know what we did on the pool deck?"

"She does ... or at least has a pretty good idea."

"How?"

"The security system."

"Oh my god!" The blood began to drain from Sharni's face.

"It's fine. No one saw it. She deleted the recording as soon as she found out we were locked outside."

"How do you know this?"

"She told me."

"I'm pretty sure I just had a mild stroke." Sharni shook her head.

Alex chuckled as she held the house door open for her.

"You don't care if someone saw us?"

"I seem to recall asking if you wanted to stop, and you saying you didn't care where we were." Alex shrugged.

"A momentary lapse of judgement," Sharni laughed, shaking her head.

Alex closed the door and walked up to her. "We're all alone."

Sharni grinned and stepped into her arms with her hands joining at the back of Alex's neck. Their lips teased each other in a sultry kiss. Alex spun around, holding onto Sharni as she backed her up against the door. Sharni ran her hands from Alex's shoulders, down the front of her chest, groaning against her mouth when her hands slid over the material of her shirt.

Alex pulled back from the kiss to look at her.

"I like your suits better with no shirt."

"Is that so," Alex said with a raised brow.

"The night we met ..." Sharni bit her bottom lip as she grazed her fingers over the soft skin where the first two buttons of Alex's shirt were open. "I've never looked at someone and instantly wanted ..."

"To fuck them?" Alex finished, claiming her mouth once more as she grabbed Sharni's hands and held them just above her head against the door. Sharni's lips quickly parted, allowing Alex's velvety tongue to brush teasingly against her own. She nipped at Alex's lower lip, chasing as she pulled back, breaking the seductive kiss.

Sharni stared at her with a raised brow, silently protesting the kiss's end. Alex was right. She did want to fuck her and get fucked by her. She'd wanted that ever since she saw her in the ad on the side of the bus.

Seeing Sharni's eyes heavy with desire made Alex's knees weak. She stepped back, pulling Sharni's hands down by her sides. She let go of one and interlaced her fingers with the other as she led them through the house to the staircase.

Halfway up, Alex backed Sharni against the wall again, this time tracing kisses along her neck, tasting a hint of salt on her skin, and smelling the remnants of a light floral perfume as she ran her lips down to the V at the front of the dress and back up to the side of her neck below her ear. Sharni moaned, running her fingers through the short hair at the back of Alex's head. She tugged gently, causing Alex to lift her head enough for Sharni to press their lips together in a ravishing kiss.

Alex reached behind her head, grabbing Sharni's hands as she pulled back, breathlessly. Her eyes scanned Sharni's face, landing on the deep dark pools staring back at her as her chest rose and fell with every heaving breath. Keeping hold of one of Sharni's hands, Alex dropped the other and turned to continue up the stairs, tugging her alongside. She swung the door open when they arrived at their shared room, then closed it with her foot as she spun Sharni around and unzipped the back of her dress. Sharni kicked her heels off just as Alex undid the clasp of her halter top. The soft fabric slid down her body, pooling around her bare feet. Stepping up behind her, Alex swept Sharni's hair over her shoulder and pressed her lips to the side of her neck as her hands ran along Sharni's sides, around to her stomach as they slid up, cupping her bare breasts.

Sharni moaned, leaning her head back against Alex as her lips roamed along the top of her shoulder. She closed her eyes, reveling in Alex's warm breath on her neck and her hands kneading her breasts, until Alex's clothing began to feel like sandpaper on her skin. Sharni grabbed her hands, pulling them from her body and letting go, kicking her dress away from her feet as she turned around in her arms. She met her eyes as she leaned in, placing a soft kiss on her mouth, teasing her lips open with her tongue as her hands ran up the front of Alex's body under her suit jacket, pushing the material off her shoulders and down her arms. Alex shrugged the rest of the way out of the jacket as Sharni's hands worked back down the front of her shirt, opening the buttons one by one. She playfully bit Alex's bottom lip and moved her hands lower, opening the clasp of her pants and sliding the zipper down. Alex kicked her shoes off and let her shirt fall free as Sharni's hands inched their way back up her torso, grazing the sports bra covering her small breasts. Ending their lascivious kissing, Alex pulled her sports bra over her head and tossed it to the side.

Sharni's mouth watered and curled into a lustful grin at the sight of Alex nude from the waist up with her pants open, hanging low on her hips just below the wide waistband of her underwear. Blood coursed through her veins, settling in the pit of her stomach, leaving her lightheaded and ravenous as Alex lowered her pants and underwear at the same time, pushing the clothing aside with her foot. She watched Alex's eyes follow her panties as she slid them down her thighs, letting the satin material fall to her ankles before kicking it away. Stepping forward, Sharni closed the distance between them, running her hands up Alex's chest, stopping above her breasts. She pressed her mouth to Alex's, tasting the last remnants of champagne on her tongue as she pushed her back towards the bed.

Their kiss ended as Alex lay on her back. Sharni crawled on top of her, straddling her waist. She grabbed Alex's hands, placing them over her head on the bed as she leaned forward, looking into her eyes while her tongue snaked out, licking Alex's lower lip before biting it between her teeth, claiming her mouth libidinously.

Alex moaned against her as her hips thrust up involuntarily and her hands gripped Sharni's, desperate to feel her in any capacity. Sharni pulled her lips from Alex's mouth and sat up, bringing Alex's hands to her breasts as she lulled her head back. Looking down once more, her eyes searched Alex's. She pulled her right hand from her breasts, bringing it to her lips. Alex's breath hitched as Sharni licked the length of her finger, then took it into her mouth. Alex moved to sit up, but Sharni put her hand in the center of her chest, pushing her back down. She leaned forward, kissing her deeply before flattening her body on top of Alex and sliding lower, tracing a path with her lips and tongue until she settled between her legs.

Alex's hips thrust up and her body arched at the first touch of Sharni's warm mouth. She reached down, tangling her hand in the long, dark curls draped over her thigh and down Sharni's back. She gripped the bedding with the other hand and dug her heels into the mattress when Sharni slid two fingers inside of her, matching the slow, steady rhythm of her tongue. Sharni's other hand moved to Alex's stomach, feeling the muscles tighten beneath her palm as they squeezed the fingers of her other hand. Panting, Alex clenched her jaw to keep from crying out like a wild animal as the orgasm tore through her body. When the tongue and fingers assuaging her finally stilled, her body went limp.

Sharni traced a path back up Alex's torso all the way to her mouth as she crawled up her body. Tasting herself on Sharni's lips and tongue sent Alex's libido back into overdrive. She watched Sharni's eyes as she sat up, straddling her hips and waist once more.

"Who are you? And what have you done with Sharni Dinjavi?" Alex whispered.

Sharni's mouth curled into a grin. "You've awakened a part of me that lay dormant for years," she said softly, leaning forward and kissing her once more.

Alex wrapped her arms around Sharni and rolled her to her back with Alex now on top. She broke their kiss, teasing Sharni's mouth with gentle touches of her lips, and looking into her dark eyes while dragging her hand along her body, cupping her breast.

Sharni's stomach fluttered as Alex's hand moved lower, gliding over her taut abdomen, and grazing the soft skin on the inside of her thigh. She held her breath in anticipation, staring into the golden-brown eyes looking back at her as Alex's fingers inched closer and closer, almost agonizingly slow. "Touch me, Alex," Sharni whispered breathlessly. "I need to feel you."

Alex parted Sharni's lips with her own and touched their tongues together as her fingers swirled through the wet folds, encircling her clit before pushing inside of her. Sharni moaned, parting her legs further when Alex pressed her thumb against her pulsing center while working her fingers back and forth. Her mouth slipped from Sharni's, sliding down her neck to her chest, licking a hard nipple with her tongue before sucking it between her lips.

Sharni's back arched. She gripped the sheet with one hand and tangled the other in the back of Alex's short hair, inadvertently urging her lower. Her eyes fixated on the ones gazing back at her as Alex continued dragging her lips and tongue down her body until she replaced her hand with her mouth. Sharni's hips rose nearly off the bed when Alex's tongue lapped through her wet folds, slipping inside of her.

Alex kept one hand wrapped around Sharni's thigh while the other slid from her stomach to her breasts and back again, feeling as much of the body writhing under her as she could, until Sharni gripped her hand, stilling it as wave after wave of orgasm washed over her. She pulled her mouth away, kissing the inside of her thigh before dragging her tongue back up the center of Sharni's torso as she crawled up, stopping to claim her lips.

When Alex ended the kiss and slid off her to the side, thinking they were going to sleep, Sharni pushed her to her back and rolled onto her. Their mouths met once more in a lascivious kiss, leaving them both breathless. Thoughts of ending the night left her brain as Sharni's hand began sliding down the front of her body.

# Chapter 35

Alex's eyes slowly opened as she stretched on her stomach under the thin sheet, feeling her nude body ache in all the right places, reminding her of the night. A soft hand grazed the center of her back. She smiled and turned towards the dark eyes looking back at her.

"Can we stay like this forever?" Sharni mumbled, also feeling the aftermath of the night in her sore muscles.

"I wouldn't mind it, but I think Max's family might have an issue."

"Holy shit, it's ten o'clock!" Sharni squeaked, looking at her phone. She sat up quickly and swung her legs over the side of the bed.

"What time does our flight leave?" Alex asked, also getting up.

"Not until four-thirty, but we should probably be at the airport by two."

Alex nodded as she padded across the room, still completely nude. Sharni couldn't help raking her eyes over her, immediately wanting more of the body she'd ravished all night. When the shower spray turned on, she contemplated joining her, but there was no way they'd ever make their plane if she did. Instead, she sent a quick text to Tracey to let her know she'd be home the next day and got out the clothes she planned to wear for the long trip.

It only took a few minutes for Alex to shower. She saw Sharni texting on her phone in the other room as she toweled off. If someone told her eight days ago that she'd answer an ad to pretend to be in a relationship with someone and accompany them halfway around the world for a week-long trip, during which time they'd actually fall madly in love with each other for real, she would've told them she had a better chance of tattooing the word boobs on her forehead. She chuckled to herself and shook her head as she set the towel to the side.

"What's funny?" Sharni asked, standing behind her and kissing the back of her shoulder as they stared at each other in the mirror across from them.

"Just thinking how drastically life can change in a week," she answered, turning around and putting her hands on Sharni's waist. She ran them up her back, pulling her closer.

Sharni draped her arms casually over Alex's shoulders and leaned in, kissing her softly. "You smell good," she murmured when they parted.

"So do you," Alex replied.

Sharni laughed. "I smell like sex."

"Exactly." Alex grinned.

Sharni rolled her eyes, shaking her head and smiling as she backed away.

After finishing in the bathroom, Alex packed her bag and took one last look around to make sure she had everything, just as Sharni got out of the shower. She waited for her to towel off, get dressed, and put product in her hair to tame her curls. Then, they headed down the stairs, walking together with their hands intertwined.

The smell of food wafted through the house, leading them directly to the dining room where trays of food were displayed on the table. Max's parents and grandmother were sitting there having a conversation.

"We were wondering if you two were still alive," the grandmother said. "You must be famished." She waved her hand over the table. "It's all yours. Another pot of coffee will be out in a minute."

"Was Leo coming back today?" Alex asked.

"No. It's just us. The rental service was here early to pack up everything, so we're just lazing around today," Orphea replied. "What time does your flight leave?"

"Four-thirty."

"Mama and I are driving you," she said. "We'll need to leave by one-thirty. It'll take close to an hour to get there, and you'll need to be two hours early to get through security."

"We don't want to put you out. We'll get a taxi or something," Sharni said.

"Nonsense. We're driving you," the grandmother stated with a smile. "Now, eat up. You have a long flight."

They both smiled and obliged as the family went back to their conversation about the wedding and how Neesa and Max seemed so happy when they called this morning before boarding the flight for their honeymoon. Thad got up from the table to call his family and make sure everyone made it home safely. Then, Orphea followed, also needing to take care of a few things. As soon as Sharni was finished eating, she headed upstairs to pack her bag, leaving Alex and the grandmother at the table.

"I'm glad you two worked out your differences yesterday," she said.

Alex nodded. "It has certainly been an interesting week."

"At the end of the day, you two love each other. That should be all that matters."

"Thank you."

"No thanks needed," she replied with a smile.

"Actually, there is. You and your family have been so open, so kind and generous. The world needs more people like your family."

The grandmother smiled again. "Speaking of ..." She stood from the table. "Come with me. I want to show you something."

Alex nodded and got up from the table, following the older woman down the hall to a room she'd never seen.

"My late husband, Levi, this was his special place. Call it an office, a study, a library, a cigar room ... whatever it was, it was his."

Alex walked inside behind her when she opened the door. The room had a large antique desk opposite the door with a bookcase along the wall to the left and a fireplace across from it on the right. A worn leather sofa sat in the middle, facing the fireplace.

"Leviticus Nikolaidis was a stern, but kind and loving man. He doted on his two children, our son Konstantine Alexei, whom we called Kostas, and our daughter Orphea Athena. Kostas was very much like his father with a strong personality, which caused them to butt heads from time to time."

Alex nodded her head, listening, but unsure why the grandmother was telling her all of this.

"His father wanted him to marry Thalia Antonopoulos, a girl Kostas had courted all through college, who was also the daughter of one of Levi's business associates. My husband wanted a business deal, my son wanted love." She smiled, thinking back. "Kostas went to Athens with some friends and met an American girl who was passing through on her way to Santorini for the summer." She paused, sighing slightly. "My son, the hard-headed, gentle, loving soul that he was, went with her on a whim and fell in love."

"Oh, wow," Alex muttered.

"When Kostas told his father, it did not go well. When the girl went back to America, Levi made our son see that his life was here. His family was here. Levi strongly believed our son was trying to defy us, but really, they were defying each other because they were so much alike. Anyway, Kostas moved on, and six months later, he and Thalia were married. On their honeymoon, they took a helicopter ride and it crashed, killing them both, along with the pilot and another couple."

"Oh, my god," Alex gasped. "I'm so sorry."

The grandmother smiled softly and patted her hand. "Eight weeks after we buried our son and his wife, a letter came for him from America. Inside was the picture of a newborn. The letter stated the woman wasn't trying to trap him and didn't want anything from him. But she did want him to know they'd had a baby girl that she'd hoped he'd one day want to meet, and he knew how to find her when he was ready. It was signed Your American Girl. There was no return address, and we had no name, other than the baby ... Alexei Anna Nikolaidis."

Alex's head tilted like a dog when she heard the name the grandmother had been calling her all week. She stared at the floor, still uncertain why she was hearing such a deeply tragic, personal story.

"Anyhow ..." the grandmother went on. "The postmark on the envelope was smeared when it was stamped, so we were unable to make out the city or state. We were grieving the loss of our son and kept the news of the baby to ourselves. Levi blamed himself and carried the grief of losing his son and robbing him of his only child, heavily until the day he died." She paused and sighed. "A year after the letter arrived, we made the decision to tell our daughter and together we did everything we could think of to find the woman and the little girl, including hiring a private detective. All of it failed. Not long after, Orphea was married, and our grandsons were born. Then, my husband died of cancer, almost ten years to the day we lost our son. The day before he passed, I was sitting next to him as he lay on the hospital bed. He said, she'll come home one day. Kostas is leading her to you. He said it so strongly. I'll never forget it. He slipped into a coma that night and was gone the next day." She shook her head at the memories. "Kostas was a little younger than you when he died, but his daughter would be around your age now."

"I never knew my father," Alex said. "My mother died in a car accident when I was four. I was sent to live with her parents, whom I'd never met. They never spoke of her and refused to answer questions when I asked as I got older. They were religious and disowned her for getting pregnant out of wedlock and having me."

The grandmother got up from the couch and walked over to the bookcase. She pulled one of the books from the shelf and sat back down next to Alex as she opened it. The inside was hollowed out, giving it the fake appearance of a book. A worn envelope was in the middle with an old picture of a dark-haired baby girl.

"She's beautiful," Alex said softly.

The grandmother smiled and set the book to the side as she stood once more, holding her hand out to Alex. They walked together over to Levi's antique wooden desk, which reminded Alex of something she would see in the oval office of the Whitehouse. Everything was perfectly placed, and four picture frames were lined across the back of it. The grandmother urged her to walk around to the other side and followed.

Alex began looking at the pictures. The first was of the grandmother, looking much younger. The one next to it was Orphea, also when she was younger. The third was Max and Leo as little boys. The last picture was of a young man in a suit, smiling brightly at the camera.

"That's our son, Kostas ... on his wedding day."

Alex bent down to get a closer look and the blood drained from her face. It was like looking at the male version of herself. The same dark hair; the same strong jawline and cheekbones; the same shade of golden-brown in his eyes. She looked back at the grandmother, who suddenly had tears in her eyes.

"Welcome home, Alexei," she whispered, wiping the tears as they fell.

"What?" Alex stood up and backed away. "I'm not ... I can't be ..."

"I felt it the minute I saw you. Forgive me for not telling you, but when you told me about you being adopted by your grandparents and your mother passing, I knew I had to find out for sure. I contacted the private investigator and gave him your name. He was able to find your birth certificate finally because your adoption became a public record when you turned eighteen. Your mother's parents had your name changed when they adopted you. You were born Alexei Anna Nikolaidis. Your mother was Anna Mary Mitchell. Her parents are Mary and John Mitchell."

"I need to sit down," Alex said, feeling lightheaded. She walked over to the couch and plopped down with her head in her hands. *This can't be.* Everything she'd just been told was spinning around in her head like a kaleidoscope. "Are you sure?" she mumbled.

"Yesterday afternoon, just before the wedding, I received a phone call from that same investigator. Again, forgive me. I'd sent him a glass you drank out of the first day you were here. The lab he works with was able to extract your DNA. Over the last few years, we had our son's DNA uploaded to multiple sites in hopes that one day his daughter would be searching for him. You are a 99.999 percent match," she said, sitting down next to her.

"I don't know what to say," Alex murmured as warm wet tears slid down her face.

"You're finally home, Alexei," the grandmother replied, pulling her into a hug. "I've loved you since the moment I saw your picture. Even then, you looked just like Kostas."

Alex cried like a child, releasing years of sadness she never knew she was carrying. The grandmother's tears mixed with hers as she held her.

"I'm so sorry," the grandmother said softly. "We would've found you and fought for you, had they not changed your name. Your mother didn't want Kostas to feel trapped. I'm sure that's why she left him off your birth certificate. She'd probably planned to leave it up to him. I don't know if she ever knew he passed away."

Alex shook her head, still in disbelief. "Does anyone else know?"

"Orphea saw the resemblance right away, just as I did. She was the one who swiped your glass."

"Wow. This whole week ..." Alex trailed off.

"I'm sorry you weren't told. I knew in my heart right away, but I wanted to make sure I had the proof for you, so there was no second-guessing."

"Here you are," Sharni said, walking into the room. Her brow furrowed when she saw the two of them embracing and wiping tears. "Is everything okay?"

"I'll let you talk to her," the grandmother said. "I know we need to get you both to the airport soon."

"I'm sorry I have to leave," Alex replied. "If I—"

"This is home. Now, you know your way back." The grandmother smiled and kissed her cheek.

Sharni watched her walk out of the room before rushing to Alex's side. "What the hell is going on?"

# Chapter 36

"Are you serious?" Sharni muttered, trying to wrap her head around everything Alex had just told her.

She nodded.

"They secretly tested your DNA?" She shook her head. "This is crazy."

"Yep."

"So, you and Max are cousins. That makes Neesa your cousin by marriage."

Alex laughed. "I guess so."

"This is still so weird. I can barely wrap my head around it. I can't imagine what it must be like for you."

"Sad, happy, hurtful. I think I've been through all the emotions in the past hour. The strange thing is, I felt a connection to this place, these people, from the moment we arrived."

"It's crazy to think they've been looking for you for years and you had no idea about them. Then, you appear on their doorstep one day."

"Yeah," Alex laughed. "Maybe my late grandfather ... wow, it's so weird saying that. I remember Max and Leo calling him Pappou. Anyway, maybe he was right. Maybe my father had a hand in bringing me here."

"Call it kismet."

"I owe this all to you, Sharni. If you hadn't brought me with you ..."

Sharni smiled and kissed her softly. "Maybe your father brought you to me, too."

Alex smiled. "I love you."

"I love you too." Sharni looked around. "Show me this picture you mentioned."

Alex took her to the desk. Sharni did the same thing, starting with the photo on the left and working her way across until she saw the man in the suit and gasped. "Alex, you look just like him."

"I know." She smiled proudly.

"This week had to be so strange for them. It's no wonder they were so protective of you."

"Of us. You've been here all week as my girlfriend. They've treated you like family, too."

"Yeah," Sharni agreed. "I've never met anyone like them."

"Neither have I." She shook her head. "It's hard to believe I've had no one for the last ten years. Truthfully, I've had no one for the last twenty-four. Now, I have a grandmother, an aunt, an uncle, and cousins. I have a family." She smiled.

"I am so happy for you, Alex."

"Thanks. I'm still trying to process everything. It seems so surreal."

"You know, you don't have to fly back with me. You can stay longer. Get to know them." Sharni stepped closer, draping her arms around Alex's neck.

"I can't. I'm literally turning and burning. I have to be in L.A. Monday for a fitting, then I'm off to Monaco on Wednesday and Dubai from there," she sighed. "I do plan to come back as soon as things settle down. It's crazy how I went from thinking I was done with modeling to a new contract and a brand-new line."

Sharni smiled. "They couldn't let you go, and neither can I."

"I hope not." Alex grinned. "I also need to contact my attorney to start the process of changing my name back to what my mother gave me at birth, Alexei Anna Nikolaidis," she said as they parted and walked back over to the couch.

"Now we know why she was calling you Alexei all week." Sharni smiled. "I love it. It suits you."

"Thanks."

"Was your mother's name Anna?"

Alex nodded.

"I bet she was beautiful. You look just like your father, but I'm sure there's a lot of her in you too."

"I don't remember much. I was so young. Her parents kept no trace of her existence in their home. I was in my sophomore year of high school when an envelope, addressed to Alexei, came to the house one day. I always checked the mail, which is how I intercepted it. I vaguely remember the name Alexei. Being here and being called that, brought those memories back to me. Anyhow, I tore it open. There was a short letter explaining that the sender had been a friend of my mother's and had run across the photos. She thought I'd like to have them. Inside the envelope was a picture of my mother and one of her and I when I was probably two. I tried to find the woman after I graduated and moved out, but she'd passed away by then."

"Aww." Sharni wiped a tear from her cheek.

Alex sighed heavily and shook her head as she smiled.

"What?"

"I was just thinking I'll show you those photos when we get back and realized we don't even know where each of us lives," she laughed. "My new-found family aside, you and I have a lot of catching up to do."

"Yeah," Sharni chuckled. "We sort of skipped over dating and went right into a relationship."

"Zero to a hundred." Alex grinned.

"I think the lesbians call it U-Hauling."

Alex guffawed. "We sort of dated this week, as we pretended to be a couple. So ... we just fast forwarded a bit."

Sharni grinned and shook her head. "We should probably get going. Are you finished packing?"

"Yes. You?"

Sharni nodded as Alex interlaced their fingers and walked out of the room.

*

The grandmother and Orphea were sitting in the tearoom where the piano was located, when Sharni and Alex appeared with their luggage.

"I put this together for you. It has a few of your father's things in it, plus pictures of him and your grandfather, as well as pictures of all of us and our contact information." The grandmother wiped away a tear. "Alexei, you've been right here for so long," she said, putting her hand to her heart. "Now, you're here," she finished, holding her arms out to her. Alex stepped closer, hugging her. "I've loved you since you were only a picture I could hold. I'm so proud of the person you grew up to be. It's been a joy learning who you are as a person this week. I can't wait to get to know you ... as your grandmother."

"My Yiayia," Alex whispered, using the term she'd heard Leo and Max use, affectionately referring to their grandmother all week, as she wiped tears from her cheeks.

Orphea choked back tears and wrapped her in a tight hug. "I'm so happy we have you in our lives. I told Max and Leo. They're both overjoyed and had wondered why they'd felt so close to you all week. We've all felt that way. We love you and we're really going to miss you."

"This week has been a whirlwind. I wish more than anything that I didn't have to go, but know I'll be back as soon as I can and visit as much as I can. This place ... all of you ... this is home. This is my family."

Sharni dried her own tears as she watched the three of them. In a way, she envied Alex. She had seen more kindness, caring, and thoughtfulness between strangers in one week who didn't know they were related, than with her own family and she'd been with them her entire life. She was beyond happy for Alex, and for her sister for marrying into such a wonderful family.

"Sharni, you are welcome here anytime. You are a part of this family too," the grandmother said, pulling her into a hug.

"Thank you. That means the world to me," she replied, wiping more tears.

"Okay, let's get these girls to the airport before we all turn into a puddle," Orphea laughed.

Alex and Sharni grabbed their bags, and everyone made their way to the vehicle parked outside.

\*

Alex spent the long plane ride back to the States in a brain fog as she tried to digest, process, and compartmentalize the last eight days. She hadn't opened the box the grandmother ... *her grandmother ... her yiayia ...* gave to her. She'd tucked it safely into her suitcase with plans to open it once she settled at home, with enough time to let herself go through the array of emotions she was sure to feel. In the meantime, she lulled her head to the side, watching Sharni peacefully slumbering against her. Her grandmother had said she strongly believed Alex's father brought her to them, and Alex was pretty sure it was her mother who brought Sharni to her. "I love you," she whispered, kissing the top of her head.

## About the Author

Graysen Morgen is the author of several bestselling lesbian fiction titles. She was born and raised in North Florida with winding rivers and waterways at her back door, and white sandy beaches nearby. She has spent most of her lifetime in the sun and on the water. She enjoys reading, writing, fishing, watching her daughter play rugby, snowy vacations, and spending as much time as possible with her wife and their two children.

You can contact Graysen at graysenmorgen@aol.com; like her fan page on Facebook.com/graysenmorgen; follow her on Twitter: @graysenmorgen and Instagram: @graysenmorgen

# Other Titles Available From Triplicity Publishing

***Catch Me if I fall*** by Domina Alexandra. Sky returns home after finding out that her dad injured his back in a work accident. With the holidays right around the corner, Sky decides to stick around and help with his recovery, giving her the perfect opportunity to catch up with old friends. Growing up in foster care has left Eva Flowers with bad experiences and alone for years, causing her to avoid having real connections. But for whatever reason, she can't leave the town despite the bad memories. *In a Springtime Romance where opposites attract.*

***One Shot at Love*** by Domina Alexandra. Newly retired from the WNBA, 'Jazzy' Jazz Thomas moves back home in hopes of rebuilding a friendship she once lost. Tamara made the biggest mistake of her life pushing Jazz away and despite her fears, all she wants is a second chance. With nothing but time to rekindle their friendship, Tamara's secrets will come out, leaving Jazz with one question. Will they both leap forward and take their one shot at love, or will they cave under pressure?

***A Fated Love (Rogue Series Book 2)*** by Domina Alexandra. Starting over is never easy, however, Karissa wouldn't have it any other way if it meant being with her fated mate, Danni, a lone wolf whose own journey has been met with a lot of curves, starting with Hansel, the witch wolf, who turned her at fifteen and habitually shows up uninvited.

***Fae and Moon Bound (Claim Series Book 4)*** by Domina Alexandra. Less than a year as a newly awakened werewolf and Omega, Bonnie's life has yet to be boring. Surviving rogue werewolves, ghouls, and a dangerous stalker should make Bonnie feel more confident in surviving the future, but then again, she lets herself be captured to protect her pack and family. One thing Bonnie had not anticipated was being reunited with someone from her past.

***A Rogue's Redemption (Rogue Series Book 1)*** by Domina Alexandra. Forcibly turned into a werewolf, Danni's life has been trapped by her creator for years, until the Sentinel of a Sacramento pack finds her in a fighting pit next to a couple dead wolves. As the pack's Sentinel, Karissa doesn't get much respect for her position. When she busts an illegal fighting pit in her territory and finds a werewolf with a power far greater than she's ever seen, she realizes she's not only found her one true mate, but she'll have her role as Sentinel questioned now more than ever.

***New Beginnings*** by Graysen Morgen. Captain Tristan Malloy has dedicated her life to the Army and takes her job very seriously. When an unexpected situation arises back home, her world is upended. When the dust settles, she makes a choice that will change her life forever. Courtney Hewitt is a third generation Army helicopter pilot, who's been flying in and out of warzones until she gets sent to South America for a Special Forces Operation. The redeployment is a welcomed change of scenery, and the leader of the special forces team she's assigned to work with is an added bonus. Everyone deserves a chance at a new beginning in this action-packed romance.

*An Omega's Grief (Claimed Series Book 3)* by Domina Alexandra. Bonnie's life is finally slowing down, but on a weekend getaway with her mate Rikki, things quickly turn sour when a human is killed right in front of them. Worse, Bonnie has a stalker with an unimaginable power, and if she doesn't confront this dangerous individual, it might cost her pack and friends their lives. With time against her, Bonnie will have to make her toughest decision yet.

*Crossed Reins* by Graysen Morgen. Barrel racing is Carly Rae Walsh's life, until it's ripped out from under her. With nothing to do and nothing to lose, she uses her years of horse whispering skills and intuition to train a troubled thoroughbred racehorse. Allison McKinley is a world class dressage rider who has stepped back from the spotlight to mourn the sudden death of her mother. The last thing she needs when she decides to start training again for competition, is her father's impulsive desire to own a racehorse, and his bizarre decision to choose a rodeo barrel racer as the trainer. The two women have nothing in common except horses, and even that's a stretch. Can they uncross the reins long enough to see what's happening between them?

*Outside In* by Breanna Hughes. Cali Evans is a survivor. Her life hasn't been easy, but her late father raised her to be smart, tough, and dependent only on herself and her wits. On the eve of her 21st birthday she meets Owen Bray - a beautiful and intriguing young doctor who equally frustrates and captivates Cali. That fateful meeting inspires Cali to make a better life for herself. The next day, hoping to make positive change, Cali hops a bus for the West Coast but never reaches her destination. Instead, she wakes up in an underground bunker with no recollection of how she got there.

***I Love You, Nora Whispered*** by Kathy L. Salt. Love in the time of horses and polio. England, 1948. Nora Lakes suffers from post Polio Syndrome and very low self-esteem. When her sister Martha manages to get her a job at Waterhouse Acre Stables, she can hardly believe it. She had never imagined that anyone would employ her, damaged as she is. She also never imagined she would meet anybody like Katherine.

***Omega Rising (Claimed Series Book 2)*** by Domina Alexandra. A few months of peace. That was all Bonnie Collins was granted. New trouble has surfaced and go figure, this trouble came with a new pair of claws. When an unknown pack comes to town, Bonnie is forced to make tough decisions that will influence her packs future. Things only get harder when her mate is taken, leaving Bonnie in charge of a pack who still doesn't trust her. With chaos all around, it will be exactly what Bonnie needs to finally embrace what she has become. An Omega Rising. Book 2 of the *Claimed Series*.

***Loose Ends*** by Joan L. Anderson. After her estranged sister is killed when she falls onto the subway tracks in Paris just as a train arrives, Allison goes to Paris to deal with her sister's body and collect her things. But, after talking to the police about the accident and viewing the subway surveillance video, something seems odd about her death. When Allison's hotel room in Paris is broken into with only a few things taken, but not any money or credit cards, she begins to wonder if it really was an accident that killed her sister, or if it was murder.

***Real Love*** by Graysen Morgen. Leigh Myer is a trauma nurse practitioner who is not happy going through the motions of her daily life. When a friend offers up her mountain cabin for a relaxing vacation, Leigh packs her bags. She's never been to the mountains and certainly never in heavy snow. A chance meeting with a fish and wildlife officer turns her idea of a quiet, relaxing vacation ...upside down. Camden Gorely loves her job and loves the mountain she works and lives on even more. She's tired of having flings with vacationers who visit for days or weeks at a time, until she meets the elusive nurse from the city. Can Leigh stop running from her past and allow real love into her heart?

***Love Undercover*** by Domina Alexandra. Remi Stone never expected to get the opportunity to work undercover for narcotics. But, when the chance arrives, she takes it. With drugs coursing through a high school, Remi has only until the end of the school year to find the suspects responsible. Undercover, Remi plays her role, moving one step further into the drug industry. She never thought she'd be moving one step closer to the woman who would change her life and take hold of her heart. There is just one issue. Remi Stone is undercover as an eighteen-year-old high school senior. And the woman she can't seem to ignore is her History teacher. There will be a lot of challenges along the way, including one that could cost Remi her life and her heart.

***Playing the Game*** by Graysen Morgen. Randi Rojas is a professional soccer player who seemingly has it all, a successful career, a long-term girlfriend, a loving family, and a great group of friends ...until a chance meeting with an attractive woman sends her way offside, and into a whole new game. Berkley Ward lives her life to the extreme, spending her days either in the gym or four-wheeling in the woods, and her nights patrolling the streets as an officer. Affairs with taken women are easy, but after years of playing games, she's finished ...until she meets a beautiful woman and a game she can't resist. Both women play a dangerously seductive game of cat and mouse, teetering on the edge of friendship and affair.

***Rebel Sweetheart*** by Sydney Canyon. When a headstrong, country music superstar starts getting threatening letters while on tour, her manager has no other choice but to hire someone to investigate the threats and keep her safe. Haley Nielsen is as stubborn as it gets. She does things her way, and her way only. The last thing she needs or wants is a babysitter following her every move and controlling everything she does. Shane Crowley isn't your typical private investigator, or bodyguard, for that matter. She's a former U.S. Deputy Marshal with a lot of experience, and an all or nothing attitude. Tempers flare and the energy burns red hot between the two women as they spend weeks together cooped up on Haley's tour bus, traveling the country. Will they stop resisting each other long enough to see eye to eye? Or will the letter writer make good on his threats?

***A Tale of Spiders and Canned Soup*** by Kathy L. Salt. Living on your own can be hard, but even more so when you're dealing with haphephobia; the death of a twin sister; and a crush on your teacher. Mika is still in contact with her foster family who homes the loves of her life, three young children she would do anything for, when she begins attending University of Aberdeen and meets Pauline, an Australian that teaches Viking history. Neither woman is used to breaking the rules, and their way to each other is a hard one, especially when Mika vows to get custody of the children, whether she is ready to be a parent or not. *A story about growing up. A story about dealing with grief. A story about Mika and Pauline.*

**A Night Claimed (Claimed Series Book 1)** by Domina Alexandra. Bonnie Collins had plans. And being a werewolf wasn't one of them. Attacked by a rogue who was out to claim her and facing what she now has no choice of becoming, Bonnie can't let go of her human life as a Paramedic. The last thing Bonnie needs is more challenges. However, Rikki, the Alpha of Mill City will be just that. Finding her to be possessive and ruling, Bonnie begins challenging the Alpha's every breath. Finding out her attack was no accident only makes her more angry at the situation. A group of rogues are out to get her. With no clue why, Bonnie has no choice but to seek help from the alluring Alpha and her pack, accepting the new world she was forced into.

**Stunted** by Breanna Hughes. Professional stuntwoman Jessie Knight takes her job very seriously and although she works in the entertainment industry, she has zero desire for fame or notoriety. She also has a very strict no-dating policy when it comes to coworkers. That is, until she meets famous actress Elliot Chase on the set of her new film. The adrenaline rush of the stunts is nothing compared to the sparks that fly between them. After a passionate night together, a sex tape is leaked that sends Jessie and Elliot's private and professional lives into a spiral. Will the fallout be too much for them to last? Or will they find a way out of the mess together?

*Mission Compromised* by Graysen Morgen. Natalia Moreno is thrilled when she arrives in Fiji for a relaxing vacation. However, she soon discovers the overwater bungalow she's staying in has been double booked for the entire stay, and the resort is full. Annoyed and frustrated, she has no other choice but to share her hut with a stranger. Christian Garnier is sent to Fiji for what she refers to as a working vacation, until she finds out she has an ornery roommate for the next two weeks who is dead set on making her job twice as hard. Soon, all hell breaks loose, and the two women are sent around the world on a wild goose chase.

*Stargazing* by Kathy L. Salt. Lissa stared open-mouthed at the GIF that played over and over on the screen in front of her. Heat flushed to her face, igniting her skin. Her heart started pounding in her chest. *Stupid internet, it should really come with a warning label.* She's never been interested in relationships or sex and as the years have gone by she has retreated more and more into her work. Everything changes when she meets Star, a porn actress with a heart of gold and a troubled childhood. *They say that opposites attract, but how much of that is true? What chance do they have when one of them is a virgin and the other one star in pornography?*

*I Belong with Her* by Domina Alexandra. Tajel Pierce loves the thrill of being a paramedic. Every call she goes on gives her a rush. She makes no time for a personal life. No one can ruin her love for her career. Then there is Arianna Castaldi, who just transferred to her new paramedic position in a whole new state. All she needs is a new start without any distractions. Arianna and Tajel's relationship doesn't start off perfect. Embarrassed of the one-night stand Arianna believes she had with Tajel, she wants to pretend they never met and make their relationship strictly business. The only choice they have to keep from strangling each other is to go from denying their feelings to accepting them as they work through intense 911 calls.

*Nautical Delights* by S. L. Gape. Lady Elizabeth Barrington has spent her entire life trying to please her family; constantly opting for a quiet life, she utilises her profession as a doctor to keep out of her families' clutches; bar the annual two-week Caribbean private cruise, where there is simply no budge. Confined to two weeks on board the *Iconica* super yacht, she intends on keeping her head down and enjoying as much of the holiday as she can, whilst keeping her family at arm's length. Until a crew member catches her eye.

*Worlds Apart* by S.L. Gape. Hollywood A-lister Heidi Spencer-Brady is everything you'd expect of an Idol. Loved by all, the British Beauty is graceful, talented, humble and so far removed from the 'typical' LA scene. When her husband's infidelity with his new 'leading lady' is leaked, Dawn, Heidi's best friend and manager, goes all out to protect her. She arranges for Heidi to go back to the UK and stay on her cousins farm they had visited as children, much to the disappointment of the animal fearing Heidi.

**Castor Valley (Law & Order Series Book 2)** by Graysen Morgen. Jessie Henry is torn when she reads about the capture of the Doyle brothers, two young men who were part of her old gang. Unable to let them hang for a crime she's sure they didn't commit, Jessie leaves her wife and the Town of Boone Creek behind and sets out on a journey back to the one place she thought she'd never see again, *Castor Valley*. Ellie Henry watches the love of her life leave, not knowing if she will ever return. When she gets an odd telegram, nearly a week later, she fears Jessie is in trouble. With no other choice, she goes to the one person who can help her.

**Fight to the Top** by S. L. Gape. Georgia is a forty-year-old, single, Area Director from Manchester, UK who is all work and definitely no play. Having no time to socialise or spend time with her family she prides herself on being fit and well-polished. Erika is an Area Director for the same company, but in the United States. Whilst she is concentrating so heavily on the promotion she has been fighting for, she's starting to feel like her life outside of work is falling apart. The two women are exceptionally different, and worlds apart. Both of their lives are turned upside down when their jobs are snatched from under their noses, and they are suddenly faced with being thrown together by their bosses for one last major project...in Texas.

**Boone Creek (Law & Order Series Book 1)** by Graysen Morgen. Jessie Henry is looking for a new life.

She's unknown in the town of Boone Creek when she arrives and wants to keep it that way. When she's offered the job of Town Marshal, she takes it, believing that protecting others and upholding the law is the penance for her past. Ellie Fray is a widowed, shopkeeper. She generally keeps to herself, but the mysterious new Town Marshal both intrigues and infuriates her. She believes the last thing the town needs is someone stirring up trouble with the outlaws who have taken over.

*Witness* by Joan L. Anderson. Becca and Kate have lived together for eight years and have always spent their vacation in a tropical paradise, lying on a beach. This year, Becca wanted to try something different: a seven day, 65-mile hike in the beautiful Cascade Mountains of Washington state. Their peaceful vacation turns to horror when they stumble upon a brutal murder taking place in the back country.

*Too Soon* by S.L. Gape. Brooke is a twenty-nine-year-old detective from Oxford, who has her life pretty much planned out until her boss and partner of nine years, Maria, tells her their relationship is over. When Brooke finds out the truth, that Maria cheated on her with their best friend Paula, she decides to get her life back on track by getting away for six weeks in Anglesey, North Wales. Chloe, a thirty-three-year-old artist and art director, owns a log cabin on Anglesey where she spends each weekend painting and surfing. After returning from a surf, she stumbles upon the somewhat uptight and enigmatic Brooke.

*Never Quit (Never Series Book 2)* by Graysen Morgen. Two years after stepping away from the action as a

Coast Guard Rescue Swimmer to become an instructor, Finley finds herself in charge of the most difficult class of cadets she's ever faced, while also juggling the taxing demands of having a home life with her partner Nicole, and their fifteen-year-old daughter. Jordy Ross gave up everything, dropping out of college, and leaving her family behind, to join the Coast Guard and become a rescue swimmer cadet. The extreme training tests her fitness level, pushing her mentally and physically further than she's ever been in her life, but it's the aggressive competition between her and another female cadet that proves to be the most challenging.

***Never Let Go (Never Series Book 1)*** by Graysen Morgen. For Coast Guard Rescue Swimmer, Finley Morris, life is good. She loves her job, is well respected by her peers, and has been given an opportunity to take her career to the next level. The only thing missing is the love of her life, who walked out, taking their daughter with her, seven years earlier. When Finley gets a call from her ex, saying their teenage daughter is coming to spend the summer with her, she's floored. While spending more time with her daughter, whom she doesn't get to see often, and learning to be a full-time parent, Finley quickly realizes she has not, and will never, let go of what is important.

***Pursuit*** by Joan L. Anderson. Claire is a workaholic attorney who flies to Paris to lick her wounds after being dumped by her girlfriend of seventeen years. On the plane she chats with the young woman sitting next to her, and when they land the woman is inexplicably detained in Customs. Claire is surprised when she later runs into the woman in the city. They agree to meet for breakfast the next morning, but when the woman doesn't show up Claire goes to her hotel and makes a horrifying discovery. She soon finds herself ensnared in a web of intrigue and international terrorism, becoming the target of a high stakes game of cat and mouse through the streets of Paris.

*Wrecked* by Sydney Canyon. To most people, the *Duchess* is a myth formed by old pirate's tales, but to Reid Cavanaugh, a Caribbean island bum and one of the best divers and treasure hunters in the world, it's a real, seventeenth century pirate ship—the holy grail of underwater treasure hunting. Reid uses the same cunning tactics she always has before setting out to find the lost ship. However, she is forced to bring her business partner's daughter along as collateral this time because he doesn't trust her. Neither woman is thrilled but being cooped up on a small dive boat for days forces them to get know each other quickly.

*Arson* by Austen Thorne. Madison Drake is a detective for the Stetson Beach Police Department. The last thing she wants to do is show a new detective the ropes, especially when a fire investigation becomes arson to cover up a murder. Madison butts heads with Tara, her trainee, deals with sarcasm from Nic, her ex-girlfriend who is a patrol officer, and finds calm in the chaos of police work with Jamie, her best friend who is the county medical examiner. Arson is the first of many in a series of novella episodes surrounding the fictional Stetson Beach Police Department and Detective Madison Drake.

**Mommies (Bridal Series Book 3) by Graysen Morgen.** Britton and her wife Daphne have been married for a year and a half and are happy with their life, until Britton's mother hounds her to find out why her sister Bridget hasn't decided to have children yet. This prompts Daphne to bring up the big subject of having kids of their own with Britton. Britton hadn't really thought much about having kids, but her love for Daphne makes her see life and their future together in a whole new way when they decide to become mommies.

***Rapture & Rogue*** by Sydney Canyon. Taren Rauley is happy and in a good relationship, until the one person she thought she'd never see again comes back into her life. She struggles to keep the past from colliding with the present as old feelings she thought were dead and gone, begin to haunt her. In college, Gianna Revisi was a mastermind, ring-leading, crime boss. Now, she has a great life and spends her time running Rapture and Rogue, the two establishments she built from the ground up. The last person she ever expects to see walk into one of them, is the girl who walked out on her, breaking her heart five years ago.

***Second Chance*** by Sydney Canyon. After an attack on her convoy, Marine Corps Staff Sergeant, Darien Hollister, must learn to live without her sight. When an experimental procedure allows her to see again, Darien is torn, knowing someone had to die in order for this to happen. She embarks on a journey to personally thank the donor's family but is too stunned to tell them the truth. Mixed emotions stir inside of her as she slowly gets to the know the people that feel like so much more than strangers to her. When the truth finally comes out, Darien walks away, taking the second chance that she's been given to go back to the only life she's ever known, but she's not the only one with a second chance at life.

**Meant to Be** by Graysen Morgen. Brandt is about to walk down the aisle with her girlfriend, when an unexpected chain of events turns her world upside down, causing her to question the last three years of her life. A chance encounter sparks a mix of rage and excitement that she has never felt before. Summer is living life and following her dreams, all the while, harboring a huge secret that could ruin her career. She believes that some things are better kept in the dark, until she has her third run-in with a woman she had hoped to never see again, and gives into temptation. Brandt and Summer start believing everything happens for a reason as they learn the true meaning of meant to be.

**Coming Home** by Graysen Morgen. After tragedy derails TJ Abernathy's life, she packs up her three-year-old son and heads back to Pennsylvania to live with her grandmother on the family farm. TJ picks back up where she left off eight years earlier, tending to the fruit and nut tree orchard, while learning her grandmother's secret trade. Soon, TJ's high school sweetheart and the same girl who broke her heart, comes back into her life, threatening to steal it away once again. As the weeks turn into months and tragedy strikes again, TJ realizes coming home was the best thing she could've ever done.

**Special Assignment** by Austen Thorne. Secret Service Agent Parker Meeks has her hands full when she gets her new assignment, protecting a Congressman's teenage daughter, who has had threats made on her life and been whisked away to a Christian boarding school under an alias to finish out her senior year. Parker is fine with the assignment, until she finds out she has to go undercover as a Canon Priest. The last thing Parker expects to find is a beautiful, art history teacher, who is intrigued by her in more ways than one.

***Miracle at Christmas*** by Sydney Canyon. A Modern Twist on the Classic Scrooge Story. Dylan is a power-hungry lawyer who pushed away everything good in her life to become the best defense attorney in the, often winning the worst cases and keeping anyone with enough money out of jail. She's visited on Christmas Eve by her deceased law partner, who threatens her with a life in hell like his own, if she doesn't change her path. During the course of the night, she is taken on a journey through her past, present, and future with three very different spirits.

***Bella Vita*** by Sydney Canyon. Brady is the First Officer of the crew on the Bella Vita, a luxury charter yacht in the Caribbean. She enjoys the laidback island lifestyle, and is accustomed to high profile guests, but when a U.S. Senator charters the yacht as a gift to his beautiful twin daughters who have just graduated from college and a few of their friends, she literally has her hands full.

***Brides (Bridal Series Book 2)*** by Graysen Morgen. Britton Prescott is dating the love of her life, Daphne Attwood, after a few tumultuous events that happened to unravel at her sister's wedding reception, seven months earlier. She's happy with the way things are, but immense pressure from her family and friends to take the next step, nearly sends her back to the single life. The idea of a long engagement and simple wedding are thrown out the window, as both families take over, rushing Britton and Daphne to the altar in a matter of weeks.

***Cypress Lake*** by Graysen Morgen. The small town of Cypress Lake is rocked when one murder after another happens. Dani Ricketts, the Chief Deputy for the Cypress Lake Sheriff's Office, realizes the murders are linked. She's surprised when the girl that broke her heart in high school has not only returned home, but she's also Dani's only suspect. Kristen Malone has come back to Cypress Lake to put the past behind her so that she can move on with her life. Seeing Dani Ricketts again throws her off-guard, nearly derailing her plans to finally rid herself and her family of Cypress Lake.

***Crashing Waves*** by Graysen Morgen. After a tragic accident, Pro Surfer, Rory Eden, spends her days hiding in the surf and snowboard manufacturing company that she built from the ground up, while living her life as a shell of the person that she once was. Rory's world is turned upside when a young surfer pursues her, asking for the one thing she can't do. Adler Troy and Dr. Cason Macauley from Graysen Morgen's bestselling novel: *Falling Snow*, make an appearance in this romantic adventure about life, love, and letting go.

***Bridesmaid of Honor (Bridal Series Book 1)*** by Graysen Morgen. Britton Prescott's best friend is getting married and she's the maid of honor. As if that isn't enough to deal with, Britton's sister announces she's getting married in the same month and her maid of honor is her best friend Daphne, the same woman who has tormented

Britton for years. Britton has to suck it up and play nice, instead of scratching her eyes out, because she and Daphne are in both weddings. Everyone is counting on them to behave like adults.

***Falling Snow*** by Graysen Morgen. Dr. Cason Macauley, a high-speed trauma surgeon from Denver meets Adler Troy, a professional snowboarder, and sparks fly. The last thing Cason wants is a relationship and Adler doesn't realize what's right in front of her until it's gone, but will it be too late?

***Fate vs. Destiny*** by Graysen Morgen. Logan Greer devotes her life to investigating plane crashes for the National Transportation Safety Board. Brooke McCabe is an investigator with the Federal Aviation Association who literally flies by the seat of her pants. When Logan gets tangled in head games with both women will she choose fate or destiny?

***Just Me*** by Graysen Morgen. Wild child Ian Wiley has to grow up and take the reins of the hundred-year-old family business when tragedy strikes. Cassidy Harland is a little surprised that she came within an inch of picking up a gorgeous stranger in a bar and is shocked to find out that stranger is the new head of her company.

***Love Loss Revenge*** by Graysen Morgen. Rian Casey is an FBI Agent working the biggest case of her career and madly in love with her girlfriend. Her world is turned upside when tragedy strikes. Heartbroken, she tries to rebuild her life. When she discovers the truth behind what really happened that awful night, she decides justice isn't good enough, and vows revenge on everyone involved.

***Natural Instinct*** by Graysen Morgen. Chandler Scott is a Marine Biologist who keeps her private life private. Corey Joslen is intrigued by Chandler from the moment she meets her. Chandler is forced to finally open her life up to Corey. It backfires in Corey's face and sends her running. Will either woman learn to trust her natural instinct?

***Secluded Heart*** by Graysen Morgen. Chase Leery is an overworked cardiac surgeon with a group of best friends that have an opinion and a reason for everything. When she meets a new artist named Remy Sheridan at her best friend's art gallery she is captivated by the reclusive woman. When Chase finds out why Remy is so sheltered will she put her career on the line to help her or is it too difficult to love someone with a secluded heart?

***In Love, at War*** by Graysen Morgen. Charley Hayes is in the Army Air Force and stationed at Ford Island in Pearl Harbor. She is the commanding officer of her own female-only service squadron and doing the one thing she loves most, repairing airplanes. Life is good for Charley, until the day she finds herself falling in love while fighting for her life as her country is thrown haphazardly into World War II. Can she survive being in love and at war?

***Fast Pitch*** by Graysen Morgen. Graham Cahill is a senior in college and the catcher and captain of the softball team. Despite being an all-star pitcher, Bailey Michaels is young and arrogant. Graham and Bailey are forced to get to know each other off the field in order to learn to work together on the field. Will the extra time pay off or will it drive a nail through the team?

*Submerged* by Graysen Morgen. Assistant District Attorney Layne Carmichael had no idea that the sexy woman she took home from a local bar for a one-night stand would turn out to be someone she would be prosecuting months later. Scooter is a Naval Officer on a submarine who changes women like she changes uniforms. When she is accused of a heinous crime, she is shocked to see her latest conquest sitting across from her as the prosecuting attorney.

*Vow of Solitude* by Austen Thorne. Detective Jordan Denali is in a fight for her life against the ghosts from her past and a Serial Killer taunting her with his every move. She lives a life of solitude and plans to keep it that way. When Callie Marceau, a curious Medical Examiner, decides she wants in on the biggest case of her career, as well as Jordan's life, Jordan is powerless to stop her.

*Igniting Temptation* by Sydney Canyon. Mackenzie Trotter is the Head of Pediatrics at the local hospital. Her life takes a rather unexpected turn when she meets a flirtatious, beautiful fire fighter. Both women soon discover it doesn't take much to ignite temptation.

*One Night* by Sydney Canyon. While on a business trip, Caylen Jarrett spends an amazing night with a beautiful stripper. Months later, she is shocked and confused when that same woman re-enters her life. The fact that this stranger could destroy her career doesn't bother her. C.J. is more terrified of the feelings this woman stirs in her. Could she have fallen in love in one night and not even known it?

*Fine* by Sydney Canyon. Collin Anderson hides behind a façade, pretending everything is fine. Her workaholic wife and best friend are both oblivious as she goes on an emotional journey, battling a potentially hereditary disease that her mother has been diagnosed with. The only person who knows what is really going on, is Collin's doctor. The same doctor, who is an acquaintance that she's always been attracted to, and who has a partner of her own.

*Shadow's Eyes* by Sydney Canyon. Tyler McCain is the owner of a large ranch that breeds and sells different types of horses. She isn't exactly thrilled when a Hollywood movie producer shows up wanting to film his latest movie on her property. Reegan Delsol is an up-and-coming actress who has everything going for her when she lands the lead role in a new film, but there one small problem that could blow the entire picture.

*Light Reading: A Collection of Novellas* by Sydney Canyon. Four of Sydney Canyon's novellas together in one book, including the bestsellers Shadow's Eyes and One Night.

**Visit us at www.tri-pub.com**

Made in the USA
Coppell, TX
07 August 2024

35685411R00187